# The Walkers

Tina Mardel Stewart

ISBN: 978-1-964482-37-8

# Dedication

The Walkers is dedicated to my children and to a man for whom using language effectively was always important.

Acknowledgment

I offer so much gratitude to my parents, Ruth (Perkins) and Charles Mardel for practising and instilling a love of language and story-telling. Thank you to my children, Peter and Beth; my grandchildren, Alexandrea, Harris, Daniel and Duncan; my extended family and good friends for encouraging me to "put it in writing". Last but by no means least, thanks to the folks at Amazon KDP Publishing for their patience and expertise.

# Table of Contents

# Preface

One of the pleasures of living near the ocean's shoreline is my morning walk to the music of the waves and the imagery of the land. Concerns and frustrations melt away with each step, even those that require muscles to trudge through snow several months of the year. I liken the effect to a twist of rope slowly unwinding until all its tension is gone. Contentment reigns.

I have no influence on the sights and sounds of nature on this old rail-bed. The waves roll, the beach rocks rumble, the clouds float across the sky, the wind blows, the plants come to life, and the birds chatter. In my mind, all transform into words which, eventually, create a story about a walking trail.

There are communities along the shore, each with a history, a culture, and a cast of characters. Some people naturally share attributes and habits while others do not, but all are connected by their surroundings. That is how and why I chose to tell the story of Sara, Carrie, Margaret, Ben, and a rescued Labrador Husky.

They belong "to the shore", to the island, to the land and the sea, whether born and bred or come from away. I hope you get to know each of them as individuals. You may learn something new from them or, perhaps, recognize yourself in them. I like to think that there is a little of me within their daily lives.

# Chapter One

## Sara

"Good morning," in passing, as we walk the shoreline trail on this October morning.

The old train track, now a groomed path of crushed stone, stretches for miles, far beyond where the eye can see. The ocean expands from below our feet to the rocks, harbours, and hills on the north shore of the bay. The buildings are bright dots against the undulating greens and the steep clay-brown cliffs when not shrouded in fog or rain-soaked clouds. Sea birds ride the waves ducks wheel overhead before landing ungracefully on the breaking sea. After a high wind, the beach has changed shape yet again. The loose wall of rocks either laid flat or piled nearly as high as the trail itself, kept at the water's edge by strategically placed boulders. Occasionally, after really high surf, even they are no deterrent.

The scrubby salt-worn bushes are snug against large patches of multi-coloured lupines in the summer. The stunted evergreens are resigned to leaning into the bitter northeast winds of winter. The tiny red berries, low to the ground, doggedly persist through sheets of ice awaiting summer's sun. Leaves and wild grasses change from pale springtime yellows to brilliant green and then to shades of gold and amber before they, too, are frozen stiff under crystals of salty snow.

There are surprises on the more barren headlands where we step off the trail. Looking at the sponge of the moss, we see huge brilliant toadstools (yellow tennis balls to the untrained eye), tiny white cracker-berry flowers and a rare corner of tall purple irises in full bloom. Nature's hardiness and resilience come back to life when the ground thaws.

Our daily walks, in one direction or another, short distances and long, beside a quietly rolling lop or being covered in cold spray, bring exercise to mind and body. The sounds, the sights, and the emotions change as we step outward and then back home. Dogs with their people come and go, as do we. Greetings pass from one side of the trail to the other on the wind, spoken aloud, "Good morning," "Chilly today," "Happy New Year," "Wicked wind." A simple nod of the head, lift of the hand at other times and, for those walkers engrossed in their headphones, a silent passing along the shore. That is uncommon.

In the summer, his grey ponytail moves with his step. His hiking shorts nearly meet sturdy socks above his walking boots. The backpack looks empty if he's heading eastward. There is music coming from earbuds and his relaxed but purposeful stride looks well-practised and comfortable. No pause in stride; a smile and quick greeting pass from him to me.

## THE WALKERS

On damp, chilly days, even from a distance, we see his familiar silhouette as our feet take the final bend towards the shore. He wears the gear – water and wind-proof black balaclava tucked into a tight-fitting black long-sleeved jacket. The waist sits atop the same colour hiking shorts over leggings. Gloves keep the elements off his hands, and hiking boots complete his comfort.

His point of origin is unknown to me. His destination is also not obvious as he walks beyond our stopping points in both directions. One Fall morning, our paths crossed as he bent to leave seeds for the birds who frequent the trail along with us humans and dogs. The nearest grocery store is, at my speed, more than an hour's walk to the east along the shoreline trail. Westward from our starting point, we can walk for ninety minutes before arriving at an actual community.

I don't know his reason for walking the shoreline. My companion and I walk for the pleasure of each other's company, to keep my aging body somewhat agile and healthy, for the joy of hearing the waves, discovering new scents, and seeing all that is around us. It isn't necessary to see other humans. In fact, it's often nice to be truly alone. The occasional presence of this other walker is, however, a tiny mystery for my imagination.

*******************************

# Carrie

The kettle is freshly-boiled, and a tea bag in my favourite mug. It's time to permit myself a sit-down. The sun shines through my window and highlights the dust that my cloth didn't catch. The lane is quiet, with no rusty garbage trucks doing their weekly duty. Nothing but light bounces off the frosted grasses, and on the pond that bends to the rocky shore, there's a skim of new ice. That's pushed the ducks and seagulls to more open water closer to where the salt and fresh compete under the bridge.

I can't help but look back up our lane. Where it takes a bend from houses to a rocky shoreline trail, I often see the woman patiently waiting while her dog stops to explore yet another new smell. Again, today, she smiles and waits. Something is said as she looks down at her companion. To my mind, she's saying, "Okay, it's your walk, too, so sniff away." They are obviously both enjoying their daily excursion to the beach trail. I haven't looked at the thermometer outside my window, but it must be chilly out there. The wind is coming off the water, and the pond has frozen in ridges, waves that no longer move, at least not on the surface. No wonder the woman stamps her boots and pulls her woollen cap a bit lower over her ears.

This past summer, two large domestic geese shared the pond with the seabirds and mallards. The dog must have a good memory because she – I always think of dogs as ‘she’ and cats as ‘he’ - stops every few yards to gaze at the water. She obviously remembers the geese paddling to the rocks that jut askew when the pond is low. I’ve seen them brazenly and confidently strut across her path merely meters away while, on a shortened leash, the dog just watches. Those lords of the lane haven’t been around for a few months, but the dog still keeps an eye out and sniffs the air at that bend. Don’t mess with geese. I imagine her human walker would advise.

My window overlooks the brush surrounding the pond, the fancy new homes on the far side, the incline up to the trail at the end of the road, and the other two small houses on this end. Three former summer homes in times when the city seemed a long way back after nearly an hour of bumpy, dusty travel. That’s no longer the case, but we have kept standing as highways shortened the commute, and created new communities on old family pastures. Occasionally, you see a small home tucked back from the road, sandwiched between the big ones. The stories my little home could tell during years of change, more than I’ve ever seen.

I wonder from which of those homes the woman I see this morning begins her daily walk. Perhaps, a little home like mine remodelled but still holding history now brings year-round comfort to her and her dog. They always come from the same direction but not always at the same time each morning. The traffic lights at the intersection beyond my view must impose a pause and make it safe for them to go from busy to quiet, from short leash to long as trees and grasses take over from asphalt and concrete underfoot.

It's no wonder that, by the time I see these two walking past my window, the two-legged walker looks relaxed and the sniffer's nose is to the ground with her curvy tail swaying happily. The old rail-bed trail is at bridge height above their last few steps. It brings wind off the ocean, rocks rumbling within the grip of the waves, and open, clear air as far as the eye can see.

My tea is gone. No time for another. Raisin bread is on its second rise. Time to leave my window perch, heat the oven, put a load of laundry in the washer, and smile a 'thank you' to the walker and her husky companion until tomorrow, I hope. They add to my mornings.

***********************************

## Margaret

I am none the wiser again today! I'm the reincarnation of dear old nosy Aunt Maude. As children, we joked about our maiden aunt's love of her lookout spot slightly to one side of her wide living room window. She was a confirmed devotee of knowing the business of the neighbourhood and, when possible, of the community as a whole. It was never in a mean-spirited or gossipy way. More to ensure, at least in Aunt Maude's own mind, that her offers of knowledge about everyone's comings and goings would provide an encompassing blanket of protection to all she held dear. That, we children decided, really meant absolutely everyone, livyers and strangers.

Now I, in my own way, having inherited her house and habit, like to ensure as best I can that a happening would not be missed from that old rocking chair aside the window. Not to have made note of something could be a failure of some proportion. It's not that I'm a proud woman but I do feel confident in my ability to provide that sense of security.

To be prepared with knowledge of and for my fellow townspeople, I keep an eye on who comes and goes. Some people are predictable because they leave and return from their jobs in the city in a pretty routine pattern. They tend to live in larger, more modern, newer homes with one or two cars. They seldom walk anywhere, not even to the corner store up the road.

From within my little bungalow these past sixty years, I am very happy not to live a life structured by commutes. Hours tortured by bumper-to-bumper speedsters who have no idea how to make use of signal lights with, for heaven's sake, no need to roll down a window and use your hand to show a direction change. Those same people also and obviously, in my experience, have disabled all their fancy technology-driven safe distance reminders.

My observation is supported by the sounds of emergency vehicles heading out the fancy highway at least twice a day, usually more often than that. I know the subtle differences in the siren of a police car, an ambulance or a fire truck. There's nothing wrong with my hearing and while they are up the road beyond my view, their direction is easily discernible to one who listens to the world around her.

Oh, my goodness. My mind wandered atop a bit of a soapbox just then. It's time for a deep cleansing breath to rid my thoughts of distraction and any future tirades. The sun is glorious today. There's still a slight tinge of green to the bushes and grasses at the edge of my front lawn.

There he is again. I never seem to be looking in the right direction at the right time. His departure point eludes me. That lack of knowledge is detrimental to my overall protection plan. Better vigilance is obviously required. Today, the air must be somewhat warmer than this time last week. He's changed his all-encompassing anti-wind, cold and wet, very tight-fitting attire for a lighter, looser jacket, brown shorts atop brown leggings and a contrasting headband to hold back his pony-tailed grey hair. His hands are bare, and he looks quite content as he strides along.

He comes from up behind the short hill, but exactly from where, I don't yet know. His backpack is slack this morning but he has something in the small outer pocket. I've seen him stop to leave crumbs or seeds for the birds just as he's stepping off the little bridge down the way. Perhaps those are the contents I'm noticing. His step is easy, long and well-practised. I wonder if he's listening to his favourite music as he watches the waves hit the shore to his left.

I have never been one for lots of walking. Pottering in my garden, tending my few strawberries and patch of rhubarb, pulling carrots in the summer, and shovelling a minimal pathway in winter do me just fine. Of course, I hang clothes on the line any day that there's the tiniest bit of warmth coming from the sun. Someone once teased me that my laundry is freeze-dried. A clever phrase but not great on the hands when I bring it in to thaw before ironing. Old habits die hard. In my case, good habits don't ever die.

The walker, whose full story I do not know, has now made the turn away from the village. I'll have to remember to look for his return. Certainly, if one goes east from home, one must come west again. Actually, I know he does because I've caught sight of him coming towards her, backpack bulging with shopping of some kind. The bigger stores are a good two-hour walk at his pace. I wonder if that's where he's heading.

There's also a boat club and harbour way down the trail. Maybe he belongs to someone down there. His stride doesn't change, empty or full bag, straps over his shoulders. Yes, I really must keep an eye out later this morning, sometime between boiling the kettle for tea and a biscuit or two midday and thinking about what to make for supper before the news comes on at 5:30.

**************************

## **Ben**

Man, there's nothin' like *Satisfaction (I can't get no)* for a nice pace along this trail. A stroll around the garden at 7:00 this morning told me I could shed a few layers today. My gear is good, light-weight and protective all winter long but it's fun to feel less is needed against the day's elements. The wind is still out of the north, so it won't be balmy. It's so rarely balmy. No Caribbean or West Coast breezes here, but I'm not complaining. I don't need to sweat twenty-four hours a day to be content. I love the peace, quiet, and friendly solitude. People say "Hi" or "Good Morning" as they pass and, for the most part, just let me be me. No questions asked, no life story necessary.

As I leave the confines of the community, I can't help but smile at the line of washing frozen stiff from the overnight air. I give silent thanks for my wood-stove with its indoor heat for drying my laundry.

It's only October, but last week, some of the boulders just offshore were topped with crystallized sea-blue shower caps. The surf had frozen upon touching the cold stone. It was both beautiful and chilling to see. During my walk, after a night of really high winds at high tide, even the beach rocks on the trail were all iced together. I slowed my pace a little then and kept an eye to underfoot so as not to crash to what would be a very hard and uncomfortable landing.

My boots have sturdy soles, and I walk this rail-bed trail so often that I could likely stay on dry land with my eyes closed. However, the light and shadows on the far shore in the north, the islands ahead of me with their craggy sheer cliffs above breaking surf, and the birds high in the sky or bobbing nearby on the waves make closed eyes impossible.

One day last summer, as I headed east, I saw two eagles atop a nearby pole. They majestically sat to watch me stroll past. When I paused to admire them, the male took flight, and when I was farther along the trail, I saw him shepherding a young offspring back to their original perch. A family of three with one yet to grow into its magnificence.

At other times, going in either direction, I swear tiny little sparrows flit just a few feet ahead of me all the way. They dart from salt-stunted alders to cone-laden pines, moving just before I draw parallel. Their voices chatter to each other, saying who knows what above my earbud music. Definitely, for me, no walking with downcast eyes.

Several times, as I head eastward in the mornings, I come across a woman walking with a dog. Both of them seem to be really enjoying their progress. She pauses while the dog stops to sniff another new or maybe familiar smell in the wild grasses alongside the stone path. There are a couple of houses on the landward edge of the walk. They have dogs in their gardens, and the barks begin from those on tethers or behind fences.

The woman and dog stop briefly as I pass and watch the dogs greet each other from a distance with tails wagging while we humans say a brief "Good Morning." She has a pleasant voice that affirms her morning is actually good, but it brooks no stopping to chat. That's fine with me. I think, perhaps, we both enjoy being in our own space.

Sometimes, I see her in the distance, coming from the opposite direction. Her walk varies, unlike mine. If there is another walker coming near them, the woman shortens the leash so the dog and she are close. On one occasion, a small terrier took exception to the big dog. The woman walking the little dog did nothing to control it. Were the Husky ill-tempered, that nasty little one could have barked its last hurrah.

The woman stood to one side on the grassy verge, and her big dog sat as told. With a look of curious disdain, I chuckled that even from a sitting position, the dog could be thinking, 'You've got to be kidding me.' After the troublesome pair had passed by, I noticed her hand deliver a rewarding treat to a large but gentle mouth. In a fraction of time, an unexpected encounter was settled so as not to ruin a good walk for anyone, human or canine.

This morning, still a few paces ahead of me, they turn south onto the boardwalk at the duck pond. I drop some crumbs for the little sparrows to find in the grass before I cross the longer bridge and continue on my way. *Rhythm of the Saints* keeping pace with both me and the waves. My destination lies ahead.

****************************

# Chapter Two

## Sara

Mother Nature trumped my wishful thinking this November morning; not an unusual occurrence, really. The bright sun streaking through the bare branches outside the window looks mild. Last night's forecaster predicted a warm-up for the next day or two, and my memory has already discarded the bitter -20 C. windchill of that sudden change a few days ago. On an island surrounded by the North Atlantic, weather is neither temperate nor predictable. No matter growing up here, it never ceases to catch me off guard as I prepare clothing to head out the door for our morning walk.

The wind off the water yesterday kept other walkers tucked into warmer places. Along the boardwalk, even the ducks were huddled on a small patch of grass beside their ice-covered pond. With her big black nose poked through the low palings, my companion stopped repeatedly to see if any of the mallards wanted to play. With no takers and oblivious to the sting of the wind, she reluctantly moved after my gentle tug on her leash.

While still eager to jump towards the ducks, provoking them into flight, she is calmer these days as a maturing but still happy and boisterous seventy-pound toddler. My saying "good job" as my hand comes out of a mitt, reaches into a pocket, and finds a reward is having the desired effect. Being both food-keen and intelligent come together well in this dog.

We changed our route today and walked alongside the busy road of traffic heading to the highway. My theory that careful exposure to the noise and scary wheels is worth doing to create some street-wise sense for my pup rescued from a tiny community in Labrador.

There's a sharp bend in the road at the intersection. Even with an obvious crosswalk and four-way traffic lights, motorists focus on other vehicles, not on a pedestrian. Each driver must be so busy getting from one place to another, one task to the next, that they've no time or inclination to slow the two tons of metal protecting them.

To cross onto the centre island, I'm always hesitant until I'm sure no one is careening around the corner with nothing but the nearby coffee shop foremost in mind. Some drivers simply don't stop, so my young pup is close beside me and never the first to step off the curb. Her focus remains on the tall grasses on the verge of the quiet road beyond three lanes of cars. One more shoulder check behind me when the Walk sign flashes, then I sigh, and we head towards the shore.

Good smells await that big nose of hers, and motorized life is no longer beside us. There's nothing but the screeching of gulls, the rumble of rocks pulled by the surf, my footsteps on the gravel trail, and wide open space ahead. Sometimes, I walk off the path with her in an effort to lessen the noise of my boots. They can be jarringly loud within the natural peace and quiet.

At the final curve just before the trail, I can't help but notice the difference between homes. On this lane, the three small bungalows look cozy and tucked into the land. They belong here. Weathered but cared-for clapboard in gentle shades, off-white, pale yellow, and light grey with a daring deep blue or Kelly green door. Look west, and a dozen tall, brightly coloured, carefully manicured houses are clustered with narrow lawns stretching down to the edge of the pond. Off to the east, yet another even newer community of modern designs with attached garages, multiple roof angles, sidewalks edging the lawns and scarcely a tree in sight. In twenty years, those newly planted saplings will grow to break the sanitized view.

The contrast between neighbourhoods is striking, and my heart belongs to the tiny, simple lines of the older homes. Just one solid roof with a chimney above a kitchen, symmetrical windows small and efficient except for a wider one allowing light into a main room. I suspect these homes are original to this lane. Maybe farmer's homes that, despite their size, raised large families within. Adults who worked and children who learned how to work the pasture land surrounding them. In season, they'd be out on the bay in small boats catching fish to tide the family through a long winter.

Nowadays, during the food fishery, there are white dots far out on the open water. The catch is government controlled, for each boat just fifteen fish per day. Brightly coloured buoys closer to shore mark submerged lobster pots. One or two waterproof gloved hands reach over the gunwales as I watch the fishers haul the lines, tip out lobster, re-bait the trap and let it go back over the side into the waves.

When I look away from the water, back up the lane, I notice how a couple of the homes face the pond, close to the road for easy access year-round. They have lacy curtains that twitch in curiosity as we walk past. My favourite house though, if it were mine to choose, is the pale yellow square with no curtains at the front window. Although well back, maybe 300 feet from the actual shore, it looks to the sea. There are wild roses along the front. They form a prickly hedge close by the lane and, to one side of the home, two substantial beds have been dug out of the earth, waiting patiently for something to be planted.

An old-fashioned clothesline strung between two big maples stretches across the back of the garden with a sturdy pronged pole just visible, no doubt ready to lift wet clothes up off the ground and into the wind. These older houses are all on lower land than the trail itself and would have had a good view of the train when it carried people and goods around the curve of the bay. No more trains these days, but the mountain tops of the north shore, on a clear day, might be visible from an uncluttered window.

When my companion stops to smell yet another interesting item in the grass beside the pond, my eye occasionally catches a glimpse of a plain wooden kitchen chair off to one side in a pool of indoor sunlight. I don't make a habit of looking into people's homes, but as much as I love our walks each day and have a cozy home of my own awaiting our return, to sit in that spot with a cup of tea surveying this corner of the world holds much appeal. Perhaps, on a warm summer's morning, someone will be outside as we pass and offer a wave or a "Good morning, grand day on clothes."

Meanwhile, reigning in my imagination, we carry on, climb the slight rise to the trail, and turn west over the bridge instead of homeward to the east today. We'll add an extra half hour to our round-trip before finding ourselves at the familiar duck pond again. This path is higher above the rolling waves, and there will be new scents to discover while I debate with myself whether to walk as far as the big grey house, my turn-around marker.

***********************************

## Carrie

I've little energy for anything much this morning. The wind last night was wicked. It rattled windows and, I swear, shook the walls. Sleep just didn't last long at all. I found myself wondering if the garbage can would be out in the pond by sunrise. Did I close the windows on my car? Something I forget to do unless it's raining when I get home. My little car is eleven years old now and has her share of rust, but she gets me up and down the shore. Mind you, I don't go very far. To a card game or two at the parish hall or to a tea at the Legion maybe once a month. Even then, Maisie usually calls to offer a ride. She knows I hate all that traffic once I get up to those lights.

Sometime around midnight, I got out of bed, walked to the kitchen and looked out the window at the car parked in front of my place. Mind you, I couldn't really see if the windows were closed or not, and I wasn't about to go out there in that wind anyway. So, why did that keep me awake? Tucked back under the quilts made so long ago by my mother, my body said sleep, but I couldn't.

I tossed and turned til the bed was as rumpled as the wind-battered trees. Now that I think about it, though, I must have slept some because I actually came awake to the quiet of no more shuddering windows. The covers by my feet were all pulled askew, and the top quilt bunched to one side, not my usual hardly-disturbed bedclothes. I really must have been fidgety and my thinking is a bit rattled as well.

The sky this morning is a surly grey even though the wind's died down. No clothes going on the line today, says I. I'll wash the floors again, then make up a grocery list when I settle in for tea to see if my favourite walkers happen by. No, wait, a change of plan. I'd better go look at the roof. That wind might have taken off a shingle or two. Hope not. Now, where did I put my boots?

The grass is water-logged as I walk far enough into the garden to spot any suspicious shingles. I've checked on this roof for the last thirty years and, touch wood, have yet to see anything missing. Lord knows some of the storms off the bay have tried their best. The garbage can is tipped over but still close by the back step. A few willow branches, the thinner ones, are scattered on the grass, but nothing much else seems damaged. One glance beyond the corner of the roof and out over the bay tells me that a darkening sky isn't finished with us yet. There's barely a whisper in the air as I lift one boot after the other through the soggy grass and step up to my back door. It's all very weird, this calm to the air.

Maybe I won't bother with the floors. Even my cautious feet are bringing mud over the sill. Boil the kettle and sit down. A shopping list needs doing before I forget what I remembered. Things are getting low in the back pantry. I'm never out of tea bags, but it feels like I'm about to drain the last of the tin milk. That will never do. So, number one – milk for tea.

The cheapest place to get that is just up the lane at what I call the everything-you-need-except-shoes store. From towels to socks, candy to pet food, paperbacks, frozen meals, storm chips, baking supplies, picture frames, yarn and tins of milk, that's the beauty of the place. And they give a discount for seniors if you remind them.

Goodness, pet food. I haven't watched for the lady and her dog this morning. Checking the roof and squelching around the garden have really distracted me. I wonder if she chose not to tempt the high surf after last night's storm. The waves must have been fierce. The trail might be damaged. Sometimes, I'm told, whole sections of the path can be under newly thrown rocks. If the surge is still strong, it's not wise to be up there anyway.

Keeping my feet on solid ground until the time I'm put under the ground, that's me. Perhaps she feels the same way today. I'll just boil the kettle fresh, have a sit, drink my tea, do my list, and see what that heavy sky decides to do. If not today, maybe tomorrow, I'll do the floors and keep my eye on the lane.

*************************************

## Margaret

Thank heavens, my place is sheltered by two other homes. Last night's wind was insane. The weather person on television warned of gusts up to 100 km per hour, but I shrugged her off. Predictable is not how our weather works. I have to admit this morning, she was right. I woke a few times to remind myself that a tornado or hurricane, like those I see so often on the mainland news, isn't likely. Besides, my little house survived a couple of surprise tropical storms a few years back. Being low to the ground, much like myself, can be useful.

I noticed this morning that everyone around was out checking their roof and making sure neighbours were okay. I parted the curtains on my front window to wave my survival to Max next door. He righted my garbage bin with an all's well head nod. A few steps, and he'll be in another yard. No flies on Max when it comes to checking on everyone. It's not that I mind being checked on. Of course not. That also means any missing roof bits will be noted and probably repaired with an easy "Do that for you tomorrow, Margaret." If I drop dead some morning, I'll be found before long. I hope to god that doesn't happen before I've put my day clothes on, mind you.

So, what will I do today now that the storm's passed? I thought a load of laundry might be needed but I don't much care for those angry grey clouds to the north. If it can't happen on the same day, I'm not one for hanging clothes and then leaving them until they eventually dry. I'd sooner do a hand-wash and string it on the line above the wood stove. If anyone drops in, they'll see socks, shirts, and maybe a tea towel, but nothing too personal. Those will be draped on my old wooden clothes-horse. It's dried many a pair of drawers and a bra or two in the spare room, well out of anyone's view but my own.

I see, up the road, that more folks are taking stock of any wind damage. The big new houses, to my mind, don't stand up to the storms the same. Siding hangs off one or two, fancy fences look wobbly, early Christmas lights hang off gutters, and wreaths on front doors are bedraggled. I figure those flowery decorations might work well someplace else but even fake flowers don't much care for our weather.

The big box stores that sell them must be rubbing their hands together if they had hands. You know what I mean. Another bunch of House and Garden shoppers will be on their way for replacements. I'll cut pussy-willows or flowers from my yard because there's always a vase in my cupboard somewhere. That will give them a cozy home on my kitchen table. So much more sensible to my mind.

Here he comes, the chappy with the ponytail. Didn't I miss, again, where he starts from. Never on my toes enough to catch which of the lanes he leaves before he hits the main road. For heaven's sake, Aunt Maude would tut, I'm falling down on the community protection job. It's not like there are tons of roads branching off that I can see from my place. There are only three up along and a couple down where the river bends under the little bridge. He always comes from up the way, so unless it's beyond the hill at the store, I really ought to catch sight of him stepping onto the road.

Ah, well, he's fine. Doing his own thing, in his own way, with a backpack, boots and walking gear. It's about 9 o'clock now. That's about the usual time, so last night's wind didn't change his schedule much. He looks so relaxed and comfortable as he strides along. He'll give the nod to return a wave from someone, a slight smile on his craggy face, friendly enough but doesn't lend itself to more than "good morning" as one foot moves ahead of the other. I sit back a bit as he comes near and then passes by my window. My place is back from the lane, but I wouldn't want him to feel I'm overly interested.

If I peer out a bit more once he's gone by, I can just see him cross the bridge down by the last few houses before the shoreline trail. Once there, my walker is on his own. Even if I manage to catch sight of him on his return a few hours from now, his destination in both directions is lost to me. Empty or full backpack, no clues. His pace doesn't change much, whether going east, coming west, going uphill, moving down, crossing the bridge, or stepping onto the trail. Unlike some people I see around here, he's very fit, tall, slim and straight-backed in an easy sort of way. I'd put him around mid-life, forties or so, but that's mostly because I can see that his ponytail is a telling salt 'n pepper grey.

It's just as well that I'm not one for letting my imagination run wild. I like good solid details. No point in making wild guesses and then having poor information. However, I wouldn't mind knowing just a little more about him. Who does he belong to? Where's he headed? He walks most days in all sorts of weather. Doesn't seem to both him. Never see him in a car. I'm not about to ask anyone. That's not me. Hey, Aunt Maude, it's your rocking chair after all.

************************************

## **Ben**

I'm wondering how the trail will be this morning. Last night's windstorm was a good one. Not unaccustomed to hearing sounds outside my windows after years in warm climates, I slept well. A quick look around the open land in front of my place shows no damage. There's a cardboard box that's come from somewhere and a few branches off one of the trees. The big line of sturdy evergreens along the back acts as a great windbreak, so all's as it usually is to the east.

My little house, low to the ground and with a solid frame, barely reacted to Nature's onslaught through the night, but I have learned not to gloat. Instead, my thanks are silently offered that my initial inclination won out over more common renovation advice. I suspect some of the more rapid construction techniques in new neighbourhoods took a beating.

A short chat with my daily port of call down east says they made out fine. The wind gusts had been anticipated, so things had been tied down and brought well above the high-tide line, if not inside the breakwater itself. I'll head out as soon as I've had a coffee and tried my new molasses brown bread slathered with homemade raspberry jam topped with a slice of good strong cheddar. The bread and jam are courtesy of a friend who loves pushing me out of my comfort zone with new recipes and his preference for garden-grown preserves. Neither was common in my life before I came here, so it's fun to learn from him and share the anticipation of an often surprising end result.

The barometer on my wall says things are on their way back up after the wind and rain. That low pressure has gone out to sea and is heading towards Greenland. I hope it swerves away from hammering England. They've had a really tough couple of weeks with flooding in the south. Waterways through several villages have swelled to overrun fields and crack apart ancient floodgates. Not the kind of weather most common in the Midlands where man-made reservoirs are needed to provide open water for sailing.

I'm thinking of a lighter layer of gear this morning. The temperature isn't bad, hovering just above zero Celsius. It will keep me warm enough to be comfortable but not burdened so much as to break a sweat after an hour's walking. My days of living in a constant state of dripping perspiration from morning through night are done. Gone are those times when even a brief good morning lift of the arm brought yet another burst of clamminess to an ever-present sheen.

Living with next to no clothing, bare arms, legs, head and feet was glorious for the first few years. It quickly became an assumption. Showering at the end of the day, once the water in the above-ground hose had warmed but wasn't too hot, became par for the course. Checking for land crabs and centipedes lurking in the shower stall was also rapidly habitual.

Each evening, with a drink in hand, I'd wade into a green-blue ocean just cool enough to bring relief from the late-day sun as it sank rapidly below the horizon at 6:00 o'clock. Each day's end brought the promise of a consistent 25 degrees by breakfast time and 30 or 31 degrees for the rest of the day.

No one ever greeted me with a comment on the weather, so unlike here, where it's the first topic mentioned. The weather off the Pacific was one thing that never changed much, barring an approaching hurricane offshore. The sudden short spasm of warm afternoon rain would catch newcomers and tourists. We who lived there knew it was coming about 4 o'clock every day. In its passing, the steam would rise around the potholes in the old tarmac roads, and you'd know not to step out of your footwear. Drying off a bare foot on the pavement was one-trial learning at its finest.

During a shower, it was common to call a warning to visitors ignorant of the manchineel tree. Those huge trees with thick branches spread wide look like a massive umbrella, a quick doorway out of a shower. The unwary would run to take shelter under the drooping foliage just as they might do under a big maple in their home climate. Luckily, those I warned were never badly burned by the poisonous sap that drips when a leaf is touched.

The tree also taunted shell collectors who would spot classic sand dollars in the sand at its base. Those shells and anything living inside them were well protected from marauding seabirds until high tide could wash them safely back to sea. Intricate white spheres stayed just so because even birds knew to give the manchineel a wide birth.

My mind really has gone off on a tangent. Back to a bygone life while I look at the temp outside and decide on today's walking clothes in this very unpredictable climate. I've no regrets. It just takes some intricate planning before heading out the door. More accurately, going out the door from one hour to the next. My friend laughs that you can look out your front door, see one type of weather, then turn and look out the back door and see something quite different.

It's easily the case that the weather can change in less than an hour's walk. Some days, the winds shift from north to northeast, come right off the water and chill to the bone. That's why I don't want to create sweat under layers of clothes. I feel warm, remove a hat or gloves, and suddenly I'm freezing. No one from my former days could possibly wrap their minds around our weather up here on a very much larger island 5000 miles away surrounded by the North Atlantic.

Okay, check my list and I'm ready to go. Earbuds, music on the phone app, backpack, hair tied safe from the sea breeze, appropriate clothing and footwear, a few crumbs for the sparrows if they're around today, and hit the lane down to the main road and onward. I've no real time limit, so I might stop and watch the seabirds ride the waves. I try to keep different birds in my mind's eye. No pelicans, flying fish or lumbering albatross in sight here, but there's often something for me to identify when I get back home. Whether it's flying, swimming or walking, I enjoy coming across anything that shares the shoreline trail.

*******************************

# Chapter Three

## Sara

Literally and quite remarkably for November, is the lack of any wind this morning. We take the traffic route to the shore and, for the first half-hour along the trail, there isn't even enough breeze to ripple the ocean beside us. The surface could neatly reflect clouds above, but the sky is clear. Close to shore, just below us, I can see individual rocks through the calm water.

Pup slides with canine glee along the tops of the snow until some small hollow catches her attention. I wait while scrabbling paws dig a larger hole until her complete face, from nose to ears, is happily jammed into the soft white powder underneath. Her back arches into the air, tail-tip swaying as she folds herself into the perfect Downward Dog of a yoga practitioner. The tail wag excepted, of course.

Moving on, we meet a burly man walking a very small dog who sports a tiny red sweater. We both shorten dog leads and my "I agree" answers his "Nice, there's no wind." He's another walker pleasantly surprised by the still air. Greetings are barked from the usual fenced gardens as we head east and he turns to the west.

To our left, groups of black and white seabirds float on the calm ocean. These are more slender creatures than the ducks on the pond. Striking black wings, each with a single large white patch, sit below a black neck, showing a choker both wide and white. Their heads are small with a very visible sprig of feathers that stick out high enough for me to see through them to the countryside beyond. Even if we don't pause to admire them, they either see or sense us and immediately disappear underwater, resurfacing several meters away. This morning, I see four different groups, half a dozen to two dozen in each, at different points in our walk.

Just as we stepped beyond a more sheltered section of the trail where gnarled evergreens block the ocean view, the calm air is gone. We are next to open water again and the wind, not present half an hour ago, is strong on my face. The tide is still making its way towards shore, so the lone area of sandy beach exposes possible treasures. Turning sideways to the wind, we sink into the bare sand. Curious about the water rolling towards us, pup cautiously wades ankle deep before returning to sniff for any good discoveries on our way back up to the trail just minutes later.

While she doesn't find anything of great interest, I find three beautiful sea urchin shells. Each a different colour than the other and, surprisingly, all unbroken. They have avoided being ravaged by hungry sea gulls, saved from being fished out of the shoals, carried high above the rocks, then dropped to smash open for the morsel hidden inside.

My treasures are all slightly different. One is a deep green, another dark burgundy and the third a soft sage. Each has dots and pattern lines that fan from the top centre hole down to the edges that curve into themselves on the underside of the shell. I smile because, beyond the obvious advantage of my jacket pocket holding a supply of bags to clean up dog deposits, those bags also serve as a ready receptacle for more pleasant fragile contents.

My face is cold and the headland that would take us off the groomed path seems too far for today so I turn, glad to have the wind at my back from here to home. It will still be an hour-long walk, so not without some merit. As I switch the leash from one hand to the other, I glance back at the headland. Out of the side trail, he steps. Clad from head to toe in his customary black gear, the other walker. His long stride would bring him into our space fairly soon as he, too, is walking from east to west. I cross the bridge where the sea tide meets the duck pond and choose to retrace our route avoiding the cluster of ducks waddling down the middle of the quiet road.

My instinctual glance for traffic shows that the walker has paused to lean on the bridge rail and look out to sea. My companion isn't keen on having someone behind us as we walk and, making use of the long leash, she keeps twisting herself around to check. A few paces on, when she next takes a look and I turn slightly to dissuade her, I can see out of the corner of my eye that the man has also paused, possibly tying a loose lace, one foot propped up on a boulder.

Not wanting to disrupt his walk or mine and to allay my pup's distrust, I pick up our pace. Soon enough, we turn into the nearest neighbourhood and continue on our way, one of us smelling the air for any hint of last week's squirrel.

I can't help thinking about what I've just seen. At this time of the morning, when I do see that other walker on the trail, he's coming from the west, his backpack hanging slack. From the east, later in the day, the backpack looks full. Just now, with his backpack limp against his back at 9:30 on a Sunday morning, his presence surprised me. He was walking not *from* but *to* the west.

A Saturday night spent away from home, perhaps. Not that I'm truly all that interested. It's just curious how this walking trail brings habits to mind and it's of note when something changes from ordinary to extraordinary.

****************************************

## Carrie

As if that windstorm wasn't enough to mess up my routine. My fingers darn near froze as I hung clothes on the line early this morning. The wind is strong enough to shake the water out of the laundry, but it doesn't feel cold enough to turn it into chunks of coloured ice. My fingertips, though, will be holding my mug carefully until they thaw out. Tea and toast, old hands warmed up, then I'll go up the lane to the store. I found a spare can of milk hidden behind the tomato soup last night, so no need for panic this morning.

One of my neighbours was keen to tell me about her new car when she passed by a little earlier. I was hanging towels, so I didn't really pay her a lot of attention. She did go on about how she is able to start her car from her phone. That threw me, I must admit. What and why would you do that? Surely, you'd be dressed in no time, go out, and turn the key to start the car. Something about warming up the seats and getting the windows clear of ice, she said. There's not enough ice to worry about that today and my hands will have thawed out enough to use the scraper if I need it by the time I decide to go.

I like Maisie, but she's the one who laughed at me when I moaned about power windows a few years back. I still don't see how important it was to get rid of just rolling the window down using a handle. I suppose it's like when my father, god rest his soul, was told to stop sticking his hand out the driver's side to signal a turn he was about to make. As a teenager, I probably laughed at him when he didn't just flick the stick on the side of the steering wheel and then flick it again if it kept ticking after he'd gone round the bend. Just another of those so-called improvements that get more vehicles and lazy drivers on the roads, in my opinion.

Anyhow, my car gets me from here to there whenever I want it to, and what more do I need. Nothing is the answer. The only time I'm irritated about a car thing is when I've got to remember to have the guys at the local garage take off the studded tires. It's all well and good if our weather is predictable and the roads aren't going to get slippery again. May month does not, around here, guarantee that.

It matters not what the government rule makers think, I prefer to change my own tires like my father taught me years and years ago but I can't. They're too heavy for one thing and, for another, the guys use some sort of high-powered wrench to tighten the nuts. No way I can loosen them, not even if I get a flat. At least there's a government discount for seniors for the license and change of tires twice a year. That's something.

Maisie said she doesn't have a spare tire, on her car, I mean. She's got something like the tire patching kit we used to have for our bikes when we were kids. If that doesn't work for her, she has to touch a button that calls someone who will ask her a bunch of questions then call someone else who will send help from the nearest station when they locate it. Not great if you drive across this island and are a couple of hundred miles from the nearest town that has a garage. To my mind, not nearly as efficient as being able to change one's own tire, pitch the busted one into the trunk, and carry on to wherever you're going.

Okay, give it up, girl. Time to move on because my list is on the table in front of me, my keys are in my pocket, my phone, whether I need it or not, is in my purse. I'm good to go and, what's even better is Maisie went on without me. She won't see me duck in the back way to the parking lot. No need to bother with those crazy traffic lights at the intersection. I sure hope her fancy new car doesn't get dinged by some coffee-starved fool running the red light. Out the door I go and give a pat of trust and encouragement to my little car before we drive the two minutes up the lane.

The lot is kind of full this morning. Sundays, after church, bring everyone out. That's fine because I'll park on one end away from the crowd and once they remember I'm a senior, someone will help me bring my stuff to the car. They're good that way and I always have a Toonie tucked away to say thank you. I don't have a lot to pick up. The extras for Christmas baking are long gone and won't be needed until the next bake sale or birthday comes around.

Basics like milk go into the basket as well as oranges (always good at this store), flour, a tin of tuna and maybe one of baked beans (although my mother would roll her eyes because, to her, only home-made were good enough), butter (which is really margarine), cheese (plain old rat-trap), some biscuits as a treat, and half a dozen eggs. I just passed by the toilet paper (bathroom tissue to Maisie) and don't have it on my list but I'll get it anyway. Not something to run out of when you most want it. There's an old joke about catalogues and the outhouse.

The cashier is very young. Mind you, most everyone is very young to me.

"Nice to see you. Did you find everything you were looking for"? I nod and say all that's on my list, plus one more, thanks.

"Need a hand getting it to your car"? I appreciate that, thanks. "You got your 10% seniors discount, by the way".

A nice young man, must be in High School, carried all the bags to my car and smiled when I slipped the coin into his hand. Hope it buys him something. Now, out the back way again, down the lane, and take my own sweet time lugging things into my little house.

****************************************

## Margaret

I didn't see him at all this morning. Mind you, I was busy making tea buns for the church bake sale after I came home from the early service. Not so many folks attend that any more, the service, I mean. They go to the bake sales. I miss seeing quite a few old friends in the pews. We'd always have a chat on our walk to the gate after the service ended.

This minister is fairly young, maybe in his fifties. Youngish to me. He's soft-spoken and gives the scriptures a today sort of meaning. I don't doubt my upbringing or even attending church but I think my outlook has mellowed a bit over the years. I still hold my belief and feel a connection to my grandparents when I visit their graves in the old cemetery, but no longer do I think of them as actually being underground. It's been a very long time since that soil was turned. Although, there's a comfortable peace in that quiet place, especially as the season turns from the harsh winter to the beginning of Spring and I see new life in the grass that grows around the headstones.

Today's air is crisp and cool enough for my heavier coat, gloves and hat. A wool hat that will be removed once inside the church would never have happened when I was a child. Easter week brought a new hat for me and my younger sister. My grandmother didn't help matters when she'd provide a purple hat with frilly edges for a red-headed eight-year-old tomboy like me. I hated to see myself in that hat and, to this day, I am not a fan of wearing hats for decorative purposes or to satisfy some ancient rule made, I'm sure, by men.

Just before 9:00, I make my way up the hill to the big white building on the crest. A smattering of cars are already parked in the lot. I cross it and go up the dozen wide, well-worn steps to the heavy wooden double doors. Ralph, one of the vergers, holds the door ajar for me with his big hand comfortably around the fancy metal handle. Ralph's been around for a long while. The story is that he once thought of getting ordained. He even went away to Divinity School, but something changed. He returned home and chose to remain involved as a lay person. His is a pleasant face and welcoming presence whenever I do get to a service.

I'm home again before 10 o'clock and eager to make those tea buns. I make half the batch with raisins and the rest plain. I'll put a mix of buns into freezer bags so that whenever my tongue is twisted for one, it will be handy for a sit-down and cup of tea. Again, I glance up and down our lane, but there's no walker in sight. I cannot imagine him as a church-goer. He strikes me as too much of a free spirit for something so controlling. I think it's his pony-tail and loping gait that leads me to imagine him living in a warm climate with beaches, huge waves and surfer dudes. If that's true, what on earth is the man doing here?

Maybe he's more like my father was. Just to aggravate my mother and get a rise out of her when Mother was readying to take us to church, he would heave a well-rehearsed sigh that she was meant to hear. This was quickly followed by a pronouncement that being outside in Nature was his religion.

I can hear him now, "The most religion I feel happens as I stand waist-high in a river and cast a line to float a hand-made fly as temptation to a hungry salmon."

Without fail, Father's words brought a rise out of mother more often, certainly, than the fly brought forth a salmon.

"Ye gods and little fishes," she'd mutter.

I never have understood what she meant. I began to wonder, in my adulthood, just how much of my mother's reaction was to convince herself, as much as us children, that we needed to go to church.

All these thoughts ramble through my mind as I remember Sundays with church, a midday meal and either a family stroll around town or, with apologies to my long-dead grandmother, a board game to while away the afternoon. If there was unfinished homework that had to be done before we all ate a light meal in the early evening. We'd then watch something on one of the two black-and-white television channels or simply read our favourite book until we went off to bed.

When we were on holiday in the city, Sunday afternoons often included an afternoon of tea, unusual drinks, small cakes, and having to be on one's best behaviour. These happened in a big drawing room in an old four-storey house owned by friends of my parents. Gatherings that were not really meant for the pleasure of young children, my sister and I went for the cake, fizzy drinks, and adult watching. To us, they were an odd mix of people, the combination of which changed from one time to the next.

Some of their mannerisms were perfect for the mimicry that we and Father would perform as we drove to wherever home was during that holiday. I remember Mother trying to admonish us but her stifled laughter always added fuel to our fire. We laughed so hard that by the time we neared home, our legs were tightly crossed and we pleaded with Father not to drive past any running water.

Oh my, haven't I gone wandering down multiple memory lanes while those tea buns fill my kitchen with sweet smells. In the comfort of my little home, that seems to be happening a bit more of late, the wandering not the baking. Good times are good to remember, I say. As I bend down to look through the glass window of the oven, I'm pretty sure that one or more of those buns won't make it into freezer bags today. No big Sunday lunch when it's just me. Hot off the pan, they really are calling out for a chunk of cheese and a freshly-boiled kettle. My chair beckons and my window awaits.

****************************************

## Ben

I woke to the sound of motors revving and a jumble of voices. Listening more intently, it was obvious that preparations were underway to get out on the water. I'd slept well as the waves gently rocked the boat and was more than ready to head back home on a clear but cool Sunday morning.

Tidying up the galley, checking the moorings and not wishing to wake anyone else, I gather my things together. Books, phone and charger, gloves and a small bag of stale hamburger buns get tucked into my backpack. I climb onto the dock and, with a nod to the face appearing in a window alongside, I set off for home. It has been a welcome change of scene but spending more than a day without walking quickly wears thin.

I join the trail just beyond the mouth of the harbour where the gulls are already keen to follow the wake of boats heading out the bay. Bits of bait or, if they're really in luck, fish guts might hit the waves. Their competing cries break into an otherwise peaceful morning. The sun is doing its best to make its way through the grey clouds and, if it holds any warmth, I'll not really need my balaclava or a spare layer. However, it's often a wait-and-see game from one end of the walk to the other.

Within an hour, I'm on the eastern headland with half an eye on the calm ocean and the other on the lookout for ancient tree roots unearthed after last week's high surf. I know that the ground underneath the turf can sometimes be eaten away by a particularly strong current, so that keeps me at least a few inches away from the ragged edge. Roots are easy to negotiate, a sudden sink-hole hidden by scrub and grasses, not so.

Walking this path off the groomed trail makes me feel that I'm the only human around. The houses are a good hundred feet on the other side of the trees. There's nothing but me and the shoreline next to the rolling waves as I breathe in the clear air.

The beach on the ocean side of the duck pond bridge is uncovered today. I imagine someone is bound to feel the urge to look for treasures washed ashore or dropped from the sky by the birds.

As I approach, a group of black and white seabirds float and then dive under the salt water. They disappear instantly and pop to the surface as if pulled by some invisible thread. This morning, the sharp contrast of their plumage is even more striking as they swim next to their dull brown-grey companions. Their heads are smooth without tufts of spiky feathers, although their body shape and size are the same. Males and females of the same species, I assume.

Across the road, the trail starts again, but my boot feels loose. Conveniently, there is a machine-placed row of half a dozen large boulders, one of which is at a perfect angle for tightening my lace. It's also the spot where I like to scatter breadcrumbs for the tiny birds that frequent the trees lining this section of trail. My fingers find the bag of old bread in my pack and it crumbles as I pull it out.

My lace tied, I straighten up and notice the Husky up ahead. Her walker has paused to let the dog burrow into what's left of a snowdrift at one edge of the path.

It's amusing to watch. She pushes her snout deeper into the soft snow beneath the sea-salt crust, then folds herself close to the ground until nothing but her ears are visible above the snow. Her shoulders and chest curve down, but her rump and tail arch skyward. It's all done with obvious canine glee and, from her body language, the walker must be laughing as she stands with the leash fully extended.

We're all heading west, so I wait for a few minutes to let them create some distance. I prefer not to overtake on this part of the trail. It seems an invasion of space, both theirs and mine. What's a couple of minutes after an hour's walk and a couple more hours to go before I reach home.

Once again this Fall, I've noticed Christmas decorations hung here and there along the middle section. Most of the trail from here is bordered on one or both sides by trees and an occasional patch of headland. Since Christmas last year, my eye has been caught by a silver ball, a red ribbon, a sparkly star draped onto the sprig of an evergreen bough.

Someone puts them there and no one takes them away. I smile to think that people are wishing Mother Nature a merry holiday season or simply adding a tiny bit of colour to balance out the sameness of sky, snow and path. If my mind isn't off on some tangent, I find myself having a quick look as I walk between these trees. Last week, I counted eight ornaments in a twenty-minute stretch between the duck pond in the east and the next pond further west.

At that second bridge, the trail rises higher above the ocean and, for a few minutes, runs alongside large new homes. Those homes have fabulous wide-open vistas, but for eight months of the year when the prevailing wind comes off that water, their heating costs must be something else. I appreciate the appeal, the sounds of the surf coming through open windows in June or July, and the wide open sky to the hills with communities on the far shore. However, I'll continue to enjoy the cozy protection of the trees surrounding my place. I can soak in all else as my feet carry me along this shore every day.

I've no need to keep track of time. The familiar tunes in my ears, punctuated by the sounds around me, provide all the company I want right now. Three hours pass quickly and, almost always, I'm a bit surprised that one foot following the other puts me exactly where I want to be.

******************************

# Chapter Four

## Sara

I delay our morning ritual today so that we can combine our walk with a stop at the community mailbox. Those red metal doors will remain locked and items won't be placed inside until sometime after 9:30. Even later than that, if there's been high winds in the Gulf or through the Wreckhouse on the west coast just beyond where the ferries dock. We know, about nine hundred kilometres east, that those high winds stop the trucks bringing mail from the mainland to all of us along the way.

Between 6:00 and 6:30 each morning, seven days a week, my dog wakes to greet the day. No matter how late she's been up the previous night, that's her routine. Out the door for maybe fifteen or twenty minutes to check all is well in the garden, then back inside for a teeth-cleaning treat. She used to jump onto the couch with that bone in her mouth but, in the past few weeks, before I can climb back into my warm bed, she's bounded onto it and claimed her own space. A twin bed occupied by seventy pounds of Husky leaves very little room for much else, her human companion and the owner of the bed included.

Today, when I finished breakfast but didn't begin to put on walking boots, she lifted her head out of her food bowl to take a long look at me. Her expectation was obvious and in response to her puzzled expression, I found myself voicing my rationale but being very careful to avoid using the magic word "walk." She settled for another round out in the garden, sniffing for any wayward cats while I put a load of clothes into the washer, checked my emails and social media, and started a fresh cryptic crossword. All fills in the necessary time until I'm ready to take us down the road away from houses to the trail with a mailbox stop on the way back home.

Our pace heading past the elementary school is much more efficient than the progress of the parents and children sitting in a long line of cars. That I don't have to wait in traffic to get children to school and probably then get myself to work feels very nice as the trail comes into view. When the big buses negotiate the sharp turn out of the school lot, we move further off the road into a driveway because neither dog nor I wish to make anyone's life more stressful. If I happen to look up into the cab, a couple of the drivers will smile their acknowledgement.

Beyond the school, we reach the shelter of the pines and I feel just the slightest hint of warmth in the morning sun. The lady with the cranky little dog hasn't passed by us in recent days but today, there are new walkers. A young couple are coming from the West, taking two children to school. They also have two dogs with them. One is a calm, older-looking English Setter, its leash held by the man.

The woman quickly shortens the other lead as we near each other because that dog, a possible Husky-Shepherd cross, lunges towards us with a deep growl. Most of the woman's strength, no slack in the leash, and a strong "No" manage to keep its aggression on their side of the path. For her part, my companion gives a determined stare towards them but holds her ground beside me. After they are past us, I allow her time to sit and look in their direction before we continue on our way.

There are children and teachers playing on the sports field as we walk past. When my pup first came to live with me, she was four months old and had gone from one home to the SPCA shelter, out to a second family, and back to the shelter. Through no fault of her own, her start in life has been tough. I adopted her after just one look at the website posting, and we've learned to live together for the past year and a half. Walking on a lead without being in sled-dog mode was a challenge for her but is now, more often than not, accomplished with mutual agreement.

She was extremely frightened of loud machinery and loud children during our first trail walks. Those fears were difficult for me to isolate until I eliminated a few factors. Was it the wind, the moving water, the cries of seagulls, just too many new scents assaulting her nose? She's a very curious and intelligent dog with a four-month history of experiences not known to me.

These days, she loves to be in her safe space behind the chain-link fence that surrounds my garden while the little children next door play outside. These toddlers, their quiet dog and my loud one, are happy to play on either side of a protective barrier.

However, the loud laughter and screams of older children, like those in the school playground this morning, still bring my companion to a dead stop. She will either get as far from them as quickly as possible or she will bark what I now recognize as her scared bark. It's in a higher pitch and persists as the fur along her spine stands on end even as she backs away, keeping her eyes on the offender. Not generally nervous and always happy, some fears still remain but are now under better control.

She is also wary of anything that's a solid dark colour – a person in dark clothing, a black compost bin in a garden near our path, a discarded garbage bag in a ditch and anything on wheels that makes a metallic sound when it moves. That movement might be as innocent, to me, as a child's wagon being pulled along the street or a bicycle travelling along the road. I have yet to determine whether it's the actual movement of the wheels or the sound they make.

One day, for example, in a very welcoming pet store, a metal trolley was being moved along an aisle to offload a pallet of dog food. My pup was terrified even after we stepped well back and the clerk stopped moving. Until he had taken that trolley out the door, she froze beside me, shaking from head to tail. To their credit, the staff recognized what was wrong, got down to her level and coaxed us to them until, with pats, soft voices, a treat, and the scary thing gone, she was back to her happy self.

I can only surmise that the sources of her concern began in a time before she came to live with me. At least for the year since, I'm aware of her fears and can provide close physical contact, calm words, and even avoidance. I owe her that much and more for the laughter and companionship she readily offers every day.

The mail ought to be delivered by now. We pass the familiar duck pond, step onto the sidewalk to push the traffic button, walk onto the zebra crossing and turn into the last ten minutes of our walk. As per her sense of routine, she leads me into the mailbox parking area and guides me around the wall of metal as I extract the key from my pocket.

********************************

## Carrie

Wouldn't you know it? As quick as I figure all my grocery shopping is done for a while, the broccoli has turned to an ugly yellow and the one green pepper that I bought two weeks ago is wrinkled and slimy. I suppose that's what I get for buying so-called fresh vegetables that weren't grown here, maybe picked in California or Mexico but not anywhere close by. Until my garden gets going this summer or there's some stuff from Ontario, I guess it's back to the can opener. I suppose I could make the effort to go down the main road to that vegetable stand.

There's always a few cars not quite pulled off the road on Saturday afternoons. People who don't know how to park getting their honest-to-god fresh veggies for Sunday dinner. This is Tuesday so it shouldn't be as bad. I know all that produce is grown right here on the shore. It always tastes so much better than anything in the stores. Turnip, potatoes, carrots, beets in season and, my favourite, parsnip. Put all of them into a pot of soup except the beets, and I'm in heaven. I can eat it for days, especially with lots of butter on nice thick slices of my homemade bread.

Now, I'm even more bothered that I was foolish enough to try my luck with what's in the produce aisles in that big store. So, I will haul on some clothes and hope my car chooses to get me from here to there and back again. One more chance to avoid the canned peas and mixed veg. Maybe I can buy potatoes by the each. Even a five pound bag goes soft with only me eating them.

That darned intersection looks busy. Don't rush me, mister. I'll go when I'm ready. I'm just putting on my indicator and making sure no one's about to step off the curb. There's the woman and her dog. I'm glad I looked both ways. Sure as hell, buddy behind me wasn't watching for walkers this morning. As I drive past, there's quite the line-up at the coffee place. It's not very nice of me, sorry Mother, to take some pleasure that Mister Hurry Up and Go will have another bit of waiting before he can satisfy his craving this morning.

The school traffic is done, so it's easy driving down past the eye doctor's, the pharmacy and the old folks' home. No one sitting outside having a smoke this morning, just the one guy who shambles his way along having a conversation with himself. One more stretch until I'm at the yellow bus and the vegetable lady. She works hard, so I'll buy from her instead of the other stand farther down the road. Besides, the stand is on the right side of the road for me to just pull off with enough room for me to turn the car around. That's all the more reason, I tell myself.

She comes out front to greet me as I pick a smallish turnip, half a dozen fresh carrots still with their green feathers on one end and four parsnip.

She smiles, “Half a dozen potatoes is no problem.”

I’ve brought my own bag, but she puts the spuds in a brown paper one for me. I haven’t noticed until just now that she makes her own pickles. I don’t. I’ll make jam from my raspberries and gooseberries, but pickles are just so much work. Slicing all those vegetables, mixing the right amounts of vinegar, salt and sugar. No, thanks.

“I’ll take one of your mustard pickles too, please.”

She passes things to me with a “Thank you. See you next time.”

A nice break in the traffic, swing the car west again and we’re on our way home. Eyes peeled for idiots pulling out of places in some mad tear to get someplace else and I’m soon back at the traffic lights. Turn right onto my lane and I’m safely in the driveway again. Thank you, little car, for getting me some decent vegetables. It’s garbage day tomorrow, so I’ll make sure that awful broccoli and bit of pepper are out the door in time. I can’t abide the smell of rotting vegetables.

That’s my response when someone like Maisie goes on about the glory of compost bins. They have a small bucket in their kitchen where the peels and cores go until the container is filled. Even with a lid on it, by the time it gets outside into the bigger bin, there’s a smell. Don’t get me started on the whiff off the stuff that’s been sitting all summer each time you lift the hatch to add new contents to the bin. Oh my, no, I'm fine with turning the soil in my beds and adding cow or sheep manure. That's a nice, clean, healthy smell if you breathe it in. Just ask my rhubarb next September which it prefers. I absolutely believe those sturdy red stalks like old-fashioned natural encouragement.

My raspberries along the back fence were really good last year. The gooseberry bush, the same old one, gave me ten or twelve cups. I thought that was pretty decent for a single bush. Those that didn't get stewed and eaten right away went into my little freezer to make jam and desserts during the cold winter months. The smell of sweet fruit on a dull winter's day sure is nice.

I've put away my purchases and now that I think about it, I'll put on a pot of soup later today. There's a chicken carcass in the fridge from three meals of chicken earlier this week and I made bread yesterday, so I'm all set. Time now for a cup of tea and something sweet. Glancing out the window as I cross to the sink to fill the kettle, I catch a glimpse of the woman and her dog crossing the bridge. They must have walked west instead of east while I was gone. Now they're on their way home. Perhaps tea for her and a treat for her companion.

****************************************

## Margaret

Four cars pull out of our horseshoe driveway. Younger members of my family all heading to work this Tuesday morning. As the oldest sibling, I've long since been retired, but my three brothers, two sisters and their husbands and partners still face that working grind. My house is closest to the road although still a nice ways back. They'll wave or give a gentle honk of the horn as they pass my windows just to let me know that my job has begun for the day, keeping an eye on the cluster of houses and land in between. I know that if no one catches sight of me, there will be phone calls to make sure their old sister isn't dead on the floor.

Our grandparents and then our parents worked hard on what used to be pastureland rotated for crops. Slowly, as the kids needed homes of their own, fallow ground was upended to build homes. None are as large or fancy as some in the new neighbourhoods up the road, just large enough for a couple of adults and, later on, a kid or two. All in all, when I take the time to tally up, we are now twenty, about the same number as the cows in Dad's herd. That's a funny thought. I could waste time for a laugh and figure out who could be which cow but I won't.

Anyhow, I count the beeps as vehicles stop and then swing onto the narrow road. A couple of the in-laws work along the shore but most everyone heads into town. They'll join the bumper-to-bumper madness on the by-pass in a few minutes. Twenty minutes or more to get them to their workplaces and, eight or twelve hours from now, they'll do it all over again. It's a life that I do not miss, having done it for so many years. I'm fine with being the older sister who is no longer at the beck and call of others. It's going to be interesting to see how the two next in line, sister and brother, settle into retirement. That day isn't long off for them.

Last night, I dreamt about warm weather. After work on a summer's evening, the little kids run and play while the older folks sit around the fire pit. The teenagers wave as they go off to do their own thing. Those adults not working night shift will pull on sweaters or grab a rug to keep warm even though their faces might be red from the heat of the flames.

Some evenings, when we're not hogging the pit that's been made and remade over the years, the nieces and nephews bring their friends. It's all about the height of the flames with that crowd. I keep my cautions unspoken because they all know someone is on the lookout for too much foolishness and I love to hear their laughter and strange music as I head to bed.

There's a calendar on my kitchen wall, a gift from a friend. The old cranky woman on each page has a remark to make every month. Thanksgiving month was giving thanks when another year of big family dinners and awkward conversation is over. In another family that is probably true, but when our crowd gets together, squeezed into the largest house available, it's amazing how little we disagree.

Not that we don't because there are heated discussions between bites of turkey and "Pass the cranberry sauce, please," but none ever last very long. Someone always says, "Give it up." We're okay with agreeing to disagree and I avoid talking politics with one particular brother-in-law at any time.

Now that I think back about these gatherings, my thoughts go back to our childhood. Mother had six of us under the age of ten. It's no wonder that she was a great one for adapting clothes so they could survive for the next in line. Ever practical, except for Sunday church clothes, there were no girls' clothes or boys' clothes. If the shirt or pants or coat were still good enough for a refit, it passed from me to you. Tears were darned, holes in the knees were patched with back pockets, lost buttons replaced by those taken off other clothes, and I even watched her make a new coat out of two old ones. By the time it got to the next kid, it felt new.

Once a year, a huge parcel would arrive filled with really good shirts, pants, coats, hats, sweaters and some Sunday-best clothes. A cousin of Mother's used to send an enormous cardboard box clear across the country. That family lived in British Columbia and, I remember thinking, must have lots of money. Someone was about my size, so it was like I'd died and gone to clothing heaven as my mother showed me each thing.

The youngest kids didn't pay much attention. All they wanted was to play in the great big magical box, but two of us would sit on the floor and watch each piece come up to the surface. After a few things were okayed for immediate ownership, the rest disappeared until we grew a bit more.

Funny how, sixty years later, I remember one particular dress. It was a really deep green with tiny white flowers on the top half. A summer dress and, in no uncertain terms, a party dress. I loved pulling off my shirt and pants, slipping into this stylish soft fabric and fancying myself in the bedroom mirror. There was just enough dreaminess in that ten-year-old me to enjoy feeling glamorous like the models in the magazines on the corner store shelf.

I should stop thinking about ages ago and come back to today. I've dreamed enough. There's a couple of birthdays coming up this month. When my pension cheque comes in, I'll run out and get cards, but gifts are almost always something baked because no one in this family has time to enjoy being in the kitchen when they get home from work.

Some of the nieces and nephews will come over to help me bake a special request, and that will be our gift to the birthday person. Muffins for work or school snacks, a cherry cake fancied up by the tube pan, a dozen chocolate chip cookies or, for one sweet tooth, a lemon cake with lemon filling and icing fit the bill. No doubt, someone will stop by in the next week or two with a suggestion.

There goes the walker. He's halfway down to the bridge already. The sun must have some warmth in it because his head and hands are uncovered. I hope he enjoys his outing today.

****************************************

## Ben

I'm going to head out into the sunshine in a couple of hours. The sky, as far as I can see, is that gentle shade of blue, so the trail will be especially pleasant. In its own way, cold, warm, dry, stormy, walking keeps me grounded, but, for now, the flea market find demands some attention. Pretty much all my furniture has been scrounged or cost next to nothing but came with a promise to renew its life in some way. The two kitchen chairs with their old wooden rungs wanted a touch of sandpaper, a new coat of paint and some fresh glue. They look good sitting on either end of my barn wood table in a pool of light this morning.

My table long discarded and buried under a pile of rotten planks, for example. I couldn't have found a happier project than repairing and refinishing that table. Scrubbing years of neglect off the pine, sanding the ragged but surprisingly warp-free top, and replacing a couple of struts underneath all brought her back to life after years of being buried under debris in the old shed out back. Little did I know, this time two years ago, what my new home would provide. The magic of giving back some love, especially to old wood, feels really good.

So, next on my list is to sand and refinish the arms, legs and back of an armchair. The fabric is very worn from many hours cradling people but the frame remains sturdy. I'll do the messy work first and leave decisions about how to recover the seat and backrest for another day. Simple lines will make for simple restoration, wood and fabric, I think. Unlike that old wing mirror dresser, there are no curlicues and intricacies needing a toothbrush to clean tight corners.

Sandpaper in hand, the roadside market seller comes to mind. He stood by his chair and laughed that his grandmother was a no nonsense kind of woman. This piece of furniture obviously reflects her attitude and, being a no-fuss sort of guy, that chair and I are going to be the best of friends. I'll even keep an eye out for a partner to keep her company when Spring flea markets start up again during weekends in parking lots and yard sales in driveways.

Now, it's time to grab a shower to get rid of the fine wood dust that covers me. The creases in my hands are brown and one look in the bathroom mirror at my hair reveals more pepper than salt. Definitely a clean-up for me before getting out into the salt air. I need a few things that can be found in the corner store up the main road, but walking the shoreline has become a pleasant routine. Whether I discover something new or simply move along to the tunes in my ears, it doesn't matter. Life's good on the trail. The dial on the outside of my window reads in the low single digits, so depending on the wind direction with no rain or fog or snow, an easy walk lies ahead.

My place stands unto itself on this tiny lane. It's such a drastic change that former mates cannot comprehend where I am. More a path than an actual road. It's really unusual when anyone thinks to come this way, which allows the birds, squirrels and smaller critters to live unmolested and without too much fear. The crows and an occasional sparrow hawk need to be watched for but I'm the only two-footed noise around. My finding this little bit of peace tucked away on land surrounded by forest has been awesome.

A time of colleagues, pressures, crowded spaces and noise is long gone in favour of a revamped former summer cabin in a faraway place. Here, life is distant enough from the shore road for plenty of privacy and that suits me well. I'm not anti-social. I just like people on my own terms and, thus, avoid any obligation to share. It never was a consideration for me to live in a neighbourhood with homes barely an arm's length apart. I'll happily pass them by on my way to elsewhere, thanks.

Someone honks a good morning as I cross the little bridge. It is one in a short line of four vehicles, two cars, and two trucks crossing over the river that runs to the sea. Both the water under the bridge and the ocean beyond look fairly calm right now. A couple more bends in the road and a short clamber down around the swimming hole bring me up onto the groomed trail.

Signs of habitation disappear quickly because homes are no longer visible from where I now walk, unlike the little community that hugs the road. It will be well into the afternoon before my feet return to this spot. If the weather holds, my stride may lengthen with any wind behind me most of the way home. I make no predictions, though. All this can change as quickly as I turn a bend in the coastline. It's so unlike what filled my days not so very long ago.

************************************

# Chapter Five

## Sara

I had to make a run into town before our walk today. Pup happily occupied the back seat and stuck her head out the window while I made a quick stop in a couple of places. Leaving the city behind twenty minutes later, we come atop the final rise that pulls your eyes to the vast expanse of ocean beyond the communities below. It was windy on the highway, blowing a snow squall out of the west and shuddering the car as I drove. The far shores of the bay were obliterated by a wall of grey, an impressive shroud of wind-blown snow. If you didn't know there were hills and homes over there, you could be forgiven for thinking it was nothing but wild ocean.

The sun burst out of a blue sky in between each blast of swirling white, a typical January snow squall. I decided to take a chance on a walk after we got home. The sun was out. The sky was clear. We'll make it. Dog patiently waited while I layered my clothes, adding to rather than removing what I already wore, I pulled fleece-lined snow pants over my jeans. A t-shirt already underneath my warmest hoodie was covered by my down-filled jacket. I wiggled my warmest woollen hat to sit snugly over my head and ears, then arranged the dog's gentle leader before working my hands into weather-proof mitts.

We step out into the -10 C. wind and say a small prayer that the next squall will wait until we get home. All is good until I near the shore ten minutes later. Beyond the trail, the sea is more white-caps than water with the wind whipping it into a fearsome frenzy. Any idea of walking on the trail this morning is whisked away on that angry sea.

“Sorry, pup, not happening,” as we turn back to go down a lane parallel to the trail. The houses and trees on either side of us block most of the wind. Down at the pond, the ice has been blown to the far side, and the ducks are hunkered down on a tiny patch of open water close to land. Not even they are venturing very far this morning.

It’s a shorter walk and the gale is mostly at my back as we turn towards home. Literally, two steps later, we are suddenly engulfed in blinding snow. Its force stings my face and plasters the front of my snow pants and jacket. We have no choice but to continue into it, one careful step at a time. Unable to see through the white-out, I keep pup on a very short leash by my side, away from the road.

I can feel her body against my leg as we make our way onto a short stretch of sidewalk. The traffic is invisible until it is right alongside me. I really hope they can see that we are on a sidewalk and not in their path. About fifty feet along, I know we have to cross the two lanes because the cement path ends only to begin again on the opposite side.

I lift my head enough to make sure no cars are close and hope that neither I nor my companion slip on the freshly fallen snow as we hurry across the half dozen steps to safety. The force of the wind and heavy wet snow make even my Husky turn her head away from the worst of it once we're back on familiar footing. Her look is a desperate plea for edible encouragement, so I freeze my left hand outside my mitt to offer her a treat. As rapidly as it descended, the squall passes and the sun returns. I think we both breathe a huge thankful sigh. Ten more minutes and we'll be home after a not-so-pleasant outing.

Not so fast, roars Mother Nature. We turn the final corner for the straight stretch along our own road. The sudden grey cloud overhead is a very brief warning. I take two more steps and we are in the midst of another blast of wind and snow coming from the other direction. Our street, a side-road off the main shore route, is without traffic so we make it to our garden gate, cold and battered but without incident. Once off her harness, pup makes a happy run for her bedraggled soccer ball, barely visible in the middle of the garden. The squall moves eastward as the ball and dog come toward me. It is time to play despite the weather.

What a morning. What a walk. Of course, we both survived

and while not very comfortable at times, it was a welcome change after driving on the highway to run errands in the heavy traffic of town. I leave my companion alone to play her version of soccer, take myself indoors and peel off layers of weather protection. The kettle soon begins to boil for hot chocolate and a partridge berry muffin goes into the microwave. As I sit to think about my next task, pup comes indoors, shakes off the snow, and settles down for a snooze on the doormat. The weather can do as it wishes, as it will, without us directly in its path for the rest of the day.

My hot drink rests beside me on the end table. I think of a good friend who moved to the mainland last year. She was selling her belongings before her departure day, and I bought her grandmother's old armchair. It sits in a corner of my living room and, now, reminds me that it needs a new cover. So, perhaps that should be my next rug-hooking project. If I use strips of material instead of yarn, it will withstand the wear and tear of those who sit in it. Muffin, cocoa and creativity, it's amazing what walking in snow squalls will generate.

I have never hooked a chair cover despite more than fifteen years since creating my first little mat. There have been nearly 140 wall hangings, half a dozen floor rugs, dozens of Christmas ornaments, a few mug coasters and table mats as well as a case for a throw-pillow but no actual upholstery. However, I wouldn't ordinarily choose the snow squall method of inspiration.

## Carrie

I made soup for lunch today and have leftovers in my freezer for another easy meal sometime when I don't feel like cooking. Not that meals are a big deal. There's only me to feed. I occasionally watch cooking shows on television and think I should try to make what I see on the screen. Then, the inspiration fades and old reliable meals come to mind, things I've cooked since I was at my mother's apron strings. Pretty basic by the crazy standards on those fancy shows. Their concoctions sure do look full of delicious calories, though.

There's something to be said for doing a cooking badge in Brownies and taking Home Economics in high school. I'm glad I wasn't stuck doing Chemistry, Physics, Latin and Advanced Math like my older sister. How many times did I get her angry by going on about how much fun I was having without needing good grades? People used to say she was the fast cruiser needing to tear across the tops of waves to prove that she could. I was the rowboat that lolled along, not caring if the tide was on its way in or out.

Two girls, four years apart, we were completely different in looks, attitudes and, later in life, skills. Happy enough in our own way, except that she didn't like her long blond whip-straight hair and I hated my very curly, untamed red hair. Gosh, I miss her now that she's no longer around to tease.

I remember how she'd wail at me to leave her alone while she crammed for some test or other. By the time I reached high school and Kate was in junior high, Mother wasn't always patient with us. I remember convincing myself that it wasn't actually our behaviour that angered her. I surmised that it was because she'd married outside the family norm.

"Your father is from mainland Canada," Grandfather would grumble.

Stationed here during the war, Father took up with Mother, and that didn't sit too well with people. Then, our parents added fuel to the fire by moving to the west coast where his crowd lived and where we two girls were born.

Sometimes, we'd hear stories from Father that he and Mother never quite fitted in on either side of the country. They liked to travel. Most of our lot just wanted to stay where fathers, grandfathers and even greats before them had always been. His crowd had their noses up in the air about Mother being from a small east coast farming and fishing community. That was, somehow, less than acceptable for their son.

Years later, we showed them they were wrong when we drove across the country to here and built a home on old pasture land near the seashore. For me, it's a very good thing we did that because I'm here ever since and wouldn't want to be any place else. Thanks again, Aunt Maude, for sticking up for Mother when we needed a place to live.

The weather's gone foolish today. It was good on clothes earlier but now it's like we're back in winter again. One minute, it's great, five minutes later, before I've even cleared the dishes away, the wind is throwing sideways snow against the windows. I'm glad I got my shopping done yesterday. My car isn't moving anywhere in this nonsense.

I was about to go out and rescue the clothes off the line but there's not much point. It irks me, but they'll have to suffer in that wind until they're dry. As long as they don't disappear through the air into the fancy new neighbourhood across the pond. My goodness! Suppose those folks sit down for supper only to see some old lady's unmentionables stuck on their fence-post. Wouldn't that just brighten the end of someone's long day?

I noticed the walker and her dog come round the corner a little while ago, but with that squall, she turned away from the shore. Can't say as I blame her. That sea has to be nasty with this wind. She must really love that dog of hers. She walks in all sorts of weather. I've had a few cats in my day but cats don't need to be walked. I've let them out the door and prayed to god they'll come home. There's been a time or two when they've looked a bit scruffy after being out all night when they didn't return before I went to bed.

I felt sorry for them, briefly. If you're going to live with me, you better live by my rules, cats or people. I suppose that's why I've never married.

This is a good day to get started on those little baby caps. One of the ladies at the church social last week was talking about making them. It's for a donation to the children's hospital in town. The tiny babies need to keep warm and wearing a cap holds in their body heat, she said. We passed around copies of the pattern and it's dead simple to crochet. Not everyone knows how to crochet. Mostly, knitting is more popular. I have lots of different colours in my yarn box left over from the lap throw I made last winter. I gave that to the church sale and someone said it went for a nice price.

I can make a dozen or more of those little caps in no time and then I'll phone the number on the bottom of the pattern. If someone picks them up from me, that'll be great. I can deliver them anywhere along the shore, but I'm not going into town with them. Now, the sun's shining again but it won't last long, I don't think. Where's the basket that holds my leftover yarn? I don't suppose I put it in the spare room closet.

Sometimes, I do things that really make sense. Other times, they make sense in the moment, but then I forget why I did it that way. My mind is just so full of useful information. I do think the newest stuff occasionally pushes some of the older bits out somehow. They didn't explain that in Home Economics. I wonder if they did in Chemistry or Physics.

There it is, just as it should be. Basket and bag of scraps in the closet beside the boxes of Christmas decorations and the tub of summer clothes. There's only one tub of clothes. Our summers just aren't long enough for more and, besides, who needs more than two or three changes of clothes before they go in the wash and onto the line.

Now, the Christmas stuff is another story. Friends and family think it's a good idea to give me house-decorating things as gifts. I suppose I have half a dozen strings of lights for my tree which weigh it down every year, and by the time I put out all the things that need to stand alone on tables and windowsills, I have no room for anything else. They mean well, both gifts and people.

Okay, basket, bag of yarn and off we go to my chair by the window, weather be damned. Forgive me, Mother. I'm making little caps for teeny tiny babies. Perhaps that will erase the curse words. It does, in my mind. I almost let another one slip because it would have been good if I'd remembered to look for the case of crochet hooks while I was in the spare room. Put the basket and yarn down, woman, and go back for the hooks. I also need to see the pattern for which size hook to use.

Now, what did I do with that?

****************************

## Margaret

This is definitely an indoors sort of day for everyone who doesn't have to make their way through bouts of god-awful weather to get to work. I worry about my crowd until I know the younger ones are safely on the buses and I can breathe a sigh of relief when texts come from those driving. They all reached work okay but the going was rough with blowing snow creating white-outs over patches of black ice on the highway.

I won't be far from my front window at the end of their day, watching and waiting for them all to make their way off that road and back to their homes before dark sets in. The only ones I won't see will be a couple of in-laws who work night shifts this week. By morning, when they get off work, this weather should be gone out to sea.

I potter around the house all day, every now and then, trying to look through the snow plastered against my window. Don't know how but lunch dishes are done before I know it, and I see the number three bus drop the last two kids at the end of my property. I'm surprised that they're not heading through the snow and wind to their own homes. They're coming straight here.

That can mean only one thing. Young minds with ideas for birthday gifts. The baking cupboard is well-stocked, always is, and the old chest of drawers in the front room still has plenty of craft materials left over from last year's Christmas creations. We should be fine for all possibilities. If not, their houses are a quick walk away for whatever I don't have.

I pull a baggie of peanut butter chocolate chip cookies out of the fridge freezer. They'll warm up nicely in the microwave if the kids want some.

Emily is the first through the door, "Hi, Auntie," with Liam close on her heels, "How was your day?"

I remind them to hang up their outdoor clothes on the pegs along the wall and to put their snowy sneakers on the mat.

"My day was all indoors and a little boring, so it's lovely to see you," I say as we walk down the hall.

In all honesty, although I don't tell them this, and the adults don't get the same treatment, it's no big deal if my floors get a bit wet. The hardwood is old and worn from lots of feet, both clean and dirty, dry and not. Having them choose to spend time with me is pretty nice. While I love their parents, with no kids of my own, the young ones get away with an occasional misdeed.

We all agree that the weather today is the pits.

"It sucks that we had school", comes from my nephew, fourteen years old.

All I can do is laugh because, despite his comment, Liam

really doesn't mind school and there aren't too many weekends when he's not being transported by someone, friends or family, to after-school sports of one kind or another. Last summer, during vacation, it was softball. I went a few times when his team played.

This time of year, activities have moved indoors. Boxing is his newest thing and it came with a need to buy new size 13 gym shoes, special protective hand wraps and remembering to eat an early meal. The other day, he told me it only took one evening to learn that running around the gym with a stomach full of food is not a good idea.

Cramming two warm cookies into his mouth and stacking a few more nearby, he announces that his gift idea is to make a couple of birthday cards and a puzzle game he's seen online. I hear him rummage in the chest before he puts an armload of supplies onto the kitchen table and begins poking through it for whatever he needs. His cousin and I are working at the counter, so that table is all his and I have a feeling he'll use every inch of it. At a glance, I see coloured paper, glue, glitter, markers, old magazines and scissors at the ready.

My very modern eleven-year-old niece, Emily, dons an apron in my presence. Not a frilly one that ties at the waist. No way. This material covers from neckline to knees. She and I had a sewing weekend with some old denim one day last year. Back then, the apron grazed her ankles. Not so this year.

Wearing an apron while baking in a kitchen is somehow safe with me. I like to think she's okay with her old aunt's views about labels being thrown around by some people. If you're not harming anyone and whatever you're doing is bringing you joy, what odds, I think. An apron, to me at least, is not a sign of being under someone's thumb. It's saving on laundry.

I see the tin of cocoa, flour, baking powder, vinegar, oil and sugar coming together on the counter. My biggest bowl, the best for rising enough dough for six loaves, comes out of a lower cupboard and the whisk from the drawer in front of her. She's decided on cocoa cake, usually just called chocolate cake. It's an easy egg-free recipe that a work colleague gave me, lord, thirty or more years ago. The little recipe card itself is grubby and bent at the corners.

That friend was a young nurse at the time. We lost touch when she moved away, and the next I heard, she'd started her own business. Something about auras that surround a person, some good, some not, some to grow and others to limit. She used to make noises about such things back when we knew each other. I just let it go because that nonsense aside, I liked her. Wonder how her business went? Her cake recipe is still perfect.

I remind Emily to preheat the oven and rub the cake pan well with margarine before she's too far ahead. I do as my mother did, save the paper wrappers when the block of margarine is gone. They're perfect for greasing bowls and bread pans. Seeing her get ready, I'm reminded of something. No one needs to know this, but when I made those cookies last week, I pushed the wrong button on the stove. Thinking I'd turned the oven on to heat up to 350°, I was all set with the first batch on the pan. I opened the oven door, but no heat fogged my glasses.

My first thought was the old stove had given up the ghost at a very wrong moment. Then I noticed the oven light was on. I do that only to check if something's getting too brown. Dear lord, woman, you're losing it was my next thought. I'd turned on the light and not pushed the Start button. Thank goodness it was just cookies. They didn't suffer for waiting. The cookies won't tell and neither will I.

Bringing my attention back to here and now, Emily is telling me about the bus driver's poor taste in music and her cousin is elbowing her aside to get to the sink because the finished card isn't the only place showing glue. His creation is very clever, but I find it a bit confusing. He informs me, quite pleased with himself, that it's a collage of magazine pictures and letters. A bit of a jumble to my old eyes at first glance, but after he shows me why he's chosen certain images, I can see how he has his father in mind all along.

Inside the card is done like those old-fashioned bank robber notes handed to the teller, cut-out letters spelling a demand. This time, of course, it reads *Happy Birthday, Dad!* I respond to his high five and add my own approval. He sniffs the chocolate in the air as his cousin reaches for her share of the cookies. An empty plate, a dozen cookies gone in less than three hours. Thank god I don't have to feed youngsters every day.

Cars turn into the driveway soon after that, so they get ready to head home. The card, puzzle and cake will stay with me until the celebration on the weekend.

"Put on your hats." "Do up your coats," come out of my mouth as their feet squirm into footwear whose laces remain tied.

I get a hug sandwich before they take off out the door. The wind is still howling, but it's easy for me to watch them because they time their run to match a lull in the squalls. Out the back door window, I see them safely enter side-by-side homes.

Clean-up isn't much after that. The card maker has put things back into the drawers but a few sticky spots on the table need a wipe. All the baking supplies are returned to the cupboard, but not all the chocolate stayed in the bowl. Nothing the dishcloth can't remove before I heat up leftover chicken and veg from last night's supper. I never seem to manage to cook just enough for a single meal. I guess it's just as well leftovers suit me day after day and, for that matter, year after year.

First, I'll have a little sit-down in my chair. Having the kids here was more activity than usual. Don't get me wrong, I love it. Looking at the white swirling outside my window, it occurs to me that I haven't thought about the walker all day. A blurry shadow inside a wall of snow is all I might have seen. I can't imagine that even he would be wanting to go out in today's weather, if he has an ounce of sense to him, that is.

****************************************

## Ben

There is no doubt at all about where I am living. A while back, I overheard someone say, "If you look out your front door, you see sun, but turn and look out the back door, it's pouring rain." I laughed to myself at the time, thinking it was a great example of exaggeration about the weather in this province.

The last laugh's on me today. I can, literally, look out at the woods behind my place and see blue sky and sunshine through the tall trees. A dozen steps from there to the front door and I see nothing but a raging blizzard. It's unbelievable, except that I've been here long enough to know it's very real and folks weren't making it up that day in the hardware store.

The weather was rarely a topic of conversation before I came here. Bordered by the Pacific Ocean, warm rain, drizzle and fog meant Spring and, oftentimes, Summer as well. Later on, in my next life, the sudden afternoon downpours were a relief from the hot sand underfoot. Neither place held danger unless out on the water with lightning on the horizon. Only fools tempted that. On dry land, to sit and let the warm rain wash over you brought a kind of peace, a confirmation of being at one with the world around you.

If I go out in today's weather, I'll be at one with Nature in no uncertain terms, her terms. In between the snow squalls, the wind still howls, but the sky is brilliantly lit by sunshine.

"More fool you," says Mother Nature, "go get on your gear and head out on your walk. See what happens next."

Sorry, My Lady, I'll wait for a while and see if you continue past us to churn up the great Atlantic beyond. I'm in no rush.

There's an untouched canvas sitting behind my chair in the corner. An idea has begun to germinate during recent months of walking the trail. Maybe I'll pull out my sketchbook and see if that goes anywhere today. The walls shudder just a little when the wind hits us, but they're solid. If the electricity goes, I have the old tin kettle, another shed discovery, and the wood stove, so a cup of good coffee is never far away.

I chopped another load of wood into splits and half-junks the other day when I got home, so the repainted tin bucket on the hearth is full. At worse, I can bundle myself up enough to go cut more. Snow, wind or sun matters not. The stack is only feet from the back door.

It really is tempting to head out. Although I fight against too much routine, my walks for supplies or coffee with a friend are a nice start to most of my days. Looking at the wind this morning, though, I think the trail will be less than comfortable both underfoot and on my face. That's the only part of my body that ever feels the bite of the wind. My gear is great with nothing but my eyes bared to the elements if necessary, so I'm pretty much cold-proof.

The effort of facing a strong wind never bothers me. It's a challenge I'll accept. Keeping an eye for a rare rogue wave occasionally brings back memories of warmer, much larger waves and a good shorey before the whitewash hits golden sand. Gosh, those two terms popped into my brain from a time and place in the past.

Routine be damned this morning. It's cozy in here. A Northern Flicker just landed in the dogberry tree. He's all puffed out to stay warm but, otherwise, looks unperturbed as the gusts push him around. His red flash caught the corner of my eye when he bobbed his head to loosen a berry on the branch near the window.

Looking through the swirling snow out there now reminds me of the tracks I saw in yesterday's soft powder. The drag of a rat's tail was obvious, but off to one side behind the wood-pile, there were definitely signs of a rabbit and, all around the garden, plenty of little bird's feet had made delicate patterns. That evidence of life is blown into oblivion today. I hope the animals themselves are safely tucked into hollows and the crooks between boughs.

I put my mug and sketchbook on the little stool beside my old armchair, straighten the blanket draped over its back, give the wood a nudge to keep the fire going, and tell myself it's okay to resist routine. Ingrained from too many years following other people's rules, I have to fight that urge when it rears its ugly head.

A couple of deep breaths and a careful sip of hot black caffeine while music fills my snug room are just the incentives I need.

The springs inside will unwind, I know. They always do, whether on the trail, digging a new vegetable bed from my patch of land, bringing old wood back to life or, like now, reaching for my sketchbook and drawing lead. I'm here in this new life, my third shot at life. I push my hair off my neck, close my eyes and wait for an image, any image of the trail. Each time I walk to either east or west, my mind's eye is always busy. Something will take shape and find its way onto the open page.

The fire is down to glowing embers by the time I look up hours later. Several pages have snippets or full-page sketches. My body is telling me it's time to move, to stretch out of this position. My neck is cricked. It crunches as I slowly move it side to side. The pencil is warm from my grip, and the tip worn to a nub.

I let the book close, lay both it and the lead onto the stool and push myself up out of the chair. The mug is empty, a brown ring on the white porcelain proof that I drank the contents in the interim. The residue will get removed in the old aluminum sink and the mug reused with lunch.

It's been quite a while since I last allowed myself to "waste my time" like this. Unbidden but not unexpected, my father's words from long ago come to mind. They were frequently thrown in my face when I hadn't done a chore on time, his time. Today, though, I am so unwound that it's very satisfying to discover four hours have passed. The wind still rages outside, but I am really happy. My long legs work out the stiffness by walking from window to window. I stop, bend down to the tin bucket and lift a junk of wood. It will rekindle the flames in the burner. Mentally, I give this morning's change of routine all it is due. I may look through those pages tonight. I may not.

After a grilled cheese and chutney lunch, I pull on my jacket and boots to clear the doorways of drifted snow. I will probably need to do it again before supper rolls around, but without my usual physical exercise today, any food beyond lunch is not really necessary. As I dress for even a brief time outdoors, it continues to surprise me how lighthearted I feel. I'm aware that I'm humming and, all alone in this room with firelight bouncing off the old wooden walls and ceiling, I'm smiling.

An old past-time, a return to a path not taken, has brought as much pleasure to me this morning as does walking the shoreline on any given day. It's been years, too long in the coming, although buying that canvas a few months ago obviously started me thinking along these lines. No pun intended. Said out loud that makes me laugh as I reach for the shovel.

********************************

# Chapter Six

## Sara

The day begins earlier than usual with paws tapping along the wood floor and a meaningful sigh as someone plunks herself down on the hooked mat beside my bed. My half-open eye rises from the pillow to peer at the clock, its yellow light glowing behind a series of unbelievable numbers. I groan gently that 5:45 is just too early. The determined grey and white face watching me does not understand my appeal. I guess if she has to go, she's got to go, so I push back the nice warm covers and climb out of bed.

Pup stands, does a full-body stretch, a big yawn and waits for her collar to go around her neck. She gives herself another good stretch halfway out the door with front paws on the deck and back legs on the sill, then she's off down the steps into the darkness of the garden. I slink back into bed and wonder how long my reprieve will be. Not long enough because a mere fifteen minutes later, I hear her feet come back to the door. Once more, I get out of bed to open the door and proffer the obligatory dental treat before both of us are back on or in bed again. I must have fallen asleep because the digits glowed 7:20 at the next reading.

Now, it's two mugs of tea and a slice of hot toast later, with a large canine curled up beside me on the couch, feigning sleep. It's time to check emails. The usual junk mail is quickly deleted and I make a mental note of others to which I'll reply later today. However, I am surprised to see something from a distant relative. We haven't been in touch for at least twenty years, and as far as I know, she still lives on the other side of the continent.

When we did meet, she was a Mother Superior in a religious order based somewhere in southern California. A cousin on his father's side of the family, Sister Jean, had come for a visit, after which they kept in sporadic touch until Father's death. Obviously, she had stayed strong in her faith, whereas Father liked to say, "Mine has lapsed." Despite that, he had looked forward to seeing her. I remember how they enjoyed ten fabulous days together.

Sister Jean rode on the passenger seat of Father's touring motorbike while he showed her the west coast of our island. From somewhere, he found leathers and boots for her to wear when they travelled and everyone thought they looked a fine pair. Father with his black gear, denim vest full of badges from places visited, and his pure white 75-year-old beard open to the wind above the helmet strap. Meanwhile, having negotiated getting herself actually up onto the bike, his American cousin sat upright behind him. The 70-year-old nun who became the Head of her Order enjoyed her comfortable seat as they sped along the winding highway during a week of July sunshine.

Now, on my screen, I see a subject line that asks, "How are you?" When my surprise mellows into pleasure, I respond and, for a few minutes, more than twenty years disappear. She wants to get in touch one last time and to reassure me that, although she retired and moved, my letter about Father's death had, in fact, reached her. She has emotionally relived her time with him, remembers me well and hopes that I will accept her blessing for a happy future. There's a finality to her message that makes me unhappy despite her last line that she, herself, isn't sad. She's okay with where she's soon going and perhaps will meet up with my father once again.

At times like this, I really miss the fun I used to have with my father, and it's strangely compounded by the sudden knowledge that someone who brought such joy to him is now leaving this world. I hope that Sister Jean and Father will, indeed, find each other in another realm. It isn't my belief, but it is hers, so I write back with my news, accept her blessing, tell her that I'm so glad she got in touch, and wish her peace in all that comes her way.

Surprisingly shaken, I decide to go for our walk. Being beside the ocean with its waves and salty air will settle my soul and I can send my best wishes on the wind to a gracious, adventurous woman far away. The excited response from my early riser lifts my spirits before we're even out the door. She always does that but today, it's especially appreciated as her head nudges me to get my walking boots laced. Keys, phone, pocket full of treats and poop bags, we're ready to go. The tightness in my heart will lessen with each step along the trail. This I already know.

It's late enough that the school traffic, both vehicles and children, are no longer en route. It's all quiet as we turn onto the trail and head westward for a longer walk. There's a definite smell of the sea this morning. The waves are lazy. They roll to shore with very little surf, perhaps because the tide is in. There are dark patches further out the bay and a cluster of seagulls in one spot on warmer water, maybe.

Absolutely no sign of those black and white birds with the punk rocker head feathers. I wonder what moved them to a different location. The ground smells along this part of the trail are keeping my companion's nose constantly sniffing. Now and then, she trots with an intense determination from one side of the trail to the other. Watching her and hearing the rocks rumble under the waves is working its magic on me. As one foot moves ahead of the other, my heartfelt wishes float on the currents, air and ocean, from the Atlantic to the Pacific until they reach one special person.

****************************************

## Carrie

The sun is gorgeous this morning. It's filling my whole house with a brightness that can't be taken away by a chilly breeze, not indoors, at least. Floating in the sunbeams are bright specks of fairy dust, as my mother used to call it. In reality, it's the broken dust bunnies that eluded my dustpan. I'll let it settle where it will for now. I know the sun streaming in is deceiving because if I press my hand against a window, there's no warmth to the glass.

Coming around the corner, the woman is not as chatty with her dog as usual. Her step is gentler, a bit less purposeful, as if she's lost in thought. Her pace seems to lack its normal intensity as she passes my window and heads to the trail. A walk less for exercise and more for some other purpose today, perhaps. The dog looks as happy as always with her tail curling up into the air and her nose skimming the ground. I'm glad that I'm not a rabbit or a squirrel. That nose would search me out in a flash.

Yesterday, I did the last of a dozen tiny baby caps. I plan to give the woman a call and arrange to get them to her. There isn't a specific time frame, but the sooner they get to the neonatal wing the better, I expect. It was a lot of fun making them and I used lots of colours. Some are all one colour, others have stripes. The temptation is to do the old-fashioned pink and blue, but mine have yellow, dark and light green, white, a nice pale apricot and a deeper blue as well as the two traditional colours.

They only differ in size if the yarn count of one is a bit heavier than another. I kept to all washable wool even though I doubt that one hat gets worn by more than one baby. I've seen proud new parents put pictures in the newspaper of their pride and joy wearing his or her little beanie. To my mind, a hat on a head is much cuter than a prissy ribbon wrapped around a spike of new hair, but that's just my opinion.

If I need to deliver the caps to someone, I'll swing by the neighbourhood mailbox to check for mail. I don't suppose I've turned my key in that lock for a couple of weeks now. Maisie has stopped by, picked up my key and checked both boxes because she's always on the go. She says that it's to save me driving on the slippery road. No doubt that is partly true but knowing Maisie, she also gets to have a look at my mail as well as hers.

You never know, I might get something out of the ordinary instead of a bill or two. Wouldn't it shock the life out of her if she came upon a letter from an admirer of mine. I'm tempted to write something, mail it to myself, and on the back flap, write SWAK, sealed with a kiss.

Oh my, that's not very nice of me to be thinking like that but I can't seem to stop. I'd have to keep a straight face when Maisie hands me that piece of mail. I wonder if she'd put it on top of any other mail or if she'd tuck it in between so as to pretend she hasn't seen it. This is getting worse and worse, this thinking of mine. I'm really enjoying myself. It must be all this sunshine making me foolish. Anyhow, if I go out with those baby caps, I'll check the mail myself. I won't play a trick on poor old curious Maisie.

Last week when I was grocery shopping in the big box store, they had turkeys on sale. The last time I bothered to cook a turkey for myself, I ate it for days, cold turkey and dressing sandwiches for lunches, hot turkey with vegetables and gravy and dressing for suppers. Even so, I still had enough from even a smallish bird to freeze some and to also freeze the well-picked bones for soup. That was sometime last year, probably when they went on sale after Christmas.

Well, I found a nine-pound one this time. That won't last as long, but it'll be plenty enough. I still have partridge berry sauce in the pantry from last Fall's berries. It's not cranberry sauce and, in truth, it's more jam than a sauce, but I like it just the same. I can't get through the year without making partridge berry jam and having the fruit on hand for muffins.

In my fridge freezer, there's always a bag of crumbs made from stale bread. I use it for coating fish or chicken sometimes not only as dressing for turkey. Mother called it stuffing. Most people around here, including me, say dressing. It's still bread mixed with savoury, salt and pepper and onion or a bit of apple for moisture. Not everyone puts in the onion or the apple, but I do.

All this talk about turkey is making me hungry and it's only mid-morning, for heaven's sake. The bird has been thawing in the fridge since yesterday, so if it's ready, it will be supper tonight. If not, I'll look forward to having it tomorrow night because I can't tolerate the sound of water running all day while a turkey thaws in my sink.

It's halfway through the morning and I've nothing much accomplished so far except for watching the walker, daydreaming about mail from a non-existent lover, and stirring up fairy dust. Never mind, says I, the kettle's going to be boiled again and I might just treat myself to a slice of banana bread that's calling my name. I'm going to sit in this sunshine and watch the antics of a huge flock of starlings swirling into and then out of the trees, a cloud of birds. I, for one, do not possess their sense of purpose this morning.

*************************************

## Margaret

Four of the teenagers have a day off school today. "A PD day" was the answer to my "Why?" when they appeared at my door just after noontime.

Like an old-fashioned posse, bodies all dressed in black, they look menacing, especially after their buddies join to swell their number to eight. I'm pleased that those belonging to me have come to say they're on their way somewhere and will be back in time for supper. Supper in their respective homes not here at my place. They're all good kids, and while I don't want or need to know where somewhere might be or what exactly they'll be doing for four or five hours, I don't expect trouble before they return.

Just before the lanky teens paraded through the garden, I saw no fewer than six Northern Flickers in the trees. It's not unusual to see one or two, male or female, but to see so many was quite a sight. They compete for leftover dogberries in the big old trees between my house and my brother's. Tomorrow or whenever I next go outside, there will be sprigs of red on the patchy white snow either from them or after swarms of starlings swoosh down from the electricity wires high above the road.

The other day, I actually had to look out the window when I heard an odd sound. It was like when you shake out a rug, the air makes a sort of thud. The front garden was suddenly covered in a hundred starlings pecking and chirping. My sudden appearance in the window startled them, and when they all took off into the trees, they made the sound again. It was really interesting.

As long as pecked berries are all that I find underfoot, I don't mind. It's the splats of red bird droppings that I can't stand. As a kid, I was used to cow and sheep manure sticking to the soles of my rubber boots. No longer being forced to live with that, I prefer plain old mud in the treads of my shoes, if there has to be anything extra there at all. Don't get me started on how angry I get with birds when I have laundry on the line.

I just don't know how they manage to aim their business onto clothes that are either moving in the breeze or hanging straight down on a calm day. There have even been days when my window has an ugly streak on it. That takes some sort of mean-spirited aim, doesn't it?

I remember my Uncle Tom telling us not to look up at the seagulls when he'd take us out in the boat.

If we did happen to gaze up to see which bird had made a scream at us or at another gull, "Make sure your mouth is closed," he'd laugh.

It wouldn't take more than one time to remember that warning. If you've ever seen the ugliness or felt the force of what a gull can drop from the sky, you know what I'm talking about. What a disgusting topic to be on my mind this morning! I obviously need to get busy.

Perfect distraction and perfect timing have just stepped into view. There he goes, the walker heading towards home. The posse is hanging out down by the little bridge at the bend in the road. Some of them look up as he nears and nods are exchanged. I wonder if the kids know anything more about him. I must remember to ask them if they stop in later today.

Mind you, knowing kids these days, they accept people for whomever they are. At least, this group does from any conversations I've heard. They probably don't pay my walker enough attention to know a thing. They're too wrapped up in their teenage lives, dying to get a driver's license. Finding out the story behind an aging hippy type who prefers walking to driving is not at the top of their curiosity list, unlike someone I know.

At the church card game and tea last Wednesday, there was talk of a celebration to mark the forming of the town, the amalgamation of six smaller communities. It was a controversial idea when first brought to each community council. Although on a smaller scale, it reminded me of 1940's arguments about bringing our province into Confederation. That move caused all kinds of rifts between people in the same family, never mind from one town to the next.

I remember people insisting that each community retain its historical identity. I believe that's how it was worded. So, to this day, the signs along the shore road still announce when you're entering a different community, even though they simply run together as you look at them. I guess ideas moved with the times and no longer did someone get into the family's bad books for marrying the guy or girl from down the shore. The original fierce rivalries, some causing bloodshed, calmed down as time passed. Mind you, if someone asks me today, "Where do you belong?" I'll give my community name, not the one for the whole shore.

Anyway, there's talk of an event to celebrate the anniversary of when we all joined into one larger town. I'm a bit interested to see what sorts of things will be suggested for that. I hope we, who voted the councillors into office, will have a say in how we'd like it to look. I suppose I'll put in my two cents' worth.

*******************************************

## **Ben**

This morning, I am keeping company with a lot of birds as I walk the longest section of the trail. The gulls are plentiful out on the water and wheeling overhead until they find a rock sticking out of the waves that can provide a perch. Crows fly low above me, their conversations competing with seagull cries. For whatever reason, all are having a loud morning.

When I look down the side-road beside the beach bridge, the utility wires are supporting an enormous flock of starlings. I stop to watch them shuffle themselves into some preordained order of who can stand where. Just when they look to be settled, a spacing rule must come into effect because a long section of them glide an inch or two sideways along the wire. I chuckle that I'm not the only creature who values personal space.

The surface of the pond itself is really interesting. I don't think I've seen it quite like this any other day. The white of the ice has wide caramel-coloured swirls running through it. They resemble the cream designs that baristas draw on the top of an expensive cup of coffee, only in reverse. The swirls are brown on white in this case. The surface of the pond is absolutely calm and, in its own way, the artistry is paint-brush perfect. Not knowing what or why it looks that way on this particular morning, I can't help hoping it isn't the result of some type of pollution.

My music walks me the rest of the way and now, I find the morning has disappeared with errands completed and conversation over coffee at its end. The use of my friend's Internet connection offered nothing to capture my attention, so we said goodbye, and I hit the trail once again. As I reach the end of the trail and begin to walk back into the community, I shuffle my music once again. Up ahead, there's a group of kids hanging out on the bridge.

The obligatory black gear reigns with these guys. As I approach and then step around their huddle to continue on, a couple of them give a sideways tilt of their heads, which I return. No one that age wants to break a conversation to acknowledge an old guy like me. That's all fine. I was like them a few decades ago hanging with my buddies on the corner of some street in town. It's all cool.

I carry on up around the tight bend in the old, narrow road, and my body begins to remind me that I've been walking for more than three hours. It's been a good walk with time to gather my thoughts after recent memories of tough family times. Working to live out the expectations of others used up twenty years of my young life.

When I finally threw my hands into the air, railed at the skyscrapers of glass, and walked away, it had not been pleasant. Checking out and heading south away from structure, kilometres turned into miles. It was a daunting but compelling prospect. Now, after a decade of self-satisfied existence in daily sun, sand and surf, I'm happy to walk a different shoreline, to exchange a nod with young dudes.

As I walk past the little white house nestled in the valley below my last uphill climb, I smile and cast a sly eye to my right. Will she be in her chair tucked to one side of her window today? I know she keeps a careful watch as I head east or, like now, when I come up from the bridge on my way home. Her shadow a few steps back from the window will let me know she's there.

At other times, her hand is lifting a mug off the table in the glow of bright sunlight. I'm happy to know someone is watching out for me but not pushing into my space. Her home fronts a group of houses on the same expansive property so I expect she's surrounded by family. She's never alone, which obviously suits her, but is not the life for me.

I shrug my shoulders to shift my backpack into a more comfortable spot as I crest the hill and see the road where I'll turn. My lane takes me another fifteen minutes further, and then a dozen final steps up through the trees onto the path, and I'm at my front door. Sitting on the top tread, I see a few ducks on the distant pond. They occasionally waddle up here to let me know I'm no longer an interloper. Their voices carry on a calm day like today and the short, sharp sound reminds me of laughter. The possibility that there are waterfowl jokes floating between them makes me grin.

The old latch lifts easily as I slide out of my pack to open the solid wood door. Sun streaks through the back windows and settles an instant coziness on everything. Boots off, jacket hung on the nearest peg, I carry my pack the few steps into the middle of my home. My trusty water bottle comes out of its side pocket before sandpaper, varnish, a couple of foam brushes and a few groceries all land on the counter. It's definitely time for a coffee and some leftover soup that was supper last night.

After that, I'll start a fire and decide what's next. I could work some more on the chair. I might jump into making a batch of lasagne now that I have the ingredients. I could also open the sketchbook that sits on the stool and have a look at what I did yesterday. Curiosity may get the better of me but, first things first, items into cupboards followed by sustenance for the body. It's good to be here.

****************************

# Chapter Seven

## Sara

My daily walks along the shore haven't changed much in recent weeks, other than the sun starting to provide a little warmth. We had a week of intensely bitter weather just as the first official day of Spring was announced in March. On those days and not being used to such dramatically cold temperatures, we didn't walk the shore. They were disappointing times for both pup and me, but even with protective balm on her pads, the danger of frostbite was too great. She, herself, went out into the garden but lifted her paws off the ice and snow several times before I quickly called her back indoors.

Once past that spell of weather and into May, the air became more humane. Lots of mornings, we walked in cool drizzle that blew sideways on us, but that's our norm in April. We have a long-standing saying, "We haven't hit May 24$^{th}$ yet." It's not uncommon for the start of the camping season to be cold and wet. Cold enough for those enjoying that long weekend in campers with furnaces to turn them on for warmth.

Living here, if we don't go out in all sorts of weather, we'd spend half our lives stuck inside the house. That's one reason I'm glad that my pup came to live with me. She gets me off the couch and out the door every single day, several times a day, regardless of the weather. Twenty feet of hallway simply doesn't make for very effective ball chasing. The fenced back garden has plenty of space for afternoon playtime, shoreline walk or not. It's her favourite place to be, especially the moments right after she's unhooked from her leash.

I love to watch her run at full speed, careening around trees and cutting through the gaps between bushes. I imagine she's thinking Freedom! When she's had enough, she plops down puffing and blowing but looking very pleased with herself. As long as winter's snow remains below the top of the fence, there's no tempting escape route. This pleases me if not her because she'd love to race up our side road into potential traffic to play with Rosie the Rottweiler three houses away.

There are more walkers, with and without accompanying canines, during our shoreline walks now that the weather is warmer. A few little guys still wear their sweaters as they trot along on tiny legs. Walking in this morning's rain, we meet a woman with her very handsome and well-trained German Shepherd. That dog looks to be older than my pup and is a good hand taller. Keeping to our own sides of the trail, we, on two legs, lift our heads enough to smile and greet each other. "Nice to see another crazy dog owner out in the rain," she laughs.

I notice something new on her dog that I've never before

seen. All four of its legs are covered in sleeves of some sort. They join onto a swath of the same material that covers the dog's belly, held in place by a couple of straps that come up and around him to clips on his back. It's like a harness but in reverse and with leg coverings.

We continue walking in opposite directions and with a glance down at my pup's undercarriage and legs, I understand what that dog is wearing. The usual white and grey of my Husky's belly and legs is a very noticeable muddy mess. She'll be in quite a state by the time we arrive home, whereas that Shepherd will be relatively clean.

The thought of dressing my dog in that very practical but rather comical contraption makes me comment to her, "Did you see that? What do you think?"

I get the usual look that asks, "Did you just say something I need to know?" as we walk around the next bend towards the duck pond and beach.

The rain is heavier, but the wind is behind us as we turn, so below the hem of my raincoat, the knees of my pants will be slightly protected from here to home. I dress myself against the rain and mud as best I can. Perhaps dressing my dog, while unusual, is not such a crazy idea after all.

Despite reasonably good winter walking clothes, it is so nice to feel less than frozen. As the days get longer, we'll be able to walk in the late afternoon and, eventually, with Summer's arrival, we can walk in the evenings after supper. Slogging through snowdrifts and negotiating ice underfoot is always a challenge for such a large part of our year.

There will be a nice spring in my step and less wear and tear on my body very soon. While I shall enjoy that, I know that my cold-weather companion will disagree. She wilted and panted on hotter days last year. Maybe, this year, she'll choose to cool off in the kiddie pool that sits in the basement waiting to be brought into service.

I didn't catch sight of the walker this morning. He has the right clothing to be comfortable in this horizontal rain. I expect, even in this weather, he will walk to wherever it is that he goes. Our timing just isn't similar on this particular day.

We're back home now after a quick stop at the mailbox. A rub-down with an old bath towel removes some of the accumulated mud from pup's body. My wet outer clothes will drip dry from a peg beside the door and, soaked through to the skin, my damp slacks and socks are replaced with lovely warm dry substitutes. It's certainly time to put the kettle on and think some more about that image I drew for the chair's upholstery.

I suddenly remember that I had quickly stuffed a small envelope into my inner coat pocket before we stepped out of the sheltered mail pavilion. It has remained dry, thank goodness, and I lift it out with a watchful eye to drips. The stamp is colourful and from the USA. I'm puzzled as to who would be writing to me. Stepping away from my wet coat, a gentle tug on the small flap that seals the envelope reveals a simple white note card with a crest emblazoned at its centre.

The hand-written script tells me that my father's cousin, Sister Jean, has died at the Convent House in Santa Rosa, California. She spoke of us quite often after her sabbatical visit, the letter says, during a life dedicated to her Lord and her Sister family. The writer has honoured her wish that I be told about her peaceful passing six weeks ago. My heart hurts a little but I smile with very good memories. I tuck the note into my writing journal, then turn and walk towards my old pine trunk.

The stash of used t-shirts under that lid offers a good selection of colours. Which I choose will influence the image that I hook. On one side of the trunk there's a small supply of leftover yarns, on the other, t-shirts, some already cut into strips, some still intact. My cutting mat is tucked into the space under my bed as is the big bag of burlap awaiting a purpose. I've already cut a piece for the backing so unfolding the leaf in my two-person table, I set up my sewing machine. I need to use a zigzag stitch around the edges of the burlap to prevent the open weave from fraying while I'm hooking. It's a task that takes the few minutes needed for my tea to steep.

Well, it would have taken only a few minutes if I had thought to check the bobbin before sewing. That particular stitch uses more thread than a straight stitch, and I made a rookie mistake despite many years using that machine. The feeder runs out of thread and ought to be refilled but, in truth, I decide to cheat. The thread won't be seen on the finished product because it will be tucked under itself, so I simply use a filled bobbin from a previous project. It doesn't matter if the top and bottom threads are two different colours. At least, it doesn't matter to me.

Edges now stabilized, and while pup is having a well-earned nap, I sip my tea and draw my scene onto the burlap. It's a very simple stylized version of clouds in a sky above an outline of hills with the ocean coming to the shoreline at the bottom of the image. I've used three different French curves to shape both the clouds in the sky and three pools in the ocean. Those coloured pools can be darker or lighter water, or I could hook them as mirrored reflections of the clouds. It's not representational so I'll decide as I go along if the ocean will be rough or calm, without or with reflections.

******************************************

## Carrie

Well, Deanne, the lady who gave me the pattern for the baby caps, came by a week or so after I'd finished the first dozen. Since then, while our weather slowly turned away from the cold of Winter, I've made another two dozen, and she's swung by to get them from me.

"They're being used all the time," she told me, so that makes me very happy.

As she was leaving, I mentioned that the store up the way had a Dollar Days where you buy one ball of yarn and get another one free, so my yarn basket has been restocked for future projects.

A few of the lunches for seniors were cancelled in the past four months and I don't have a plan for what to crochet next, so I've been mostly pottering around the house and looking at the seed catalogues that come in the mail. Each time I get one, I have to laugh because, for places other than here, folks are getting ready to plant.

In my garden, not far from the water, I'm only beginning to hope that the ground will thaw and we won't get a snowstorm in late May month. There will be no seeds or little plants ordered by me for a while yet, I'm afraid. I can look and dream, dog-ear the pages for possibilities, and then tuck the magazine away next to my armchair for future reference. If I repeat my usual habit, I'll unfold those corners and order nothing, relying once again on my steadfast perennials.

The phone is ringing now and the number is familiar, but I let it go to voice-mail. I follow the press this, press that routine and see Deanne's name. I'm not busy and if she's just called me, she is also free, so I dial her number.

"There's another project on the go for the hospital," she tells me.

We chat for a few minutes until I have all the details and agree it's something I'm interested in doing. That I had restocked my yarn bin makes us both chuckle, "Perfect timing."

The project is called Snugs 'n Hugs. People are making 4-inch squares that will be sewn together to create colourful afghans and lap blankets. They'll be available to comfort those who spend time in the mental health unit, the chemotherapy clinic or the children's hospital. While the size of each square is specified for ease of constructing the larger blanket, the colour is not. That's my kind of style, and I thank Deanne for contacting me. I'm keen to get started as soon as I hang up the phone, and I'm going to keep an eye out for more yarn sales. I might even have a look in the thrift stores for some good quality second-hand supplies.

The past few months have really flown by. I've seen the walker change her clothing from a heavy-duty coat, hat, mitts and footwear to more medium-weight gear. Her companion is oblivious to the change although, in yesterday's rain and wind, she didn't look any too pleased. I suspect, given her breed, she prefers cold days. The rain was practically falling sideways in the strong wind, and as they stepped onto the trail, the woman seemed to wish herself further down into her raincoat. Even at a glance, I could see that from the bottom of the coat to the tops of her boots was already dark with wet. The sides of the lane looked to be a sea of mud, so I expect that was none too pleasant for either of them.

Today, the sun is out, and while I doubt it's as warm outside as it is here behind my window, that gives me hope. The ducks are enjoying open water on the pond these days, and during weekends, I sometimes see clothes hanging on one or two lines in gardens on the far side. Life is starting to venture outdoors and people walk with a lighter step.

Mind you, I've also noticed that some drivers equate sunshine and bare roads with an increase in speed. When I went to get my hair done one day last week and the sun was shining from a beautiful blue sky, my sticking to the speed limit was obviously annoying the driver behind me. I'm sorry to say that it was a young woman, not a good role model. Then, I thought perhaps she was on her way to an after-school job and she hadn't left herself ample time for that day's increase in sun-loving traffic. Still, that's not my problem.

I think I'll grab some balls of wool now, sit down with a cup of tea and make a start on a square. I like the bright light in my little house today. It suits my mood, so instead of a fast car, I'll wield an efficient crochet hook and see how long it will take me to make one four-inch square. The good thing about crochet work is that it's so much easier to rip out than knitting. If I decide the colours aren't right or I get distracted and lose count, all I have to do is pull on the end and out it comes. So simple to redo or change until I'm satisfied. This is going to be a really nice project until my garden is ready for carrot seeds.

****************************************

## Margaret

The land around our houses is good old farmland, so it has plenty of drainage for the Spring runoff. This week's rain has tested it big time, I must say. The kids threw fashion and peer pressure to the wind so as not to spend all day wearing rain-soaked clothes in school. They ran to the bus as it began the climb up from the bridge rather than standing with friends on the road's edge. The wipers on every car were going full tilt as folks headed to work and I know we're all thinking the same thing. This is the middle of May. The May 24th weekend has not yet arrived. It's foolish to expect good weather before then and even more foolish to expect it on that particular weekend. There's a long-standing prophecy that's a joke but not a joke for those who live here.

I remember planning a fishing trip as a teenager to one of the bigger ponds out the highway on one particular 24th of May holiday. My boyfriend and I were going with another couple. None of us were old enough to drive at the time, so my father took us fifteen or twenty minutes from home to our chosen spot. We had the usual spinning rods and can of worms, a backpack with a lunch and drinks, an old tarp, a blanket to sit on and not much else. It was already drizzling when we left and Father told us we were crazy. Being invincible teenagers firm in our conviction that our plan was a good one, we clambered out of the car on the roadside before Father made a U-turn and headed for home.

The idea that the fish would rise to the bait as well as the raindrops, kept the four of us flicking lines out into the pond for a couple of hours or so. To a person, none of us was willing to complain about getting wet to the bone as the drizzle turned to actual rain. We girls were certainly not about to admit defeat if the two guys didn't, so we held out.

When "Time for a break" came from my boyfriend, we reeled in the lines, propped the rods against trees, strung the tarp overhead between two evergreens and squeezed underneath it. The shelter was a relief although not great for providing warmth. That came from arms around shoulders and bodies sitting close as we ate and drank whatever that backpack offered.

Pick-up time was only an hour away, and we had a twenty-minute walk to get back to the road, so we just whiled away what was left of our outing. The rods remained against the nearby trees until it was time to brave the rain once more.

As I remember it, my father kept his "I told you so" somewhat under his breath as we loaded the wet tarp and fishing rods into the trunk and then climbed our damp selves into the warm, dry car.

We all laughed at the complete lack of anything resembling a catch until our driver allowed himself to chuckle, "except maybe a cold."

We'd had fun but knew that a hot shower and dry clothes back in our homes were the next part of our plan. That's the $24^{th}$ of May weekend that I remember best.

Isn't it funny how one thought triggers another? I went from watching my family's departure in this morning's rain to that particular Saturday in May long ago. Last evening, I started a crossword puzzle that calls out to be finished but for now, I'm loading the washer with clothes while the sun still shines. There's bound to be enough warmth out there to dry lighter things.

This is another month with multiple birthdays, so I take the calendar off the kitchen wall while I wait for the washing to finish and look at the pen scratches in the squares.

My sister has, for years now, given me a calendar that has photos of family members, events, people and places atop each month. Usually, on New Year's Day, I open the new calendar and, with the one just finished for reference, I go month by month until everyone's birthdays have been transferred from the old to the new. I know I could put them in my phone but I'm not in the habit of checking that. This way is better for me. Besides, with them all noted on one page right there on my wall every day, it keeps me organized.

Since I've retired, the days of the week or the exact day of the month is not always foremost in my mind. Actually, when someone has a long weekend, it throws me right off for the rest of the week. I keep thinking the day off is a Sunday, so from then on, I'm one day behind until someone kindly corrects me.

I think we must have had a few years of bad winters because in this family we have a lot of birthdays happening between April and August. All the more reason for my baking cupboard to be well-stocked, my craft supplies kept up to date, and a few spare pieces of material for possible gifts needing to be sewn. I think I'll have a cup of tea and a sandwich, then do inventory and prepare a list of anything needed.

The card my nephew made for his father was a great hit and the cocoa cake was happily demolished in no time at the birthday supper. I didn't see if the puzzle worked because, as always happens when so many of us are in one place at the same time, conversations turned to long-standing recipes. I assured everyone that I still have a number of our mother's and grandmother's cookbooks and hand-written recipes. That led us to question where the old family dishes are stored and in whose attic.

A rambling discussion soon followed of ancestors, from where they originated both within this province and before they even settled here. I found it interesting that a number of the nieces and nephews hung around with us older folks. They seemed genuinely interested. Before the evening was over, people were letting it be known whose birthday was next and it didn't go without a reminder that time is closing in for the birthday person who is expecting a fortieth year of lemon bliss.

Isn't it just like us to be talking about cakes when we walk out the door not long after we'd all complained of having eaten more than was sensible. Here I am now, smiling to myself at the tangents of thought and conversation that bounced around during that gathering. Goodness knows where it may all lead as this month's celebrations take place.

Oh my goodness! There's a robin out on my lawn. As much as that gives me hope, I have to say out loud from this side of the window, "You are one very misguided little bird." Doesn't he know that we haven't yet had the $24^{th}$ of May weekend?

****************************************

## Ben

The morning greets me with chickadees singing in the tree outside my bedroom window. Now, that's a sure sign that our weather is turning. I lie still and listen to the five syllables of their song floating back and forth on the air. It's such a cheerful sound that not even the chill on my bare feet as they hit the wooden floor gives me pause. One of these days, I shall figure out how to get the wood stove heat aimed toward this back room. Until then, a couple of extra quilts are worth throwing aside, especially if it means I wake to a happy birdsong.

This is definitely a day for a walk. I haven't missed many days during the past few months, and the shoreline has suggested several potential images that might eventually find their way onto a canvas. The light on the water changes every few seconds. The colours in the trees and even in the beach rocks are starting to hint at Summer's approach. The official start of Spring is, I've learned, not really very applicable to this neck of the woods. No one plans changes to their trail-walking wardrobe by the meteorological clock.

The other day, I could see down through the blue-green of the water nearest the shore. It was so clear that I stood for a few minutes and just looked at the colours in the rocks on the sea bed. By comparison, on the far edge of that particular pool, the sea was impenetrable. Its dark grey-blue gave no hint of what lay beneath. There are so many shades within a relatively small area, and even they change with the wind, current or a passing cloud.

The sun is almost up as I pull on my usual layer of clothes and the kettle comes to a boil. Coffee and cereal with dried fruit get me started today. A nose out the door gives me a sense of the temperature so I can decide on which layer comes next. I think there's going to be a little more warmth in the sun after months of having to avoid getting chilled. Sitting at my old wooden table and emptying my cereal bowl, I think about what to wear en route to my destination. If it's a bit warmer out there, I'll carry my bottle of water. It can always be refilled at the other end of the trail.

My planning is interrupted by a sound not heard for many a month. Do I really hear a robin? It's a bit early for one but I welcome it just the same. What a great start to my day, both chickadees and robins. This is going to be one awesome walk along the shore. A quick look at my phone tells me that it's only 8:00, so I'll have the trail to myself for a while, at least. Breakfast finished, dishes in the sink, all appliances turned off, I turn to glide myself into my walking gear. No need for the neck warmer or balaclava today, but I put my gloves into the outside pocket of the backpack already by the door.

I lift the latch with one hand and give a final look around the place. The sun is shining through the windows in the east and I'm itching to get moving. The cracker berry leaves are turning pale green, and there are the tiniest buds on the birch tree as I move down to the lane. No more animal tracks in the snow, at least for now. I remind myself we'll see what the 24th of May brings. The road itself is muddy, so it must have rained last night, although I didn't hear it.

My legs work into my usual stride and I shift my weight to match. The treetop branches of the evergreens sway just a little but the air is quite still down here at ground level. A couple more bends in this lane and I'm at the main road. It's quiet even along here. School buses and folks starting their commute are a few minutes away. I pick up speed and lengthen my step as I head down the little hill to the bend and onto the bridge. The river is lazy this morning.

Half a dozen more homes, down past the swimming hole and I'm at the trail. The sky is hazy on the far north shore. It might even be rain. Here, though, it's a so-called chocolate box sky with puffy clouds above the gentle ripple from the surface breeze touching the water. I turn on my music and let favourites carry me along the trail.

I'm all alone and loving it.

Just past the bridge where the pond and sea compete for entry and exit, I see a family with two dogs ahead of me walking eastward. The adults hold the dogs' leads while the two children skip from side to side, their backpacks swaying with each hop. Just beyond the children, there's a large pile of compacted earth on the seaward side of the trail. Two pairs of young legs run up and down the mound with the confidence of having done it many times on their way along this part of the trail.

The family turns up the road towards the school and I carry on, once again, music in my ears as I pass the beach, the duck pond bridge and then the picnic tables across from the parking lot just before the headland path. Not at this hour, but at other times, a few cars will park in that space between houses and shoreline. Those in the vehicles have an unobstructed view of the bay, the islands offshore and high surf during a good storm. I imagine it's a peaceful spot to sit in a car, drink your coffee, gather your thoughts or even enjoy a clandestine meeting.

There's a sudden change in the air. My hair moves on the back of my neck and my face tingles. A quick glance out over the bay tells me that what was hanging over the north shore hills has now picked up both energy and moisture. I'm likely to have a wet walk home in a few hours. I pick up my pace again, step onto the headland and into the last half hour of my walk in this direction.

I'm looking forward to a welcoming coffee, a home-made muffin and enjoyable conversation to catch up with a friend who has been away for a month or so. My gear, which has proven to be well worth its cost, will keep me dry whatever the weather when I decide to walk westward to home later today.

*******************************

# Chapter Eight

## Sara

Yes! There's a tingle of warmth in the air this morning. The rain has ended and maybe, just maybe, we're on the way to fewer layers of walking clothes. I'll not hold my breath, mind you, because we haven't yet made it beyond the end of May.

There are two cushions on my small couch. I sit on one while on the other, and with her head strategically placed atop my thigh, a bundle of fur keeps her nose just inches from my toast.

My mother's eyes would roll, and if she were here to look at this setup, "You've made your own rod" would come my way.

Yes, I have created a spoiled pup. She knows that if she waits patiently and continues to feign disinterest, there will be a tiny corner of my breakfast added to her bowl in the kitchen when I've finished eating. She will find and eat that morsel before she deigns to sample the kibble itself.

Her routines have become more obvious during the past twenty months. I know, for example, that she will eat more of her food while I lace up my walking boots. Then, she will plant her body between me and the door to emphasize a point. I went out that door without her yesterday. That it won't happen today is loud and clear.

The sky is many shades of grey this morning. I hear a small

provincial commuter plane somewhere overhead, a bird of a different kind well hidden in the greyness. We walk uphill past the fire station with a really strong wind breaking my step. Pup's ears stay flattened in displeasure until we turn and start down the lane. The saving grace is that the fast-moving air isn't overly cold. My phone registered -3 C. That's a wonderful improvement from -30 not so long ago.

Undulating is the first word that comes to mind when I see the water. One wave rapidly follows another with hardly any space in between. They don't have a chance to break before they hit the shoreline. The white caps are short and brief then the surface wind erases them. The roar of the wind is all I can hear from every side. I pull my jacket hood up over my hat and am very thankful that, as we turn east, we're walking with the wind at our backs. Looking down, even the short fur on the dog's back is blown against the grain. Neither a dog low to the ground nor a human, somewhat higher, is immune to Mother Nature's fury this morning.

The couple with the children and two dogs come towards us into the gale and we pass without incident. In the near distance and also facing into the wind is a woman with two dogs on leashes attached to a waist belt. Between the wind in her face and her dogs pulling in our direction, she has trouble keeping her balance. I doubt that I can help her because her companions don't seem overly friendly. We stand off to one side of the path and my pup sits down.

I'm pleased to see that she remains still and isn't returning the aggression being sent her way. We wait and watch as the woman rights herself and then continues to a car parked in the lane below the trail.

A little further along, he strides towards us. This morning, the black-clad walker smiles, and we both make a quick comment about the strength of the wind. His stride doesn't falter as he heads west directly into its force.

The last half hour of our walk is peaceful with things for my walking partner to smell and tall grass for her to plow through now and then. I notice tiny bright green tips on the fir trees and a few cones trying to pop open in the warmer air. On this short stretch of trail, I can push my hood off my head. At the edge of the beach, a large group of seagulls is hunkered down together. Maybe if the wind eases, they'll check the waves for food.

We turn away from the sea and stop to watch all the ducks paddling at the opening where their pond moves under the bridge. Again, I'm pleased to see how my companion stands calmly to peer through the boardwalk palings. She simply watches with no attempt to startle the ducks into flight, then turns and moves on to explore a grassy patch beside the road. The wind is picking up again so I opt for the protected lane. There are three wayward ducks a couple of metres ahead of us, so we pause on the little hill to let them disappear into the safety of low evergreen branches in a corner garden.

I have no idea how many times my feet have taken us up this lane, past these homes. Hundreds, I suppose, and yet, this morning, I notice something new at the edge of the second driveway. On the trunk of a big birch tree, beneath branches still bare of leaves, are four birdhouses. Each is designed purposefully misshapen with a curving roof above a tilted house or a straight roof atop an hourglass home.

All four are brightly coloured, and although each home is different in size, there's a small round entryway just below each roof line. I'm surprised that I've not seen these works of art before now. Their vibrant red, yellow, blue and green with white trims are in distinct contrast to the muted green siding of the three-bedroom bungalow built for human habitation on the opposite side of the driveway.

In the second last house on this lane, I look up to see a handsome black cat watching us from a window as my pup pushes her nose into some scraggly roadside grass. To my right, an old tree is in danger of losing its topmost branches. They hang precariously by a single limb. If the split continues, there will be a significant crash, and the driveway will be blocked. I suspect the next windstorm will create a job for someone's chainsaw.

At the crest of the hill, our walk joins the main road that leads to the school. We cross in front of a house that has been unoccupied for months. Walking past the empty home often reminds me of one particular day last summer.

We were on our way to the trail, and I happened to glance up at the big front window. An arm was raised slightly above the sill and, person unseen, a hand waved at me. Of course, I returned the wave and added a smile. For a little while after that day, whenever we passed on our way to the shoreline, I'd glance in that direction. One morning, the light in the window was just enough to make visible the side rails of a hospital bed. There was never another wave, and recent months have shown nothing but an empty house. I'm thankful that I shared that greeting with whoever had been but is no longer in that bed. I like to think we brightened each other's lives that morning.

A couple of houses further along, there's often a group of large dogs who greet us loudly. All the dogs look much alike in terms of breed, although their colouring differs. I think what we see is a litter of siblings. They've grown as the months have passed, but today, as my pup looks for them, the garden is quiet. No loud barks or big paws resting along the fence rail. She's disappointed until her head turns to the right and sees the usual cats in their wire and wood outdoor space. There's a cat doorway in the basement window through which they must come and go. We stop for a minute to watch them, all six unperturbed by a dog's calm curiosity.

At the end of the road, I shorten the lead, push the crossing button and wait to see if anyone is going to actually stop. This morning, we not only have a car stopping in one direction but one of the fire trucks slowing to a stop as it rolls down from the station. My hand lifts a thank you to both drivers as we head down the road to home past half a dozen houses, each with their own canine or two.

In through our gate, off with the lead, and my companion begins her romp to freedom. Her massive rope toy gets dragged a few yards, and then it's on to kicking her soccer ball before getting it into her teeth for a vigorous shaking. Meanwhile, her human locks the gate, pulls a roll of small plastic bags out of a pocket and begins the twice-daily search and collect mission. I know there is one fewer because that patch of grass near the duck pond received a perfectly-timed deposit this morning that went straight into the community bin. Back to the job at hand, our family always refers to this task as DSP. The two letters on either end of that acronym stand for dog and patrol.

Indoors again with my hands washed and outdoor clothing removed, I plug in the kettle, put a chai tea bag into my mug and return to thoughts of hooking that chair cover. My preference is bright colours. The greys of today's walk would be too boring so I check the quantities in my stash and can always cut more strips, if necessary. Grouped into varying shades of single colours, they'll sit in clear bags within my canvas bag, easy to see and easy to find.

I love that larger bag. It was a gift from someone special. On one side of the bag, there's an image of a ball of yarn resting beside a rug-hook. Above that graphic, it reads *I'm an amazing hooker. Be jealous*. Slung over one shoulder, that bag has travelled with me through a number of airports and train stations, occasionally drawing a curious look or two.

*****************************************

## Carrie

It's so like me to go hell-bent for leather when I'm keen on something. I'm doing it again with this crochet project, of course. My hands, wrists and arms are complaining bitterly enough that I am forced to take my friend's advice to heart. She has a number of aching body parts that can only tolerate a few minutes of movement at a time. Whether she's weeding her strawberry patch or knitting a pair of trigger mitts, there has to be a change in both posture and activity every fifteen minutes. To remind herself, she sets a timer on her phone or, better yet, on her stove. The bell forces her to stop whatever she's doing, rest the working muscles and move her stiffened joints by walking from the living room to the kitchen or from one part of her garden to another.

It's maddening that I have to do that because, most often, the discomfort happens not while I'm doing the task but after I've done it for too long. My body, not my mind, demands that I stop.

As my friend says, "It is what it is."

If we ignore the signs, we'll be really sorry when the damage is done becomes irreversible, so we can no longer do our favourite things. We laugh when we're together for a coffee or tea that the adage spouted by some, "age is just a number," is only true if your aging body permits it.

So, I've stopped crocheting for a few minutes to pull on a light jacket and have a little stroll as far as my rose bushes. It looks as if they've survived the freezing winds of Winter and the glitter of a silver thaw. The sun today has a hint of warmth when the wind stops, and I believe I see new life in the stems. They look less bedraggled somehow. Still no buds and only a few of the old hips clinging to sprigs. They are the ones that, for one reason or another, I didn't pick last Fall.

For the first time in my life, I made rose hip jelly. It was very labour-intensive clipping the stems and not knowing that it wasn't absolutely necessary, I spent hours scraping off the scraggly flower ends, too. These are not cultivated nursery-bred rosebushes. My hedge is old, and all summer long, it's full of very small pink, white and red rosebuds. Their scent is wonderful, especially when the windows are open and the breeze blows through my house.

The finished jelly made from the hips is a beautiful soft pink colour. A bit too sweet for my taste but bottled in small jars, it made for great gift-giving at Christmas time. If I do it again this year, I won't bother fussing over the scraggly bits. Such is the advice, after the fact, that I received from my friend, Jane.

It's still chilly and kind of grey out here this morning. Time to head back indoors now that the body has been given a break. Looking up from my inspection of the bushes, I see the woman and her dog coming down the lane. She has on a lighter jacket, no longer the puffy blue one of winter walks. Her salt 'n pepper hair is short and uncovered. We catch each other's eye and smile when she stops to let her companion sniff the greenery at the corner. Braver than I, she'll walk in the wind off the water this morning. I hope she brought a hat. I leave my shoes by the door, hang up my jacket in the hall closet, and head back to my chair. As they enjoy their walk, I return to making more squares and setting a timer.

Yesterday, I decided to make some flowers that can be sewn into the centres of the squares. Making the petals so that they sit nicely requires keeping a count of the number of chains in each round so it takes time. The stitches themselves are combinations of single, half-double and treble over seven rounds for both front and back petals. Once I had two or three full flowers done, I had the routine down pat, and, of course, that's when the ding of the timer told me to stop.

I'm making as many different coloured flowers as there are squares so that they can either be colour matched or be a bright spot in the middle of a contrasting background. If black is okay as the main colour for a blanket, each square could have a red five-petal flower in its centre, for example. I'll give Deanne a call before I start on that just to be sure a dark blanket is acceptable. If that turns out to not be a good idea, I can still make one and maybe offer it to the Legion as a fundraiser for Poppy Day.

Some of the flowers I started were just a single colour, but that soon became boring, so I now have the petals one colour and the beginning centre something else. I'm even thinking that because there are two layers of petals plus the centre, all three might look good in a mixture of shades. My roses, for example, vary from one plant to the next and also from one flower to the next on the same bush.

Lots to think about and plenty of fun to do. I don't watch much on television, but when I am into a program, my hands like to keep busy. If it's not with a crochet hook, it's knitting socks or mitts or hats. Last winter, I used up all my scrap yarns and ended up with a blanket that easily fits my twin bed. It will go with any decor because the colours are so haphazard, just the way I like it. I'll do a couple more flowers, then stop to phone Deanne about the black yarn.

For supper last night, I made fishcakes from salt fish that I'd soaked overnight. I like to boil the fish, potatoes and onions all in the same pot. Once I'd mashed black pepper and savoury into the fish mixture, I had enough for a dozen cakes. Most are in my freezer, but I devoured three last evening with sweet mustard pickles, then kept two more for lunch today. The house smells fishy because it's too cold yet to open the windows but that's a small price to pay. I do love my homemade fishcakes.

Once in a while, when I've gone to town with a friend or two, we'll try different restaurants to check out their fishcakes. These particular friends have eaten mine, so we can make honest comparisons. There's one older restaurant-pub that has, to my mind, fishcakes just about as tasty as mine. Other places have fishcakes on the menu, and a couple of times after the first bite, it's obvious that they've been made with fresh fish.

We all agree that's a big mistake. Salt intake be damned if we're only eating them once every few months. I don't fry up scrunchions for myself but I do love it when a restaurant puts a few on the side.

All this talk of good food is making me hungry, even though it's only 10:30. I've been ignoring the few clothes that need to see an iron, so maybe I'll set up the board and do that instead of sitting to crochet. I ought to call Deanne, too, before I completely forget. If black is an okay colour, I'll have to scoot back up to my favourite store and hope they have some in the cubbyholes along that back wall.

If not, it will have to wait until I feel like starting up the beige bomber for a drive down the shore to the fabric and yarn shop.

****************************************

## Margaret

Frankie, my sister-in-law, stopped by on her way out the driveway this morning. She'd been thinking about the conversations during that birthday supper last week and is now wondering if I've ever looked up in the attic of my house for old family dishes, grandmother's recipes or anything else like that.

"Not for years, but I can have a look," I agreed as she gave me a hug then hurried back to her car.

A very live-in-the-present sort of woman, it's unusual for Frankie to be thinking about things from the past. She herself grew up in her aunt and uncle's home after her parents died in a car accident when she was five. Her brother and sister, both older by a couple of years, lived with other relatives, but all three were always within easy distance of each other in adjacent communities down the Northern Peninsula.

Her siblings have since moved to other places in the country, but Frankie went to university in town, then trained and stayed on this side of the island. She and my next younger brother met as university students and decided to get married before he went away to graduate school in the States. My niece, their daughter Emily, is the chocolate cake baker.

Anyway, I've no other plans for today. The sky is kind of grey behind the trees at the back of our land. It doesn't look like a snow sky or even one threatening rain but still not a day for the clothesline. I downloaded a couple of mysteries from the library last night, so they're on my reading list for later today. It took me a while to get used to the Internet but it's amazing what you can learn once you get past uncertainty.

The kids and their parents are way beyond my knowledge, but always give me a hand whenever I ask. I'm really wary of fraud and when those phone calls or emails happen, it leaves me a bit shaken. That's when those in the know show me how to block a number or check the email address to see if it is actually from the name shown.

I was awake before 6:00 this morning. It was a good feeling when I woke though, none of the unease that often lingers from some confusing but rarely remembered dream. Today, it felt as if I'd had a really peaceful, uninterrupted sleep except for the usual bathroom visit in the wee hours. My body had no difficulty climbing down from the bed and my hands didn't feel stiff, something noticeable simply because it happens so rarely.

Some days, my brother's arthritis is really bad, a condition maybe inherited from our mother. Max does his best to not let it stop him from staying active and he doesn't like it if anyone passes a comment about seeing him struggle at something. "Getting old ain't for sissies" is about as much of a complaint as he'll utter. Years of playing sports like soccer, hockey and baseball take a toll on joints, I think, no matter one's genes.

Breakfast was over, and the dishes stashed in my little dishwasher earlier when Frankie stopped in. So, now, I'll pull on the old rope that lowers the attic steps and go up to have a look at what's been there for as long as I've lived alone in this house. As the six steps unfold, I'm surprised that the mechanism works as well as it does. They're dusty but solid enough to take my 125-pound body, so here goes.

I don't suppose it's truly an attic as much as a crawl space. Even at only 5 foot 3 inches tall, I can't stand up to my full height. I can, however, crouch down a little to avoid the rafters and their cobwebs. I didn't think of bringing a dust cloth with me.

There's a pull chain next to the opening that lights a bulb in the middle of the space. It lets me inch forward to see in three directions. I remember now that we had insulation packed into the eaves and a partial plywood floor laid across joists to support things in storage after Mother died. I see her oval burgundy hat box with her initial engraved on the lid. If memory serves me correctly, that box is no longer serving its original purpose.

We put small items that none of us could bear to give away but no one wanted to take as mementos. I know there are bits of costume jewellery from when we kids spent our pocket money on her birthday gift and, from her childhood, a fancy hairbrush and comb set with a tortoise-shell decoration. She also had a couple of small prayer books and a little locket with a silver rosary coiled tightly inside. An item that never got used, it was a gift from Father's mother and, on the rare occasion when Mother let me hold them, I was intrigued by both.

A few feet further along on my left is a reused margarine box. The company that manufactured that product and another like it used to operate in town. Although I don't exactly remember when the business and its fish oil margarine came to an end, I think it was gobbled up by its parent company sometime during my university years.

I turn the box so the side without the logo is facing me, and there, in faded black marker, I see 'Old patterns and Recipes.' Still in good shape, I slide the box back towards the open trap door but I don't feel like ending my search just yet. Edging forward a bit farther, I want to see what else has lain forgotten.

There are a couple of very old metal and wood trunks. One is rounded on top with a large keyhole on the lower edge of the lid. I don't remember there being a key, certainly not one that large, so it must never have been locked. Beside it, there's a more modern longer green metal trunk. Even without touching it, I know it's too much for me to manage today. If there's anything in it that's destined for the ground floor, the kids will have to take on that job. I think I'll have a look inside it, just the same.

What was it Frankie mentioned besides recipe books? I scoot a few feet further into the attic and put my fingers under the metal lid. It creaks but lifts quite easily to reveal a layer of blanket. I really don't think we'd have squirrelled away a blanket, so now, I'm really curious. Closing the lid again, I edge the trunk into a space with more headroom so I can open it completely and lift off the blanket. One end of it has those three wide coloured stripes that signified a company up north, I think. Heavy and not bothered by storage, it lifts easily to reveal more precious cargo.

Here are the special dishes that we were all talking about at the birthday party. My heart skips a little beat as I look at the crest on the top dish and the gold that runs all the way around the rim. In the centre of this platter is an image from the coronation of King

George. The date emblazoned in red and gold reads 12 May 1937, with an inscription in Latin below the numbers.

I don't know if I've ever actually laid eyes on this before today. My mother spoke of it from time to time but didn't have it on display in the china cabinet. The only items on those glass shelves were the delicate china figurines that Father would buy for her, one for each child's birth and, later, for special times once children stopped arriving.

Rather than try to unpack whatever else lies inside the protective layers of cloth, I very carefully put that platter back in its resting place, lift the beige and striped blanket off my lap and lay it back on top. I'm feeling rather amazed and excited by this discovery and can't wait to tell Frankie that we need strong careful arms to bring a trunk down out of my attic. I turn slowly and think about how to carry that margarine carton once I get my foot onto the first rung. It slides easily to the edge with my progress to a standing position on the first step after I turn off the single attic bulb. Although a little awkward to lift onto the step I've just vacated, I can manage.

One foot after the other, I make my way down each dusty plank of wood, keeping the box on the previous level until both my feet and it arrive on the hallway floor. Before grabbing the rope and pulling the stairs back into the attic, I carry this treasure to my kitchen table. It's midday now, and the light is good despite the grey sky, so I can take my time removing the tape from the closed flaps and exploring the contents. All of which deserve the company of a good cup of tea. On my way to the kettle, I glimpse the walker striding past our property.

****************************************

## Ben

I spent the last two nights at my friend's house, a three-hour walk along the trail. He's planning to be away for a few months, and I'm happy to check on his home. I go there at least once a week anyway to use his Internet connection. One of my three email addresses is known to only two people, the friend who is going away and one other person from eight years ago and 5,000 miles away. Correspondence from these two people captures my immediate attention, whereas others get, at most, a minute's consideration.

A pot-luck last evening brought together not only a combination of food but also a variety of friends. To see one of us heading out on an adventure was cause for celebration. Rob has dreamed of making this change in routine since his move here. Our lives had thrown us together in sun and sand, then kept us apart and, for two years, completely out of touch. Serendipity, karma, or one of life's curious turns now sees us on this island with less than a dozen kilometres between us.

Rob is a much more social creature than I and the group last night comes together at his behest. Those six people have become my friends through him, and while I spend far less time in their company, that matters not when we're all together. Drinks, good food, great conversation and agreement on music lasted into the wee hours of this morning. I slept for maybe three hours, drank a strong coffee and began my walk home as his ride to the airport pulled up to the curb.

The morning is nothing but grey overhead and out on the sea. I've walked for more than an hour when I hear but cannot see a plane. Travelling west, it isn't long since take off. In a moment of fancy, I wish the sky were a clear blue, and that small tube was low enough to see a familiar face peering out from a window seat. We both know how far along the trail I am at this point in my walk.

The smile on my face and the laughter in my chest bring back last night's fun and how much we all want this trip to meet his every expectation. If Rob has anything to do with it, that's what we'll hear about in every email he chooses to send. I come back to the trail from the headland path and face the straight stretch that ends above the little sandy beach. The wind has suddenly chosen to make its presence felt. It is persistent and strong insisting my leg muscles do battle with it. I'm hoping it will clear my head and release unexpected tension.

There is a cluster of seagulls hugging the shoreline. The wind across the water is driving the waves on an angle and those birds think better of fighting against it for now. Once across the bridge and into the shelter of the trees on both sides of the trail, there is actually a bit of warmth in the air despite the absence of sunshine. That's a harbinger of good weather to come. Tight clothing barriers against the cold will be removed, but not just yet, as the treeline ends and the force of the wind hits me.

I don't object to the wind. It's been part of my life in one way or another for more than ten years. This morning, however, it nearly has the upper hand after a rare evening of socializing, eating more food than is usual and sleeping five hours less than normal. If this is against me from here to home, I'll earn whatever reward I desire. 'Reward' reminds me of the incredible email that consumed our conversation the day before our party.

My very private email address had an unexpected message for me. The name in the sender's address wasn't familiar, so I hesitated before my finger tapped the mouse.

The subject line used language that startled me and was enough to bring Rob from the kitchen behind me to ask, "You okay?"

I nodded a reply, then opened the message. Fearing a scam that had somehow hacked into this unused and highly protected email, I began to read. The sender introduced herself as the representative of a law firm in California. Leaving that message idle for a minute, I searched for and verified both the business and her.

The email went on to explain that without a postal address for me, she had been given permission to initiate contact via this email, and, it continued, permission had been granted by a person known to both me and the friend standing on the other side of the table whose face showed much concern.

"You've gone grey. What's happened?" Rob leaned forward as I said the name given in the first sentence on the screen.

Both of us were jolted back to a stretch of sand dunes and a blazing sun. On either side of that table, my laptop between us, I read the whole email into the quiet of the room just the day before yesterday.

Seven years ago, both Rob and I witnessed a horrific accident. A young dude had just successfully ridden a massive belligerent wave. We had watched from shore as he dropped the biggest bomb we'd seen all day.

As he ran up the dune to tell someone about his feat, we called, "Congrats, dude!" and laughed at his glee. We both knew that incredible feeling.

As Rob and I stood to ride again, an awful thud rolled

through the air. We both tore up to the crest of the beach as people began screaming. The dune buggy lay on its side, one wheel spinning wildly against the sky, a shattered board and the wreck of that awesome young dude sprawled on the sand. We dropped to our knees on either side of him and held his hands until the medics arrived. Even today, it's too easy to recall the look of shock in those blue eyes.

This email asked me to respond as soon as possible and to provide a phone number for further contact. We had planned to spend the day getting ready for a celebratory send-off the next evening, but this needed to be done. Once my hands stopped shaking, I confirmed receipt of the email and included my cell phone number.

A glass of chilled white wine appeared in front of me. It was noon on the other side of the continent but another message immediately confirmed my reply and asked if I could immediately take a video call. There was a nearly tangible sense of foreboding hanging in the room when my laptop rang. I motioned for Rob to stay where he was, both of us going back through time as the woman on the screen introduced herself.

Unbeknownst to us at the beach that day, the young surfer was a blonde-headed, pony-tailed kid from a very wealthy family. He had survived the initial trauma and lived through months of hard recovery, repeatedly asking for someone to find the two guys who'd stayed by his side. It had taken a lot of searching but people hired by his family had found my name on an old surfboard, then been given my email, and finally reached me and, by coincidence, Rob.

Ravaged by complications from injuries and endless surgical attempts to mend his body, his family wanted us to know that Sam had died. They and his friends had sailed off his favourite shoreline and tossed his ashes into the swells of the Pacific. His parents had lived through their son's sense of urgency to find and thank two fellow surfers who had shared his glee that day and then sprinted up the dunes to be by his side.

I told the lawyer that the second person was sitting across from me right now. She verified Rob's identity and asked me to provide a street address, to which Rob nodded his approval.

She thanked us for our cooperation and ended the video call with, "There will be a delivery by private courier within twenty-four hours."

Cleaning the house and making food was a blur for the rest of that day.

Neither of us could recall anything about the drivers of the buggy or how many other people were at the crash site. All day and evening, our conversations went back and forth in time until, eventually, exhaustion took over. Not knowing what the courier was to bring in the morning and preparing for both a party and Rob's scheduled departure led to a restless sleep.

At 8:00 the next morning, the doorbell rang, and I signed for a slim courier envelope. Coffees at the ready, we sat at the table as I opened it. There were two white, vellum, legal-sized envelopes, one designated for me, the other for Rob. We both took a breath and, in unison, broke the seals. The single-page letters inside were hand-written in classic blue ink. The words were matter-of-fact but emotionally charged with gratitude.

The top left corner held a staple, so we flipped the page. Attached to the reverse of each letter was a bank draft for a considerable sum of money in American currency. Both of us sat in stunned silence. It took a bit of time to digest what we held in our hands, what our eyes were reading. Several coffees over several hours attempted to keep us in the here and now with so much more on our minds than originally planned. That morning held serendipity, karma and, definitely, an unexpected turn in life for both of us.

Yesterday, the party ended on a high note that resonated with the two of us over and above the good vibes coming through the door with our friends. Today, Rob is on his way to points beyond this continent in that plane hidden by a grey sky. I'm facing the wind with even fewer concerns than I could ever have imagined. Despite too much caffeine and too little sleep, if the lady behind that window watches out for me today, she might notice that I'm smiling. I have three young dudes in my heart and mind.

***********************************

# Chapter Nine

## Sara

My grocery list last week included a package of locally produced salt fish. Every few months, I get the urge to have fishcakes. I don't know how others make them, but I put everything into one pot. The cut potatoes, chopped onion and fish that's been soaked overnight then drained. When the potatoes are soft, it's all strained through a colander. Black pepper and savoury added it's ready to mash together. After that, I pat scoops of the mixture into cakes. This morning, the sun is out, and there's very little wind, so I'll get it all combined before we go for our walk. By the time we arrive home, it will have cooled enough to make into cakes but not burn my hands.

My companion barely tolerates the paw balm that I put on her pads before we go out the door. She's still nervous about anyone touching her feet. The first time that I even reached to stroke a paw, she recoiled and jerked her leg away from me. After fourteen months of gentle desensitization, she is close to complete trust. Clipping her nails is still a work in progress but it gets done by me, one sitting at a time.

All prep accomplished for both walkers, we are on our way. I let her determine this morning's route. We head up the sidewalk past the fire station, gas bar and coffee shop. A plow has thrown the road salt onto the surface under our feet, which is both good and bad. The icy patches are pockmarked and less slippery, but the salt itself is corrosive on pup's paws. I'm glad that we protected them.

Today's date pops into my mind as I let the leash go to its full length now that we're away from the main road. It's the 24th of May, our infamous long weekend. There will be campers in the parks and the best aromas coming from fires in the grates at every site. Those in tents and sleeping close to the ground will have found it chilly because the forecast called for temps at the freezing mark overnight. Anything out in that air will have a sheen of frost on it at breakfast time, I expect.

The edges of the trail have a couple of inches of new fluffy snow that require my companion to stop and bury her nose as often as she can. This is the second day of the long weekend and there are plenty of paw prints from walkers who have gone before us. The gulls are quiet, only a couple soaring above the high tide and providing contrast against the bright blue sky. Off to our right, the two Australian Shepherds charge to the fence and bark their greeting. Even fifty feet away from us, I can see their stubby tails wagging.

Ten minutes along the trail and suddenly on high alert, my pup pulls on her harness. I stop and look into the trees that shelter half a dozen large new homes. It takes me a minute or two before I see a figure under the lowest branches. Sure enough, it's a cat, a large orange bundle of fur standing very still but ready to run. My hand reaches under my dog's chin and turns her head as I gently tug the leash bringing her back into a walking stance. A treat and "Keep walking" give the cat its space and move our focus back to the trail ahead.

A few minutes later, the other walker and I, almost in unison, exchange, "What a nice morning."

There's a quick smile on both our faces as we pass because, this time, we've both commented on the weather. The duck pond brings a new sight. Atop the frozen water, someone has created four ice rinks clearly defined by rectangles of mounded snow. I'm guessing that each is at least fifty feet long and almost as wide. This is the first time all winter that I've seen this on the duck pond. The temperatures overnight must have definitely stayed below freezing.

There's a hockey net twenty feet out on the middle rink, and three people are enjoying a beautiful sunny holiday morning. Two of them take a seat on the banked snow, and I can hear young laughter. We walk past a car parked on the side of the road. Its door is ajar, and a woman is lacing up her skates. I hope they all take advantage of the ice now because it won't last much longer.

We turn into the lane that takes us past the colourful birdhouses and up to the school road. The dogs in the pen beside the big green house begin to bark even before we reach there. A quick count tallies four excited auburn blurs running back and forth in the space between a barn-like structure and a very tall chain-link fence. I've noticed before today that the design and colour of the barn match that of the main house. Both sit at the back boundary of a deep lawn.

Last summer, we occasionally met a young man walking with a beautiful Irish Setter. He explained, from the other side of the road, that his neighbours are breeders. One day, he slowly walked the female.

"She's heavy with seven puppies," he said with a smile.

Our walks always provide something interesting. Not always pleasant weather-wise but rarely without something that catches my eye.

This morning, we get home and I, dutifully kick the scruffy soccer ball across the garden, watch it being grabbed by big Husky teeth and, as always, vigorously shaken. The ball's tattered pink and silver covering is barely holding its own and any ability to bounce was lost long ago. As I climb the back steps, I'm happy to see there's just enough warmth in the sun for my boots to slide a layer of ice off the edge of the deck.

Found at the side of a country road at only two weeks old, my pup, Chance, is having so much fun in the garden right now that

I head indoors to finish those fishcakes. I know from experience that this amount of mixture will make a dozen. I'll put the majority into my small freezer, but save two for the frying pan later today and a couple of small bites to upgrade dog kibble at suppertime.

As I glance out the door, my trusty walking companion and housemate has stopped frolicking and decided to lie in the sunshine on the deck, a well-deserved rest. I've finished the first of my daily two litres of water, so a cup of Earl Grey, one of yesterday's ginger-raisin-molasses muffins and a chunk of cheese make an easy lunch.

If the icicles hanging from the pergola's roof last a couple more hours, I'll break them off and throw them for Chase to catch and chomp, ice being one of her favourite things. In the meantime, I'm plotting the colour scheme for that chair covering. The clouds are not stereotypical, so they could indeed be yellow rather than white in a blue sky. If I do that, the pools in the ocean will need to be a lighter blue than the majority of the water. I think that will work, but knowing me, it will probably change as the hooking goes along.

****************************************

## Carrie

How's this for a lousy start to the day? The temperature overnight was below freezing, and I hadn't driven my car for at least a week, so after breakfast, I decided to start her up. Right now, I'm back in the house and none too happy. This is a long weekend.

There's not a garage open. Even the local guys have gone fishing or camping or just taking a day off. I'm not going anywhere for two days, even if I want to. There's no way that I'm going shanks pony, as my mother used to say.

My jacket is back on its hanger in the front closet, and my boots are on the mat. They're in a good place but I, myself, am not. I got dressed up, walked to the car, opened the door, sat in the seat and put my key in the ignition. When I turned that key what I didn't get was actual ignition. Nothing, absolutely nothing, but the engine trying to turn over.

I heard my father, god rest his soul, telling me, "Check under the bonnet," so I did. I couldn't see any loose wires or a broken fan belt. The dip-stick told me there's plenty of oil in the engine, the battery cables are all in place, and the radiator looks normal. So, it escapes me as to what's wrong with the old girl.

I'll call around to see if anyone's open, but it's not likely. I know if he's home, Brud will call back when he gets my message. He's been working on my car for over a decade and his tow truck is probably older than my car. So much for warming up the engine. I can't imagine that lying idle for a few days at the end of May has done anything too drastic. This is Sunday, so I have today and tomorrow to come up with an idea of what's gone wrong with the beige bomber.

Earlier this week, Maisie delivered a second seed catalogue

along with the newspapers she's finished reading. It's all still on my table, so maybe now is a good time to allow myself a little distraction. I always think I'll send for fancy flower seeds. The photographs draw me in every time, tall majestic gladioli in strong colours, gentle pink, white and mauve sweet peas that climb a trellis, not to mention the huge blooms of a peony bush. Sitting here in my kitchen with the morning sunshine pouring through the window, I turn down the corners one by one but don't complete the order form. I'm well aware that this is the second catalogue with dog-eared pages and an empty order form in my possession.

Thinking about planting season, I get out my old gardening book. A friend gave it to me for my birthday maybe fifteen years ago. I need to get a handle on keeping the pests at bay this summer. There's a section about how to stop slugs from eating the vegetables. Even worse is things getting down between the leaves of a plant. I babied along some lettuce plants last year, and, too many times, I pried apart the leaves only to be greeted by an earwig scurrying onto my counter. Oh, how I dislike those creatures! They look devilish to me, and they move too quickly to catch.

Spiders and daddy-long-legs don't both me at all, even though I don't want them indoors. At some point during the summer, little balls of spider eggs cling to the side of the house, but they can be brushed away with the outdoor broom. I love to see the bees flitting from one rose to another or from one dandelion to the next on the lawn, but there's nothing to like about slugs. They eat my rhubarb leaves and kill the plant at its root. I paid close attention last year and picked the slugs out of the bed each time I saw one. I also added the recommended amount of manure to my soil. I only have half a dozen rhubarb plants, but they produced a great crop for boiling with brown sugar to top yoghurt or ice cream, for jam-making in the Fall and for combining with strawberries or apples in pies.

An open plot, even a small one like mine, filled with dark, rich soil, does well. After I dug in the manure, though, I had another problem. The plants were fine. The soil was fine. A neighbourhood cat was not fine. He decided that my rhubarb bed smelled so good he was going to use it as a litter box. I'd come out each morning, and sure enough, another hole had been dug. After a couple of weeks of this, I laid a blanket of chicken wire over the bed and secured it just enough to keep out the cat but still let the rhubarb grow tall.

That's one of the reasons I won't put down poison. I couldn't live with myself if anything other than the intended target was killed. I've heard about using shallow containers of dish soap to catch the earwigs and slugs. Apparently, they climb in and can't get out again. I haven't tried that yet. Someone else mentioned sprinkling the peel of lemons, oranges or limes around the plants. I did try that. It didn't deter the roaming cats but made for a pleasant scent when I was on my knees weeding.

Well, I'm no further ahead on garden plans, but it's been nice to sip tea and daydream of the coming days when it will be nice and warm. I'll call the garage now and leave a message that my car won't start. Next in my day is to do a few more squares, a change from more flowers. Deanne liked the idea of a blanket with dark squares and bright centres but not black. So when the car is fixed, I'll pick up a dark navy. The petals already in the basket will work with navy, and when they're all sewn together, it won't be as heavy a colour as all black.

She reminded me that some of the finished blankets can be smaller, more child-size, so I'll think about how many squares would be needed for that. I also want to make sure that I have a good supply of brighter colours on hand. I, myself, could go to the store this afternoon but my poor little car can't. Nobody's going to buy all the yarn before Tuesday, I tell myself as I hear my stomach grumble.

Where's the morning gone, I wonder. It's time for another tea, a look at the local paper, and maybe a cheese and tomato sandwich. To me, that's comfort food. Speaking of comfort, the woman and her dog waved as they went by this morning. I was perturbed on my way back to the front door after trying to start the car, but I managed to return her greeting. I hope her day started out better than mine.

*******************************************

## Margaret

The family is off work for an extra day this weekend, so I'll text to ask who's available for help getting that trunk down from the attic. I'm sure there will be a ton of excited conversations from the first lifting of that blanket to the last of its protected treasures. My little living room is bound to have more visitors than usual.

I haven't seen the walker for a couple of days. I think it was Thursday or Friday the last time he passed my place. I'm falling down on the job it seems. It's a pleasant day out there, maybe even a little warmer than last week. I know because the two oldest nephews headed to the road wearing hoodies. Mind you, they aren't keen on dressing for the weather at any time, preferring to keep in fashion with their peers. The puddles at the edges of the driveway are no longer ice-covered so that's another sign of some warmth in the afternoon sun.

The margarine label keeps catching my eye. It's definitely time to cut the yellowed tape and get those flaps open. The old china jug in a corner on my counter offers up a sharp knife, and with a tingle of anticipation, I run the blade down the middle of the box. The cardboard has that lived-a-long-time smell. It's the scent of age and storage, not one of musty dampness, so the contents should be in reasonable shape. As the tape peels back, the surface beneath it is brighter than the main box. I suppose under the protection of the tape, that area hasn't had to breathe in years of dust.

The first thing I see is an exercise book, the kind we used in school for writing. This one is a pale blue and has a familiar brand name on the front. Lifting it out and turning it over, the back shows a printed timetable. Goodness, I remember filling in those squares with abbreviations of subject names: Spelling (SP), English (E), Arithmetic (A), History (H) and Social Studies (SS). Holding the edges with both hands, I turn it back to look at the front.

There, in the Subject space is *My Favourite Recipes* in my mother's precise hand. She had been taught to write in a very upright style of script. It always looked very different than the writing we were taught. The letters are more of what we called printing rather than the curves of writing. There was never any doubt as to when something was or was not authored by my mother. I could never fake a sick note to get out of school, for example.

Right now, I want to stop and spend the rest of the day turning the pages of that scribbler and reading that handwriting one recipe at a time. If I succumb to that, I'll never see what else is in this box, so I lay it to one side and turn back to what comes next. It's a small book, a faded green hardcover. The black lettering, all in upper case, says THE ART OF THE TABLE. Below that is an image of a place setting with a carafe, wine glasses and a bowl. I don't remember ever having seen this book before now.

On the first inside page are black and white reproductions of two intricately set tables. White tablecloths, silverware, centre pieces of tall flowers and crisp white linen napkins folded into pinpoint upright triangles. The opposing page lists How to Wait at Table, How to Fold Napkins, and How to Carve. The date at the very bottom is 1923. The overleaf shows the menu for A ROYAL WEDDING BREAKFAST. The smaller type below announces that its timing is for the marriage of H. R. H. Princess Mary with Viscount Lascelles in February 1922.

I am absolutely flabbergasted and don't know how or why this little book is in a margarine box of things owned by my mother. I make sure my hands are really clean before I turn another page. The Table of Contents begins on page 9 with The Dining Room and Its Appointments and ends on page 119 with Hints for the Pantry. All topic lettering is in block print.

I turn to the back of the book. On the final page of descriptive text, there are four topics, in bold and upper case type. MICE, TO CLEAN WOODEN UTENSILS, TO CLEAN ZINC, and TO MEND A ZINC PAIL. Each title has a paragraph with appropriate instructions. That's on page 126. The final two pages in the book, numbers 127 and 128, hold a General Index with topics listed alphabetically and aligned with their starting pages.

There is a wealth of knowledge inside this 5" by 7" publication. I carefully and slowly fan the old paper. Both photographic and hand-drawn facsimiles pop into sight between pages of text. I can hardly wait to sit in my twenty-first-century living room and read this household bible of information printed more than one hundred years ago. It was hard enough to not stop and read my mother's recipes. To now put this treasure aside and continue into the box is even more difficult, but persist I will as the next book looks up at me.

This is a thick leather-bound volume in a deep chocolate brown. The lettering on its spine and cover is raised, and the edges of the page have a golden tinge. I run my fingers over the letters. When people refer to leather being tooled, is this what it is? The title reads *Mrs. Beaton's Guide to Homemaking* but to explore this heavy book is more than I can fathom at the moment, so I reluctantly lay it off to one side on my kitchen table and turn back to the open box.

Next in sight is a thick layer of half a dozen publications. In magazine format, their size and style is more familiar to me. I'm guessing each measures about 10" by 12" and, while obviously read more than once, is still in good condition except for a few dog-eared corners. Now, I know from whom I get my bad habit with anything other than a library book.

The glossy-coloured covers are in stark contrast to my first two discoveries. These are obviously produced by or for companies that make baking, cooking and household supplies. Mother may have had a subscription because, looking through them, they run for a year. Twelve monthly issues through 1950. A quick but gentle look through the first couple of pages shows ads of women in aprons promoting a new frying pan or the best flour for making a cake rise beautifully.

Emily and Liam will be horrified when they see what are now politically incorrect stereotypes. I understand the context but my young nieces and nephews may not be quite as amused. The next time they are here in my kitchen baking or creating something as a gift, I foresee some interesting commentary and conversations.

When I have lifted all the magazines out onto the table there is still one item left in the carton. It's flat and soft inside a brown paper bag. There isn't anything written on the bag but, having sat under the weight of the other things, its creases are starting to fray. Very gingerly, I unfold one edge at a time and feel it fall apart in my fingers. The layer beneath the brown was once white tissue paper. Yellowed now, it too begins to crumble as I move it. With very little effort, it lifts aside to reveal one of my mother's special aprons.

My grandmother's words, "Be still my beating heart," ring true as I rest the apron's hem on the table and gently life apart the folds of material. The strings of the apron fall to one side as the body comes into the light after so many years of darkness. The white of the apron front bears cross-stitch embroidery, something my mother tried to teach me.

I read My Hearth is in My Kitchen, spelled out in tiny x-crosses, royal blue, red and sunshine yellow. A memory filled with laughter comes with seeing those words. As a child, I thought my mother had made a mistake and misspelled Heart by adding the 'h' at the end. She chuckled as her eight-year-old daughter learned the difference between hearth and heart, as I am chuckling now.

What a wonderful find this morning. I'm sure this apron can be preserved in some way that allows it to bless another kitchen in another time. My supply of gift wrap has some white tissue paper, so I'll lay the apron in that for now. There are more people than I who will enjoy the history that has been brought to life from the cloister of my attic and an old margarine carton. The trunk still to come must hold even more.

***********************************

## Ben

The announcer on the radio this morning was talking about how we'd survived this weekend without the expected wind, rain or blizzard. The weather is not just a quick report around here. It's the topic of many conversations, even when it's a glorious summer's day. I laugh at myself and wonder how long it will take for me to get used to this, if ever. My habit of checking each morning is purely to govern which gear I'll need for the trail.

I suppose, with a culture based on the sea or the land, how Mother Nature treats you is really important. Not having grown up with that concern, it was a lesson I learned soon after my arrival on this island, needing to keep the roof solid, the path shovelled, my walking gear water-proof and having both a shovel and firewood at the ready.

Last evening, after I'd come home from Rob's, my sketchbook and I spent a few hours together. I looked through the doodles and sketches made a few weeks ago. They aren't half bad. There's an idea percolating through them that appeals to me. That lonely canvas is likely to see colour very soon. What's more, going to check on the house at the east end of the trail every day brings me closer to more supplies and the potential of working on multiple canvases.

On my laptop, I have a number of files containing photographs taken during the past couple of years. Some are long shots of the shoreline and the trail going east and coming west to home. The old rail bed wound its way beside the sea, so the angles from and of the trail are often quite different. Three headlands with their natural footpaths are filled with tuckamore and wild grasses, swaths of lupines in various colours and even one patch of purple iris.

In between gnarled tree roots, I've shot tiny flowers, bright seed pods and bulbous yellow toadstools in sunshine and fog, snow flurries and rain. When memory fails me, which isn't often, I can call up these shots to find the sky or the ocean that borders the trail to finish a sketch. I haven't planned along these lines in such a long time. My face is smiling, and I tell myself to think about future drawings while walking today. I'll take more notice of the far shore, the islands big and small that lie between here and there.

My lighter jacket seems right this morning. On it goes before the backpack with the rabbit's foot key-ring zipped tightly into the inner pocket. My trusty boots, long since moulded to my feet, and I'm ready to go. The American draft in an envelope tucked in my buttoned shirt pocket sits where the touch of my hand will reassure me that it's secure. This is going to be a walk with a different endpoint. Once there, I'll take the jeep, drive down to the bank on the main road and deposit that gift. That done, Sam's family will know their mission is complete.

The lane, the road, the pace through the community pass without anything catching my eye this morning and I'm soon over the first bridge. The beach has changed shape again. Upright, rusted metal pilings are now visible, reminders of the train track that carried so many people for years. Too expensive in materials, time and labour to replace, it's now this walking trail. Intrigued by its history, I looked it up not long after I moved here.

As the narrow gauge track, which ran for 906 miles, fell into more and more disrepair, it became impossible to fix. The newer tracks were no longer made 3'6" wide, and to replace all 1,458 kilometres that linked both populated and isolated communities wasn't feasible. The train, ironically dubbed the Newfie Bullet, made its final run in 1988 after ninety years of service. Even within the distance of my walk today, there are a couple of old buildings snug to the trail and I wonder if they had former lives as the Station Master's home or even the station landing itself.

Today, just before the bridge over the big duck pond, I stop to leave some crumbs for the crows. Continuing to walk, I surreptitiously glance back to watch them come down from the tops of nearby evergreens that shelter an old graveyard. Cawing loudly in competition, six of them tuck into my offering. Their voices compete with the cries of gulls and the everyday conversations between the ducks paddling nearby.

Away from open water, I notice very well-defined rectangles of snow. They mark off four large ice rinks. On the middle one, there are three skaters. Two are sitting to lace up their skates. With the slight warmth in today's air, I hope they enjoy themselves. I suspect the ice won't stay thick enough for much longer. I can deal with massive wave curls rising out of a warm sea and pounding to the shore. Standing out on a frozen pond scares the hell out of me. My feet, here on solid ground, will carry me toward today's destination.

The clusters of beach rocks that were thrown onto the trail by the high surf a few weeks ago remind me of puzzle pieces. While they don't fit nicely into a predetermined pattern, the background colours are repeated even when the tiny surface splatters differ widely. To paint them would be very much akin to doing a jigsaw puzzle.

Objects of the same colour with just a hint of variety, enough to make one try again and again until the exact match is found. By contrast, the rocks of a breakwater are more uniform in both shape and colour, having been blasted from some quarry and then trucked here to bolster the beach against erosion. Their angles are sharp with distinct veins of solid orange or green, very different from the smooth sea-worn pebbles rolled by the sea.

I hear the engines of a jet overhead. The four white trails are clearly visible against the blue sky and the sun is sparking off the silver of the plane itself. It's on an eastbound flight path and I find myself wondering if Rob is in that cockpit. The high altitude negates a landing at the airport in town, so it must be a cross-Atlantic run. The change to longer distance hauls is what appealed to my good friend after years of short commuter runs. It's a great day weather-wise to be up there.

Back here on earth, I'm approaching the lane to the house. At a glance, all's well. No footprints in the fresh inch of snow on the walkway. The key turns easily, and it's cool but not cold with the fireplace unlit and the heaters turned down. I unlace my boots and peel off outer layers, patting my chest pocket as I head down the little hallway to the kitchen. Having promised to eat whatever is in the fridge and do my best to deplete the cupboards in his absence, I take a quick inventory. The man is both a pilot and one heck of a good cook, so everything from the mundane to the exotic fills his shelves. I'll take only what I need for a day and even that will be limited by the backpack now on the kitchen table.

The main task at hand is to open the garage door, start up the four-wheel drive and get my banking accomplished. One of the things I love about this vehicle is that it's a standard shift. Muscle memory comes instantly and given familiarity, albeit usually from the passenger seat, I've no hesitation. The drive down the lane, onto the main road and into traffic takes no time. Parking and making money arrangements are surprisingly hassle-free, and in less than an hour, I'm backing into the garage once again.

I make a coffee, lift my laptop from my backpack, and sit down at the polished raw edge table. The only email worth opening is one from Rob. His first flight to London, Heathrow, was just as he'd hoped it would be. No technical issues, no troublesome weather, no falling asleep with controls on autopilot (his favourite bad joke) and not even a lengthy hang-time awaiting clearance to land. I write back telling him how good it is to hear all that and about the jet in this morning's sky that wasn't his. I add the bank errand and a list of what I'm planning to remove from his food stock today, simply things that are at or beyond their expiration date.

Do I tell him about the painting idea that walked the trail with me this morning? He'll smile to know how I'm planning to get back into that mode. He was the one who pushed me to paint those surfboards. Selling them paid half the rent and bought us a few meals all those years ago. I decide to wait until the idea is a little further along, so I close the laptop and wedge it inside the protective pocket of my backpack. Then, with the coffee mug washed and put back on the shelf, I pack milk, eggs, bread and fruit.

It's a heavier load than usual, but if I'm to do this every day, I need to get used to it. The standing invitation to move in here won't tempt me unless we get a freak storm or super high wind and hard rain. I prefer my place and always enjoy the walk. One last check that the garage door is completely down and locked then back into the hallway and out the front door. Zipped into the little pocket, the key-ring makes a small bulge and, with safe-keeping in mind, I feel through my jacket to the pocket where completed financial matters reside until I get home.

Now and then, I move my shoulders to shift the weight a little and debate whether to rearrange the contents at some point during the two hours ahead of me. At the spot where I fed the crows earlier today, I pass the woman and her Husky. We both end up making the same comment about how nice it is to be walking today, and I feel my face crease into a smile that lingers after they've continued eastward. My step is light despite the extras on my back and I laugh, "How could it be anything else on a gorgeous day near the end of May?"

***************************

# Chapter Ten

## Sara

Yes, we're on our way to warmer weather. This is the final day of May and last week's cold snap was short-lived. We decided, well, I decided to turn west instead of east when we reached the trail this morning. Recent winds have been in our face going that way, but there's next to no wind at all right now, and it's been more than a week since Chance has had an opportunity to sniff that route. So, with a lighter jacket and no need for paw protection, we are on our way at 8:30, a little earlier than some mornings.

Now, past the school traffic on the side road, we walk by the lawns of the million-dollar homes that are wide open to the winds off the water. Five minutes later, the canine memory stops at the spot where the trees sheltered the orange cat days ago, but there's no evidence of him or her today. A fence sign further along warns Beware of Dog.

In the five years that I've walked this trail, only once have I seen a dog on that property. The door of a very large barn was open one day, probably two or three summers ago and standing there was a beagle. I didn't have my walking companion then, so it showed no interest in me, but since then, I have heard it bark from behind those walls.

My boots are noisy on the gravel trail this morning. I should have changed them for my lighter ones but despite the warmer air, there are still remnants of snow drifts where the wind hasn't cleared them. They're compacted from the footsteps of walkers and +3 degrees melted the surface during the day, but it's slippery after an overnight freeze.

My winter boots have metal ice grips built into the heels, and when needed, I can stop to flip them down for surer footing. I don't need them this morning, but that's what crunches now on the gravel path. I suppose I'm only disturbing the wildlife, so maybe it's not annoying anyone other than me.

Walking in this direction, we won't see whether the ice rinks on the duck pond have a layer of water on them. Ice thick enough for skaters may still be under any melt but it's not a wise assumption to make. Chance is picking up all sorts of scents this morning. She's antsy and crossing from one side of the trail to the other much more than usual. Long dormant under winter's cover, there must be new discoveries happening that only she can smell. For my part, there's more than one whiff of weed reaching my nose. The lack of a breeze from gardens behind the trees must allow the aroma to linger from those enjoying their preferred form of relaxation.

The air is so gentle this morning. It's almost eerie. As we walk past on the opposite end of the lane, I can see the washing on the line behind the little house on the corner. It's barely moving. Here's hoping the sun will warm up and help it to dry. My companion keeps pausing and looking up at me. She's nervous about something, but I don't see or hear anything particularly unusual. Maybe it's just an overabundance of smells on a part of the trail we've not walked in some time.

The headland off the path is just up ahead, so we'll move closer to the shore. We come back to the trail through the sheltered snow at the base of the evergreen trees, and Chance has fun shoving her face between tree roots or collapsing into a full-body roll in leftover patches.

Almost an hour has passed since we left home, so we turn around and I'm sure she knows that's what we're doing. Her pace increases and the crossing back and forth suddenly ends. By the time I open the gate into our garden, we have been walking for an hour and a half. Perhaps, in her own way, she was telling me that it was more than enough and it's only I who love this morning's warmer weather and want to walk forever.

We play in the garden until, as always, she chooses to amuse herself. That's when I head indoors to focus on other things. There are people, those who don't have dogs, who think I've gone a little canine crazy since Chance came into my life. I have friends and family whom I see whenever it suits us all, but this dog was twenty years in the waiting, the recent seven more intense.

After my partner of more than forty years died unexpectedly, I began living alone for the first time in my life. I was suddenly in a large house with good memories, accumulated belongings and a seventeen-year-old cat. It took some adjustment but, eventually, once the grief was manageable, it grew to be pleasant until responsibilities no longer shared became too much for me.

Three years later, with my old cat's ashes scattered, the opportunity to build and move into a much smaller home presented an attractive alternative. To sell the home of my childhood dreams and build my new 500 square foot place took eighteen months. The construction of even that tiny space was a steep learning curve. I had incredibly talented and caring people helping every step of the way, but, at times, even necessary decisions seemed endless. Things never before considered, layout, interior design, purchasing light fixtures, flooring, stair railing, tub or shower, style of cabinets, number of outlets, were all mine to choose.

Now, five years after that move and well settled into my new home, I am a retiree and, while not lonely, was missing something. As a couple, we travelled so much that adding a dog back into our lives hadn't been a viable option. Now it's just me with all the time in the world and no desire to travel alone. My thinking changed, and that is how watching the SPCA shelter sites for adoption dogs became a past-time until one particular 4-month-old Husky, who would eventually grow into her large ears, stole my heart.

In my defence, she isn't a sole obsession. My hands are seldom idle, especially during long winter evenings. Handicrafts of one kind or another keep me happily occupied, especially while watching a basketball or professional women's hockey game on television. Before rug-hooking, I knitted, crocheted, sewed and taught myself how to needle felt. Even before my furry companion arrived from Labrador, I was never bored. These days, I most certainly am not.

All of which brings me to another habit forming activity. I'll admit to being somewhat of an online junkie. Conversing with distant friends and family via email and on a social app, doing occasional online shopping, finding recipes or researching something like those punk feathered ducks fill pleasant hours.

Now is as good a time as any to check on a rumour that's on the go. There's going to be a celebration to mark the incorporation of the communities along our shore thirty years ago. Opening my laptop and going to a social app gives me a couple of messages and reactions to the pictures of Chance that I posted last week.

Scrolling down the page, there it is. The notice of an upcoming celebratory exhibition in the Town Hall from Canada Day to Thanksgiving. It asks for submissions from the public for the make-up of the exhibition itself and gives a synopsis of the committee's ideas about outdoor family events. Reading this starts the wheels turning in my head, but it's time to bring my sweet dog indoors and pay some attention to hooking the prospective seat cover.

***********************************

## Carrie

A friend called this morning to see how I'm doing. We don't see much of each other because she lives about half an hour away. Since I don't like driving unless it's really necessary and her eyesight is too bad to drive except in perfect weather and light, we rely on a phone chat once a month. She beat me to it today, but her timing is perfect. My phone rang just as I was about to ball up the navy yarn I bought last week after Brud fixed my car.

Oh, yes, my car. Well, that story takes up pretty much all of my end of our conversation. Barb doesn't believe me at first. She thinks I'm pulling her leg, just making it all up. "I'm telling you it's true" must come out of my mouth half a dozen times before she finally accepts it as god's honest truth.

I tell her that Brud called me last Monday night apologizing for not calling sooner. As I'd expected, he and the family had gone up to the cabin for the long weekend. Bright and early Tuesday morning, his tow truck pulled in behind my car. He already knew that she wouldn't start and how I'd checked all the possible problems known to me, so I handed him my keys and said I hoped it wasn't going to be too expensive.

He smiled and told me not to worry about that. "Wait till we see what's on the go or not on the go," as he climbed into the cab.

Then, I watched the winch take her up the ramp, the beige bomber tied down with big old chains so she wouldn't roll off the back when the truck rumbles up the lane.

"So what was wrong," Barb says as I'm telling all this to her.

It's funny this morning when I relay it to Barb because, in all honesty, when Brud had called me later on Tuesday afternoon, his voice had a laugh in it.

"Seems like you've been a landlord," he said.

I'm no landlord and what's that got to do with my car not starting.

"We popped the hood and found a fine collection of rat poop."

This was getting crazier by the minute and then he tells me there's been a rat living on the engine and, to make matters worse, it's chewed through a wire.

By this time, Barb is practically crying. She's laughing so hard, which gets me started. The bill for repairs isn't too bad and I can pay it a bit at a time. Brud also says I'm going to need the rocker panels replaced. They're rusted out so badly that he can't sand them down to patch. I told him that when they fall off, he'll be the first to know, but, for now, while they're not pretty, they're still there.

After this news, the project for the hospital blankets sounds very tame to both of us. We wind down our conversation because Barb has an appointment and wants to drive while the sun is bright and the roads are dry. As always, it does us both good to hear each other's voice. It's nicer to chat when we're in the same room, but this works if it must. I tell her, "It's written on my calendar to call you this time next month unless you call me first."

After all that talk about fixing my car, I glance out to the driveway and hope not to see any rodents. In the distance, I can see the walker and her dog head across the bridge going west. The sky is a gorgeous blue and, with a look out my kitchen window, the clothes are drip-drying, waiting for a breeze.

The papers that Maisie dropped off are sitting on the table beside my armchair, so I'll have a look at them before making some navy squares. In the thicker newspaper, there used to be a real estate section that was always interesting. Looking at the prices of houses in different places is an eye-opener and I'm so glad I'm not in the market. I certainly couldn't think about buying or even renting anywhere these days.

The local shoreline edition has news stories, commentary on different subjects, things for sale and offers for garden maintenance. Whole pages have announcements from the different town councils. Today, there are a couple of notices about zoning requests from property owners or developers. One is about a permit to have chickens on their land. For heaven's sake, we never used to need a permit for that.

Then I see a full-page story about the celebration Maisie mentioned a while back. A committee was formed several months ago to plan the thirtieth anniversary of when all the towns joined into one large council.

The story lists outdoor family events like beach barbecues, fireworks on Canada Day, events in the library and displays in the arts centre. They ask for performers to submit their names to be part of music festivals during July and August and for the general public to suggest event ideas not already listed.

There will be an exhibition of local arts and crafts, present and past, that will run from July 1$^{st}$ to Thanksgiving. I can think of a bunch of things they can display so I read on through the notice until I find out how to send my ideas to the organizers. Of course, the first option is online, which is no good for me, but phone or stopping by the events office would be okay. I think I'll just get my ideas together and give them a call.

I'm glad I sat down to read the papers before getting on with the rest of my day. I grab a pen and the little pad of paper that I use for shopping lists. If I write things down when they come into my mind, they aren't as easily forgotten.

*******************************************

## Margaret

My little house has seen a steady flow of family in the past couple of weeks, especially on the weekends. It all began with my texting about the margarine carton full of treasures. Until they came to look, I kept the contents secret. Frankie was, of course, the first to ask if she could stop by. The excitement was killing her. I told her about the trunk and suggested two strong young backs could bring that down from the attic.

Two nephews and two so-called supervisors came after school one day to do that job. The boys, Liam and Joseph, are so tall that they had to double over onto their knees to get through the ceiling door and then stay that way up in the crawl space. I could hear them teasing each other and insisting that the young women below them not take any videos of rear ends and such.

Amidst the grunts, groans and laughter, the trunk was slowly scraping along the boards. A lot of manoeuvring had to happen for the first guy to get himself back onto the ladder and still be able to reach up into the opening and get a hand on the old leather handle at his end of the trunk.

My heart was in my mouth but I kept quiet as they slowly slid it downward while he stepped from one rung to the next, continuing to support the weight balanced precariously above him. Joseph, still in the attic, had flattened himself onto his stomach and stretched to keep his grip on the broken handle at the other end of the trunk. Emily and Tara, the supervisors down on the floor, supported the weight as best they could through the open risers until both the volunteer muscle and the trunk were safely on the hallway floor. At that point, I breathed a sigh of relief and pulled the steps back into the ceiling.

Since that Friday evening, I've had a grand time making tea and coffee, filling my counter with baked goods, and enjoying an unusual number of visitors. After the initial lifting of the lid and uncovering of the Royal Celebration platter, the excitement grew with each successive visit by various combinations of siblings, in-laws, nieces and nephews.

Frankie insisted that the trunk and its contents stay in my house for safe-keeping, which pleases me. I get to have a peek every now and then to remind myself of the beautiful china dishes and the silver tea service we found inside a large velvet bag. I've polished the black tarnish off the teapot, sugar bowl, and creamer so they gleam once again. In the trunk itself, the faded brown paper lining hasn't completely peeled away from the sides. On one, at some point in time, there must have been a printed emblem because I can see just a hint of colour within a very faded design.

In the quiet of my place this morning, that old green trunk sits in the corner of my spare room. The frayed brown leather handles are held in place with metal rivets. One handle is secure; the other has torn at its halfway point, but the rivet remains. I'm very glad the trunk hadn't fallen and smashed the dishes inside whenever that handle came adrift. Max figures it happened a long time ago and something else was probably in storage at the time, which makes perfect sense.

The recipe books, especially the little green household bible, the heavy leather one and, of course, mother's own hand-written collection have been lovingly handled and carefully read by nearly the whole family. We took photos of everything and someone is going to ask about the value of those two hard-cover books just in case we should insure them or do something special to preserve them.

I was thrilled to see the looks of interest and amazement on the faces of several nieces and nephews. When the stereotypes displayed in those magazines from the 1940s clashed with present-day teen and preteen sensitivities, we adults laughed until we hurt. The kids' eyes kept bugging out more and more and their mouths uttered a never-ending litany of disbelief. My laughter bubbles to the surface even as I think of it now.

There were excited conversations about history boards and class presentations designed to shock their peers and, depending on one's age, amuse their teachers. It all proves to me that no matter what some may say, the past is not dead and an interest in our culture has not been lost within today's fast-paced but not always trustworthy online access to knowledge.

My sister and two sisters-in-law have taken their own photos of mother's recipes and I joke that I'm off the hook for the replication of old instructions. My brothers do their share of cooking for everyday meals at the end of a work day but, in all honesty, anything that requires planning, shopping for particular ingredients and so-called fancy finishes still relies more on the women in our family. Thinking about it this morning, though, no one agrees with the depictions in those magazines, the language used in the articles or the suggested role models and implied attitudes. Again, I imagine many conversations and much teasing at future gatherings.

It's nearly time to make lunch but before doing that, I decide to check my email and social media page. There are the usual marketing offers from sites I've visited, most of which I simply delete. I have a couple of emails from friends on the west coast of the island. We used to write and post letters to each other and that custom still holds true for special times or extra-special news. Later this evening, I'll read their emails and reply. For now and before I forget, I want to see if there is anything online about the town's celebration plans.

The sun is making it difficult to see my screen, so I move my chair a little to lose the reflection. Just as I sit down again, put the computer on my lap and have a look out the window, the walker is striding up the road. It's an odd time of day for him to be coming this way, but I imagine the trail is nice under this clear sky. I have yet to step outside, so I don't know if there's some warmth in this final day of May. I hope there is.

Turning my attention back to the social media site, I notice an article about that anniversary celebration. It looks to be rather lengthy, so I'll take it to the table and read while I eat my lunch.

*********************************

## Ben

In a moment of comfortable weakness, I decided to spend overnight down at the house. There wasn't a compelling reason for me to get home and having checked all the usual things that might need my household skills, I settled in. It had been later in the afternoon when I walked the trail, so lighting the fireplace and having lights on in the house was a good idea. The neighbours know that I'm looking after everything but, busy with their working lives, they would only notice if something were very obviously wrong.

This morning, I woke with a strong urge to revisit my sketches. The sun is well up into the sky, filling this bright kitchen with both shadows and light. My coffee is good and strong, alongside leftover pancakes smeared with blueberry jam. I'll give myself a slower start for a change and get home around midday today. Last evening, sitting in the fire's glow with my favourite music coming through the speaker, ideas floated in and out of my mind.

They seemed to always bring me back to one particular image, so that's where my fingers stop. Pages before have hints of a bigger image and the pages beyond this one show me different perspectives of the same. I honestly don't remember putting all of these onto paper that day, but I'm glad I did.

It's obvious that my focus has turned away from images that

flew through waves under the guidance of surfing dudes. For that, I'm relieved, grateful and pleasantly surprised. Everyday life has changed so much and I've found the peace that eluded me. The next mouthful of coffee makes me wonder if Rob has added an ingredient to make me so pensive this morning. Before I head out onto the trail later today, I'll have to add that question to my email.

I'm keen to get his reaction to my return to drawing and, soon, to putting paint on a canvas. The image on this sketchbook page isn't going anywhere, so I think now's a good time to pull out the laptop.

The one email in my inbox from my high-flying friend has a link to the town's plan for a celebration event this summer. I read through it, print the attachment and tell myself I'll check it out later. Not one for organized events and being thrust into crowds of people, I don't know if I'll attend. I let Rob know that all is well with the house and vehicle and confess to having spent last night here and to using the car the other day.

Although he doesn't really want to know what food I've used, I tell him anyway to mentally bring him back home for a moment. Mundane matters disposed of, I tell him about the filled pages of my sketchbook and add that one particular image keeps coming to the forefront. Then I hit Send. His schedule is unknown to me now that he's flying these bigger jets on long hauls, so who knows where he'll be or when he'll see my reply.

My late breakfast is finished. I close the laptop and get ready to fill my backpack for home. There's a portion of lasagne in the freezer and some homemade snack dip that will come with me today. I'll wrap them in a small towel and secure them in the outer pouch. That should make sure they don't dampen the sketchbook or the computer during their ride home.

Safety checks on the fireplace, the garage door, and the back door, and I'm ready to finish the rest of my day with a good walk. Back at my place, I'll still have enough light to expand on that sketch or maybe lightly draw it onto the canvas, making a commitment to myself.

The ocean is really calm and the huddle of gulls quite a distance out is only just noticeable. As I pass the last of the homes near the shore, there's an elderly gentleman whom I've seen before. He comes out of a small, older bungalow. Both he and his little white dog amble down the lane. The dog is off-leash but too old to do anything other than shuffle along with an occasional sniff at the ground. The gentleman's hand lifts in recognition and I wave in return. By my estimation, they may cover ten feet of ground in the same number of minutes.

I walk most of the way without seeing anyone else on the trail today but that's not to say I was alone. About twenty feet ahead is a boulder, massive enough to sit down at the water line yet reach a good five feet above me. It's a dinosaur egg but for one sheer edge and a sharply pointed tip. Each day, as I pass, I imagine a glacier forcing it from an ancient land mass with one almighty crack.

Today, sitting primed for flight, claws gripping that point, is a magnificent eagle. Before I get any closer, the black wings spread, beat the air once and lift that bird skyward.

I stop to watch its powerful flight. The sudden vacuum in the air proves that what may appear effortless is not. I watch it make a perfect landing atop a utility pole near the duck pond behind me. Yet another possible sketch or, perhaps, an addition to the bigger image roughed out in my mind's eye. Reliving what I've seen just now makes the last hour of my walk rapidly disappear.

No sign of the Husky and her companion along the path today. There's no wind, the air has some warmth, and before it seems reasonable, I've come into the community, crossed the bridge, and am halfway up the hill. Between my shoulder blades, I can feel the cool of the food. My fingers confirm the key-ring behind the zipper of the small outer pocket, and a quick pat on my hip assures me that I did bring my own key back with me.

Last week, I made an easel from some leftover strapping. Right now, I'm eager to eat, light the wood burner and lift that canvas into place.

***********************************

# Chapter Eleven

## Sara

The heavens have opened this morning. The rain is absolutely pouring down. Our walk, even in whatever water-resistant gear I have, will be a wet one. Chase isn't going to like it much, either. I already know she'll keep looking up at me to ask where her snow has gone. However, we shall get a walk into our day before I settle down to work on that rug-hooking.

Unfortunately, it's too early for mail delivery, so as we head out the front door, I decide to just make the loop along the shore, go past the duck pond and up the lane. We get back home wet but exercised half an hour later.

As soon as we step inside the door, I do my best to dry the wet mud off my companion's body, but it really is an exercise in futility. My damp clothes come off, get hung over the shower rail in the bathroom and are exchanged for a warm hoodie and clean jeans. We are ready to hunker down for a little while at least. I carry my tea to the end-table beside my usual seat on the couch as Chance jumps her wet body onto the chair that's become her resting spot. The cover on it will absorb the undeniable scent of wet fur until I next do laundry. The forgotten joys of having a dog are in the air.

My rug-hooking frame is on wheels so I move it now from

the spare room to just in front of me. It's not a large frame, the open space measuring just 18 inches by 20 inches which makes it easy to take to a hook-in. The original frame was designed with a base upon which I can sit. When I'm at home, though, I attach it to an adjustable wooden stand made to match the working height of my hands. It's the best of both worlds.

There are gripper strips on all four edges of the frame to hold the backing through which I'm pulling the loops. Those metal teeth are very sharp and I rarely manage to avoid scratching my hands or wrists every time I move the material to do another area or decide to tighten the work surface. I could put protective cloth around the frame, but after ten years of use, that has yet to happen. I've no one but myself to blame for an occasional drop of blood being shed.

One of the frustrations of living on an island that's on the edge of the continent is being reliant on ferries, trucks and planes for mail. Two months ago, I was completely devoid of inspiration for my next rug-hooking image, so I renewed a publication subscription and my membership in an international rug-hooking association.

They have great magazines and websites with articles, patterns, and ads for supplies, and they accept project submissions. Over the years, I built up quite a library of magazines, most of which went elsewhere when I moved. The only printed copies in my possession these days have been saved for selfish reasons. They are the issues that include several photos of my projects and accompanying articles.

However, there remains one main glitch in my renewed plan for rug ideas, the delivery of those publications. The four to six-week wait time for the first issue does not allow for where I'm living. I know that I can read each issue online and that my preference is a bit of a throwback, but flipping through the coloured pages still holds its appeal. This morning's weather would be a prime time to sit with tea and a muffin while I devour the imagery and words of other hookers. That neither issue has arrived after ten weeks reminds me why I let my subscription lapse five years ago.

Rather than moan and groan to no one but myself and my sleeping canine, I tighten my potential seat cover against the edges of my frame, settle my canvas bag of colours on the spare cushion beside me and pull out scissors and hook. Household chores that ought to be done and magazines missing in action shall not distract me. The first stylized cloud is going to be yellow, as will its mate on the opposite side of the 24-inch by 20-inch burlap. The larger cloud in the centre is going to be white and all will have a bright blue sky around them, as well as sunny loops peeking through here and there. That's my plan as I reach for a yellow t-shirt strip.

Time disappears when I'm pulling loops and as the image begins to take shape, the temptation is to keep going. That's when my body disagrees and I have to force myself to push the frame away from me, stand up and do something else for at least a few minutes. It was about 10:00 when we arrived home from our wet walk this morning, but now as I listen to my stomach growl, a glance at the little clock on the side-table shows me that it's, suddenly, 1:00 in the afternoon.

Whether she woke to my hunger rumblings or her own, the dog and I both need some activity. I eat a quick sandwich while she checks out her food bowl then, with the rain slowing down, we both head into the back garden for some ball and stick-throwing. I'm tossing and she's chasing but doing her Husky thing of not returning any objects until she's decided it's time.

Back inside and not as wet as earlier in the day, we play tug-of-war for a few minutes before I exchange the frame stand for my laptop. Avoiding the temptation to get swallowed up in replying to emails, I visit the Town's website. A quick look brings the article and flyer about the celebration event. The organizers have compiled a list of suggestions and given dates for submissions. Included in the events list will be an exhibition in the Town Hall with a Grand Opening on July 1st which will remain in place for several months, a number of musical events during July and August, family barbecues down on the beach, and of course, the traditional fireworks on Canada Day.

My attention is drawn to the exhibition section of the article.

The static display in the Town Hall will run from July to Thanksgiving Day in October. Celebrating both the past and present, people are asked to submit their items by the end of this month. The Arts and Crafts ideas look to be wide-ranging and I'm pleased to see requests for items knitted, crocheted, quilted and rug-hooked, one article per craft per person. The long-term exhibition will have a large floor space to display tools, equipment and supplies used in the past, along with plenty of wall space for photographs of the past and the present.

The emphasis, states the spokesperson, is on the shoreline and the communities that decided to amalgamate. People are welcome to make contact if they have questions. There's a contact person, email address, and phone number, and if needed, in-person consultation can be arranged.

Revising my decision not to get into email right now, I send a message to the contact person. I'm wondering whether a rug-hooked wall hanging and my chair cover project might be acceptable for the exhibition and if they would be considered as submissions in two different categories. I close by saying that our shoreline is home to some amazing artists and artisans who will enjoy showcasing their skills, and offer my thanks for organizing the celebration. Now, it is definitely time to continue this rainy day with some colourful loops pulled to make a scene come to life.

***********************************

## Carrie

Maisie and two of the neighbours from down the lane dropped by to wish me a Happy Birthday this morning. I was surprised that they remembered and especially grateful because they risked getting very wet as they came to my door. My friend in town called to see if I wanted to go for a birthday lunch with her, but she understood when I said the weather was too miserable for a comfortable drive. We'll do it another time.

An actual celebration with gifts, cakes and a party has been a thing of the past for quite some years. Now, I tell myself I'm not older, I'm wiser and thankful for my good health. Some friends have so many issues that prevent them from truly enjoying every day. My aches and pains don't count for much, to my mind.

Maisie's card was funny. *Like good wine and strong cheese, you age well.* If I'd thought far enough ahead, I could have had some of both on hand for today, but I didn't, and, besides, Maisie winked and handed me a brown paper bag. After she ran back to her car, I took a look and had to laugh out loud. Inside was a container of pea soup and two eclairs from the bakery on the main road. My style of comfort food fit for a birthday supper, and if the rain stops and the sun comes out over the bay, I might even see a birthday rainbow. I doubt that I'll see the woman and her dog. The weather's not fit.

Yesterday, Deanne called me to see how I was doing with

the squares. She was so pleased when I told her I now have 60 squares finished and 24 flowers that can be sewn wherever and whenever someone is ready. "I can attach them myself," I say, but she thinks I've done enough.

After we chat for a few minutes about who is making the blankets and which departments or charities need them the most right now, I remember to tell her that there's still navy yarn left in my basket. I ask if I should use it all before she comes but Deanne tells me to keep it for my own projects. We arrange for her to swing by my place next week.

I'm going to want to get out into the garden by then, so my crochet hook will be idle more than it has been recently and that's fine because it often feels more like a winter past-time. The warmer weather gets me outdoors and I might, just might, drive down to the nursery to look for some new plants. I know full well that I'll never order from those catalogues. Supporting local folks seems like a better idea, anyway.

The other thing I want to do on this lousy weather day is call the person who is looking after the town celebration stuff. There were a couple of names in the article and I think there was one on the page with the flyer, too. I hope those pages weren't the ones that wrapped up last night's vegetable peelings. I'll be really ticked off with myself if I've done that without thinking. A quick look tells me no, I haven't. The whole paper is here beside my chair. Good for me.

A few months ago, some higher up person decided that we have to dial the three-number area code as well as the usual seven numbers when we make a phone call. So, I now have to remember that as well as everything else that's already in my head and any more that's about to be added. Ah well, let's call that person and ask what sorts of craft items they have in mind for the display. There's plenty of time for me to make a blanket or knit some mitts if that's what they want.

I had a thought when I was reading the paper the other day. Now, what was it? Something to do with the exhibition, I know. Maybe I should have a little sit-down and read the article again to jog my memory.

Yes, that was it. The idea about a display of old farming and fishing equipment and supplies. In the crawl space under my house, I'm sure there are things that my father and grandfather used. I haven't looked at it for donkey's years, but it won't have gone anywhere. I could go and have a look, but I'd have to go outside to get into there, so that's not happening in this rain. The best thing is for me to ask if that's what they have in mind, and if it is, I can tell them what I own.

I've made my tea and pulled a lemon cream biscuit out of

the package. Time to dial that long number and have a chat with someone. I better swallow this bit before the fourth ring is answered. Oh, no need. It's gone to a voice-mail.

I do a quick organization of my thoughts, wait for the beep, ask my questions and remember to leave my name and phone number before I ask them to call me back whenever they get time. I'm not a fan of leaving those voice messages but I guess they help when people are too busy or lazy to get to their phones.

That's a good chore done today. The rain seems to be slowing down, the noise less against the windows. I'll finish my tea, then tidy up a bit and think about what I can do with that navy yarn. Supper will be a bit of a birthday treat, the best pea soup and the most delicious eclairs. Maisie knows me well.

**************************************

## Margaret

Wipers blurred faces earlier this morning as folks headed past my place and the kids timed their runs to meet the bus the instant it stopped on the road. Every now and then, the rain comes down with such force that it's almost a roar when it hits the roof. Not a day to walk anywhere, let alone to the trail, I expect. Not having to go anywhere, it's strangely relaxing to me, the water splashing against the windows. Sitting in my chair, trying to see through the downpour at breakfast time, I thought about the conversations we all had this past weekend.

It was another family birthday meal with extra tables and chairs arranged around the big kitchen. This was even more special because my eldest nephew had arrived home from his life out west to surprise his parents. I don't think there was a single moment when multiple conversations weren't competing for attention, even though, a lot of the time, mouths were busy chewing. Our typical family gathering made all the more exciting with that young man's presence.

The town celebration, after birthday wishes, was the main topic for the adults and even some of the older children. Everyone had read the article in the paper and most had seen the flyer there or looked at it online. Of course, given our family's farming history, the proposed display of old fishing and farming implements and supplies grabbed our attention. To have a look at what is still in two big barns behind the new homes sent half a dozen people out the back door after all the eating was over.

I expect the old books and magazines with recipes and advertisements would be considered for the exhibition. The trunk contents, with the right protection and care, might also be something our family could contribute. Thinking about that now, I'm not sure the platter should be out in the open. Perhaps there will be glass display cases for valuable and delicate items that shouldn't be handled. I've been tasked to ask all these sorts of questions when I email the organizers today.

The arts and crafts section of the exhibition mentions knitted goods and community-based projects, so I wonder if those little caps for the babies would qualify. I know that people work in the privacy of their own homes then their pieces are combined into a larger item or gathered together to meet the specific needs of charitable organizations.

I'll add that to my email, but keep in mind that they may have to limit how much is displayed by one family. It can't hurt to put it all out there and see what will work best for the celebration spaces. If our family can think of all these things and offer what we have, I'm sure the organizers are going to be inundated with possible displays.

Then, there's all the musical talent that's along this shoreline. Every summer, there are at least half a dozen music festivals in different communities with bands and single musicians galore. If people are available at the time, I'm sure they'll join the fun. I'm excited.

I have my work cut out for me today, and once I write down as much as I can remember, I'll compose a coherent email to the contact person and cc it to all the family. I don't think I have the addresses for the nieces and nephews, but I do have those of their parents who can pass along my email.

It actually took me less time to gather my thoughts and organize our family's ideas than to write this one email. I must have read and reread it a half-dozen times keeping my finger well away from the Send button until I was good and sure of what I'd written. Although I use email and, less often, text messages, the old habit of proofreading remains strong. It's ingrained in me, I'm sure, from having school essays returned to me with too many red marks for my parents' liking.

University papers didn't have those glaring red criticisms but the margins often pointed out an error in syntax or false argument. One Professor of English refused to read any further than the second error, even if only a simple typo or misspelled word. He was tough, but my papers for him were pretty darn good.

So, by the time I hit Send, I know my email has no grammatical errors, especially when the automatic spell-check insists on changing a word. My information is conveyed in clear but concise language. It's no wonder that, in my working life, I wrote press releases and educational materials for non-profits.

I've learned to bite my tongue unless specifically asked by someone to edit or critique their work. I do lament that upholding student writing to a standard that will benefit them later in life is a thing of the past. Right now, I'm laughing at myself for getting on a soap-box that has grown creaky, especially if the new AI technology becomes the norm for my nieces and nephews. They will have to bring their poor old auntie up to speed.

*********************************

## **Ben**

Half-awake, I lie in bed trying to determine the source of the running water. Steady and near my head, it makes no sense if my body isn't feeling the result of a roof leak. My brain finally kicks in and I realize the downspout of the gutter is on that corner of the house and, from the sound, it is rapidly emptying its contents.

Mere seconds later, the roar on the tin roof is deafening as another cloud bursts apart overhead. This is reminiscent of a tropical mid-afternoon downpour, sudden, powerful and, maybe, rapidly ending.

Out of bed and at the window, I see only ordinary grey sky, none of the sickly purples or greens of an approaching tornado. I can't see much at close range. The land and trees in the back are obscured by the water pouring down the glass, but I don't hear much wind. My next thought is that this is not a good start to walking the shoreline. If it's raining this hard all the way along, the path will be ankle-deep in drowning stone until it begins to drain.

So, coffee, breakfast and a break in routine appear to at least be my morning. The kettle comes to a boil as I spoon the rich brown granules into the reusable filter atop my mug. I enjoy the aroma fresh from the bag almost as much as the taste of good coffee, thanks to Rob's tutelage. The baguette leftover from last evening warms nicely in the oven while I pull on stay-in-the-house clothes. A hunk of bread with butter, a wedge of cheese and a mug of coffee will suffice while the rain waters everything outside my little house. It's all good. I'll sit, listen, watch, and think about what to do next.

Surprisingly, the room isn't dim despite the grey sky. There's a gentle quality to the light that draws my eye to the stretched canvas on the easel. It's rewarding to see the faint outline of my image from this end of the barn wood table. That last sketch pretty much captures the broad angle of the shoreline. In my mind, I'm still debating between making the location recognizable or keeping it vaguely familiar to any who looks at it. Not that I have any immediate plans to share this with anyone other than close friends who may ask.

The small beach rocks in my sketches remind me of puzzle pieces, shapes and colours that are similar but not the same, different wet than dry. The boulders each have their own personality thanks to a bit of artistic license, and once I determine a season, they will share the coast with ice and snow or with wildflowers and wind-blown grass. There are so many possibilities that, sooner rather than later, I'm going to have to narrow it down. Once that's decided and paint hits the canvas, there's effectively no turning back.

I think, before I get everything ready, a look through my photographs is a good idea. Since moving in here, I've not printed any but maybe this rainy day is a good opportunity to pick out a few that could go on my walls. More often than not, I'm off the groomed trail when I stop to take a photo. The close-ups of the new buds, the flowers in sun and shade, those incredible yellow toadstools, and, always, the ocean itself.

That I allowed myself the expense of a good digital camera when I first arrived here continues to please me. The laptop screen doesn't provide quite as good image quality as the computer at Rob's house, but to jump start colour sequences today, it's fine.

I look around my space and figure that half a dozen good shots, 14" x 18", maybe 16" x 20", will bring more colour to the brown wood. There's a great one of the sea washing over the stubborn feet of a seagull. Touch the arrow and I'm smiling at a field of purple, pink and white lupines bending in an onshore breeze. The choice of which photos may not happen today because my mug and plate are both empty, the rain sounds as if it's eased, and I really do want to get out my paints.

I cut apart some brown paper grocery bags and spread them on the table before putting my paintbox, brushes and palette up there. Sitting in front of the easel, I think about where I want to start, then make two lines, a horizon and a shoreline. My room, my space, my old instincts all come together as my brush swirls the paint and moves onto the canvas. I no longer hear the rain or think about anything other than transferring what's in my mind's eye.

When I next look up, the light in the room has changed and the muscles from my fingertips to my right shoulder blade shout a warning. I lay my brush down, stand and stretch, then turn back to the canvas. It's as if I've never stepped away from bringing something to life through this medium. The clock on the stove shows me that its hands have gone full circle four times. Muscle memory has brought me this far, now to get the body's muscles back into the groove. It's a really good start, I think, and I'm pleased. I can now see where it's going.

I stick my head out the door and smell all those freshly watered scents off the bushes and wet grass. Up in the pine tree, little birds flap the damp from their feathers and down the lane, the ducks are busy talking. It's time to take a break, make something to eat and dig that celebration article and flyer out of my backpack.

I have a vague recollection of what it's all about, but I didn't pay much attention other than to print it because Rob encouraged me to do so. Now that I think about it, that was before he'd seen my email about my sketchbook. He's so much more into community spirit than I, probably because his roots are here, and he's what they call a people person.

I'm going to really enjoy telling him about the painting that's now in the works and my decision to put some photos on my walls. He has a couple and seeing something that I've created when it's displayed in a different space feels both strange and rewarding. That someone else likes my work enough to put it on their wall or, in years gone by, stand on it to ride a wave is pretty cool. I'm daydreaming now. Sit, eat and read that article before the afternoon is completely gone.

# Chapter Twelve

## Sara

I couldn't get out the door quickly enough this morning. Daylight at breakfast and opening a window or two after yesterday's rain is such a pleasure after a long winter. The air is, somehow, both musty and fresh. More importantly, it's warm. We've made it through once again and I'm eager to get us out the door to see the changes in the plants that border the trail. Our walk comes before anything else, even checking for a response to my email about the celebration submission.

I lace up my summertime walking shoes and zip up my light red jacket. No need for mitts or a hat. Side-stepping puddles brings a ridiculous sense of freedom. No more walking with an eye to ice underfoot. We head up the sidewalk past the fire station, pause for electronic permission to cross at the lights, and head down the lane.

Chance is having a field day with all the smells in the fresh grass after the rain. She, unlike I, ignores the poor earthworms who have been washed out of the ground and onto the pavement. There are too many for me to rescue, but with so few cars on this road, perhaps they'll survive and wriggle back to someone's flower bed.

The little house on the corner already has a line of washing hung out to dry and there's just enough breeze off the land to do that today. The front border of rose bushes have fresh little buds. It won't be long before they'll be in bloom.

Surprisingly, the trail has drained well and with a few exceptions, there are no pools of water for my feet to dodge. My companion, however, finds every one available and happily splashes her way through them while I breathe in the warm air.

I don't know why it is, but there's a pronounced smell of seaweed this morning. There's none to be seen on this part of the shore, just the bare rocks on the beach. Maybe further out beneath the water, there's more than usual. Seeing all the new life in the bushes beside me, I remind myself to have a closer look at the plants in my garden today.

Each year, I've transplanted something that's thriving in the back garden and added it to the front. Last year, we had to take down a huge maple tree because it was starting to uproot during a couple of really bad windstorms. It was September and the maple was heavy with leaves on branches that wavered dangerously close to my living room window.

Since then, I've moved some of the wild rosebushes from a corner in the back garden and I've bought several Potentilla plants from the nursery. I'm hoping that the yellow, orange and white of each will bring some colour to the front lawn and, eventually, hide the stump that was once my maple tree. A root ball of heather went into a big old iron kettle once used for washing fish. Very heavy and looking well worn, it sat unused for years until I filled it with soil.

The heather, originally from my mother's garden, is a deep purple when in bloom, a nice welcome at the foot of my front steps.

This morning, as we turn by the duck pond, the seaweed aroma surfaces once again. The low tide has bared the beach, and there's a thick bank of brown seaweed all along the water's edge. I don't remember seeing this before, despite the hundreds of times we've walked this trail. As we continue to home, I also realize that we've seen no other walkers this morning.

Back at the house, Chance takes her biscuit onto the back deck while I hang my jacket on a hook, fill a big tumbler with water and sit down with my laptop. The inbox shows a reply from the celebration committee person, so it's the first message I open. She describes the exhibition space as plenty large enough to display my old armchair with its hooked seat cover and she asks that I send her a photograph along with its dimensions for planning purposes.

I read on and am smiling to see that submitting the wall-hanging in addition to the chair is acceptable. Again, she asks for a photo to ensure that the subject matter is related to the community or shoreline and asks me to include any specific details required for its installation. The email goes on to say that photos will also provide the committee with the subject matter, colour schemes and a sense of the quality of the work, so I can easily do that.

This is so exciting. A moment later, it's a bit daunting. Is my rug-hooking good enough to put out there? I know all of us wonder about that when we share our work with other hookers.

I put my computer down on the wooden trunk across from the couch, reach for my phone, and take pictures of both the front and back of the rug on the stairwell wall, the old chair with its worn seat and the half-completed new cover. Next, I check on the dog who has fallen asleep on the deck and then I write down what my ancient tape measure tells me.

I create a file and export the photos to my laptop ready to forward them to the celebration committee rep. I make myself take the time to be sure I've included all they need to know, that the photos are attached, and that my fingers haven't made any errors. I take a deep breath and hit Send. I can now move that email into a folder marked Celebration Event and stop myself from doubting what I've just done.

This is, if nothing else, great motivation for me to put the laptop away and roll out my rug-hooking frame. As of this moment, I have a two-week deadline to complete this project with approximately 100 loops per square inch. Walking, hooking, gardening, dog-time, eating and sleeping are on the agenda for the next little while.

****************************************

## Carrie

What a pretty day! I was doing my breakfast dishes when the phone rang a little while ago. It was the lady from the celebration committee returning my call. So those voice-mail things do work. I didn't say that out loud. She was pleased that I'm interested and happy to answer any questions. I told her all about making the squares for those blankets and how I often knit trigger mitts and patterned mitts as my old Aunt Maude taught me.

She asked for contact information for Deanne to see if there are any photos of the finished blankets that could go in the display. I told her that I could make some mitts, but she said someone had already offered to provide knitted goods.

When I mentioned Aunt Maude's name, I suddenly thought of the ancient tablecloth that she had crocheted. It was a Christmas gift to my mother, her sister. "That would be a wonderful addition to the crafts display," the young lady agreed. I said that I could drop it off to her and then, my brain remembered the fishing gear that might be in my basement. She liked that idea too, so I said that I'd go have a look when I went out to check on my garden later today. If I don't have anything, my memory not being perfect any more, I can ask Maisie if her husband's family has anything from their years of fishing.

We must have chatted for a good half-hour before it was all

said and done. I said, “I’ll tell Maisie to call you if she has things for the display,” and then we made arrangements to drop off the tablecloth before the end of the week. When I hang up the phone, I’m quite pleased with myself, especially thinking about letting people see something from my family. I’ve never before done anything like that.

I opened the window just a crack when I was at the sink earlier and the warmth in the air was a nice surprise. Pulling on my short boots, now, in case the grass is still wet after all that rain and grabbing my cardigan off the back of the kitchen chair, I head out the back door. I love the smell of wet grass and even though my boots are squelching here and there, it feels so good to be outside without being all bundled up in layers of heavy clothes.

The dark soil in the veggie bed will soon be ready for seeds and the Geraniums along the side of the house have a lovely green tinge to their leaves. They’re coming back to life and I can’t wait to see that long line of purple blooms. Wandering round the corner into the front garden, I look down the lane toward the trail but don’t spot my walker and her dog.

I do see that my hedge of rose bushes has new buds on the branches. To sniff their scent and watch the summer bees flit from bloom to bloom always makes me smile. That rain and today’s warm air really is kick-starting it all and my Hens ‘n Chicks in the flower beds under my living room window are the hardiest I've had in years. They'll spread themselves in no time which is the kind of gardening I love, not much work for me.

Darn, I forgot the key to the crawl space. It's on the hook just inside the pantry door, so I can carry on around to the back and nip in to get it. I'm glad these are slip-on boots, no need to fight with wet laces which might make me second guess going into the crawl space this morning. There's no leftover rainwater in the well where the concrete steps go down to the door, but the space inside might be a bit damp.

I turn the key in the knob and flick the light switch as the door swings inward. That's good, no water on the floor, so the drainage we put down years ago is still doing its job.

Now, where might father's and grandfather's old fishing gear be stored? There's not much down here and what is might be too rusty to use. Oh, my good lord! I didn't know that was down here. It's an old anchor with part of the chain still attached. It's huge, and there's no way I can lift it. I can carry those oar-locks, though. They must have come off a more recent boat than grandfather's, maybe one of my father's when he went out for lobster. I'll ask Arch, Maisie's husband, to have a look at them and the anchor. He'll know their age and might even know their story.

I wish I'd paid more attention as a kid. If I had, I'd know a lot more now. Holding this rusty old treasure in my hands, I have a vague memory of words like rowlock and spur, maybe thole. I don't even know if that last one is right at all because I didn't know then and don't know now what it means.

The only real image that comes easily to mind today is my father knitting nets. He used one of our wooden kitchen chairs to hold the starting end and even if I left the room for only a few minutes, I'd come back to see a long open mesh of knotted twine stretching out in front of him.

Grandfather used to do something the same, but there were little silver balls at the bottom of the circular net to weigh it down when it was cast out from the beach. I remember him telling me that and I think now, that kind of net might have been for caplin, but I wouldn't swear to it. I really am not a very good example of someone who is descended from generations of men who went out on the sea to provide for their families.

My cousins used to laugh and call me a 'city girl.' I objected loudly at the time, but I guess they were kind of right. Oh well, if nothing else, dear old nosy Aunt Maude's beautiful tablecloth will be a contribution to the celebration event this summer.

This trip down memory lane was nice and made all the nicer by the warmth in today's air bringing my garden back to life.

Perhaps, when I take the beige bomber down to the Town Hall, I'll stop by the nursery to see what veggie seeds they have in stock and if they're going to have any seedlings ready to go in the ground once the threat of the last frost has passed. That's definitely something I look forward to and I'll have to think about what to plant this year in my veg patch. For now, though, it's time for tea and picking up that navy yarn.

*************************************

## Margaret

"What a day on clothes!" my mother loved to say when she'd hang clothes on the line without freezing her fingers. Today, it's one of those days with the air nice and warm and the grass much greener than it was last week. The kids met the bus in sneakers and hoodies. Always the hoodies, preferably grey or black for the guys and all different colours for the girls. As much as some things change, not all things do. Having thought that, I look out at the road and there are some young guys breaking the mould with gold and green, I'm happy to see.

I'm going to carry my morning tea out into the garden now, a first for this year. My rubber boots will take care of whatever standing water may be left from all that rain and I really want to check on the front fence. When I looked out the window yesterday, it seemed to be less than upright after the plow's winter road-clearing efforts.

My path is crushed stone and, walking from the front steps to the fence, I can see that it has drained nicely. Yes, those four palings are leaning inwards from the others. I'll wait for the ground to dry out a bit more before having a closer look and assessing what I need to do to get them back in place.

Turning back to the house and sipping my tea, I think I'll continue up the long driveway because it feels so good to be out in a light jacket with bare hands and the breeze blowing through my hair. What is that phrase used when the royals are out for a stroll? A walk-about, I think. That's what I'm doing this morning. Mind you, I've never seen Their Majesties carrying a mug of tea when they do it.

The flower beds in front of the houses on my left are looking bedraggled after winter's onslaught, but they're for others to mend. Those on either side of my front steps will get my attention, as will the hedge of wild roses that defines my patch of land.

We're all on one large property, so there's really no demarcation necessary, but we each have our own ideas for what's to go in the garden. Mine is less manicured than a couple of the others. I keep my lawn mowed and, usually, my flower beds free of weeds.

However, some of the family have actual blueprints for planting. They have a hierarchy for the flowering plants according to height, colour and blooming times. A couple of the hedges are neatly trimmed all summer long, whereas my roses burst out at all angles without any interference from me.

A couple of years ago, the family got together and bought three of those Burning Bushes as my birthday gift. I love the deep burgundy foliage in the Fall and because I want to see that from both windows, we actually placed them strategically. “The first planning of anything in your garden,” they teased. I can see two out the back from the kitchen window and one in the centre of my front lawn, just the way I like it.

Apart from lining up the drills in my vegetable patch, everything else grows as it wishes. I’ll give my list of seeds and seedlings to someone and they’ll do the shopping for me. That’s the trade-off, they purchase, I plant and grow, then we all harvest and enjoy the rewards. I tried starting tomatoes from seed the other year but it wasn’t successful. I think the nursery will have seedlings in little peat pots for transplanting. The peas, beets, carrots and onions will all be seeds poked into the soil when the weather’s consistently warm enough.

Any repairs to the beds will get done with help from the older nieces and nephews before we plant anything. Last year, I was happy to see even the younger children show an interest in running the lines to support the peas, then picking and eating the edible pods later in the summer. They found great humour in the practice of caging the cherry tomato plants to hold them upright and loved squeezing eager fingers between the stalks to get at the bright red balls when the fruit was ripe.

Well, I'm back around to my door again with dreams of tall pink, white and blue Flox climbing up the walls. As I turn to look at the window boxes where the glorious colours of Nasturtiums will eventually be, I notice the walker striding up over the crest of the hill. If he glances this way during the summer after they burst into bloom, he'll see splashes of colour, and I'll enjoy the rich scent as it wafts into my bedroom and kitchen.

My mug is now empty and I'm actually feeling a little too cool, so it's back inside I go. I want to check my email this morning to see whether our ideas for the celebration exhibition have a response. A lot of the homes in this community are built on old farmland, so I'm sure the organizers will have plenty of old equipment and tools from which to choose.

Off with my rubber boots, jacket back on a hanger in the hall closet and mug in the dishwasher, I'm ready to get into office mode. I've often said that of a time and in a manner of my own choosing, office mode works for me.

My laptop sits on the little desk in one corner of the living room. It's one of those old-fashioned student desks from the early 1950s, all one piece with the writing surface coming up from the seat and an ink-well in its right-hand corner.

As students, we'd slide into the space between the top and the seat and put our books or recess in the opening below. The ink-well was never used during my time in school and the design of the desk made life really difficult for students who were left-handed. The orientation was all wrong for my good friend, Marilyn, and I recall that she had to twist her left arm and wrist at an awkward angle to write anything.

Anyway, my laptop sits there, but I do not squeeze myself into that seat nowadays. I prefer my kitchen table's broad surface. The second email in today's list is, indeed, from the young man who is co-chairing the celebration event. He is very keen to make use of the old magazines, the hardcover books, and even my mother's hand-written recipes. They will all be housed in one of the glass cases being borrowed from the museum for the four exhibition months.

He asks whether I'd be prepared to come to their office with the items to talk about how to safely display them and the amount of space needed. The committee will completely understand if we choose not to make available the commemorative platter but both it and the old family dishes will all be behind glass. He goes on to add that even when closed to the public, the building and exhibition space will be patrolled by security.

As to the old farming implements, if the family could send photos of what they'd like to share, he and his colleague will take a look, check for any duplication with other submissions, and determine exhibition space. So, with a huge smile on my face and every-mounting excitement, I reply that I'm thrilled with his suggestions but will ensure agreement with other family members before making a commitment. I add that, even though I think consent will be forthcoming given our group conversations thus far, I'll contact him tomorrow to schedule a day and time to bring our family treasures to his office, and we'll plan from there.

I re-read his email, review my own, fix a couple of small errors, give myself a few minutes to make sure of it all, check that I've copied everything to the family and hit Send. The tone of the young organizer's email is so positive that it's infectious. I'm feeling happy that our family's treasures will add to the pleasure of everyone taking part in this anniversary celebration. My attic has, I think, resulted in something that brings us all closer together.

***********************************

## Ben

I'm up earlier than usual this morning with the light pouring through my bedroom window. The forest that takes up the back section of my land means I've no need for curtains on that side of the house. I don't really need curtains on any windows if truth be told. During the more than two years that I've lived here, no one has ever come past my door, at least not when I've been home. There are distant houses and large mansions on the ridge of the hills, but this little dirt lane leads only to the ducks and me. It is absolutely the perfect setting.

Coffee and breakfast don't take long and I'm eager to get onto the trail. I'd like to go to the house, check emails, send photos to the print shop run by Rob's friend, and then have a quick look at the boat. She's been up on the crib for the non-sailing months but will be back on the water the next time Rob gets home. Leaving my place now at 6:30, I'll be back in plenty of time to work on my painting. Perhaps walking the trail will firm up some of the loose ends I felt when I put the brush down yesterday.

I lace up my lighter boots and put gloves and a hat into the backpack, hoping they won't be needed unless the wind is off waves that are never anything other than cold. Once again, I'm well ahead of any traffic except for workers heading to the highway for jobs a couple of hours east of here. They have a long commute behind the wheel every day and their fortitude amazes me. A friend laughed at me when I made that comment one night. He said that my walking a shoreline trail in all sorts of weather for up to three hours every day would be their worst nightmare, so I guess it's all about perspective. Out the door, it is for me this morning.

The community is just waking up with curtains being opened and kettles being boiled. The stream running to the sea under the little bridge and the water in the swimming hole are really full. All that rain yesterday has swollen both to the tops of the banks as I make my way past then up and onto the beginning of the trail. The groomed path has drained quickly and while there is more in the ditches on the land side, there's no standing water underfoot. That makes for easy walking, so I'll make good time.

The breeze picks up where the shore is open to the sea, but it's a pleasant temperature, neither cold nor hot. The first headland path is really bogged down with sunken pools, so I'm staying on the crushed stone for now. Even from ten feet away, there's a brightness to the grasses and moss and the evergreen branches no longer droop to the ground. Gulls are circling in the breeze and those black and white ducks bob along on the waves.

Apart from the sound of my boots on the gravel, it's very peaceful. I decide to walk past the second headland path nearer the eastern end of my walk. It, too, looks spongy and I don't want to stay at the house until wet socks and boots are dry.

I take the bend at the point where the trail skirts the basin and do a quick walk around the boat. I don't see anything amiss from down here on ground level, so I turn and cut back to the old path which will take me to the house in another ten minutes. Once there, a stroll around the perimeter makes sure that everything outside the place looks fine before I pull the ancient rabbit's-foot key ring out of my backpack and unlock the front door.

The room is cool but not cold and there are no signs of any leaks from the rainstorm. That doesn't surprise me because this place is well-built. I open a couple of the nearest windows to let in today's fresh air and make a quick cup of coffee while my laptop boots up.

First things first, I go to the shop's website and load the five photographs that I've already chosen to print, pick the finish and size and fill in the contact information. None are the same shots that hang here in this house and unless the shop is really busy, my order should be ready in a couple of days. That done, I go to my everyday email account and see a confirmation of my photo order right above an email from Rob. He's tired but making the adjustment to the demands of long-haul flights, stays in unfamiliar hotels and quick turnarounds.

Then there are a series of questions, each with an undertone of very strong encouragement. Have I looked at the event flyer? Have I thought about submitting my photographs to the exhibition? Have I gone so far as to contact the organizers to ask about submissions? If I had a dime for every time I've heard, "You really should put your stuff out there, you know," I'd be a rich man.

By this time, I'm laughing out loud and wish I could be in front of my friend when I tell him about the photos gone to print and the painting that's on its way to being the first in a very long time. I can easily imagine the next email from Rob after I tell him that none are destined for public viewing.

Coffee next to me, I type that I'm glad his change in routine is going so well back here the house and garden are both fine, as is the boat, and yes, I've looked at the celebration event information. "Guess what?" starts my next paragraph.

I tell him all about the ideas that led up to my actually setting up the easel, stretching the canvas, getting out and then, finally, using the paints. I describe where the image is as of yesterday's rainy day, where it's going when I get back home today, and how I want it to end. Just describing everything to Rob is making me feel good.

As always, I reread his email to see if my brain has missed anything and it's then that I wonder aloud about his suggestion to put your stuff out there. If all I have to do is submit photographs for consideration, frame them if they're accepted and deliver them for someone to hang, I could probably handle that.

I go back to reading both his email and my reply and then hit Send. There's enough coffee made for half a cup more, so I pour that into the mug and debate with myself about emailing the contact person while I'm already online. Another look through the website section provides enough curiosity to do it.

I formulate a short message about my photos and attach the files of those I've chosen to print for my walls. What sort of commitment do they expect and are present-day shots taken on and from the shoreline trail something that they want. I tell them the best way to reach me is by cell phone or, on a more sporadic basis, by email, both of which I provide.

The coffee is gone, so I do a check of the house on the inside, close windows, come back to shut down and repack the laptop, and prepare to walk home. My email words to Rob about the painting bounce around in my head as I lock the door and turn towards the trail. Everything that catches my eye during the next three hours holds potential. I can't wait to get home.

*****************************

# Chapter Thirteen

## Sara

The past week of walking, eating, playing, sleeping, and hooking has absolutely flown past me. The chair cover is coming along nicely and I've cut more strips of t-shirt whenever the colour stash was depleted. Right now, I feel a little guilty because I rushed our walk this morning.

Chance wasn't stopping to sniff any more than she usually does but I was inwardly impatient to get back home. I had to remind myself to breathe in the fresh, warm air, relax and enjoy your morning routine. There is plenty of time to work on the hooking. It's not yet 9:00 o'clock.

Back home and having played with the increasingly decrepit soccer ball, I'm no longer uptight about taking time out for me and Chance. I give her a rub and the touch of her soft fur on my hands brings me back to what and who is most important in my life.

My customary post-walk glass of water is on the side-table and the hooking is ready on my frame, so it's time to give it my attention. I'll keep an eye on the clock because I arranged to take both this project and my wall-hanging to the Town Hall around 1:00 today. We'll talk about where to hang *Anchored*, my image that looks from the shoreline trail to the hills across the bay with a houseboat anchored just off the near shore.

Of course, there isn't now and probably will never be a houseboat moored in that spot. The day I drew that image, I was newly settled in my little home. A definitive sense of security and belonging had worked its way through a period of grief and I had returned to solid ground, anchored, if you will. Where others might scoff at the incongruity of that scene, the story behind its creation is quite logical. I hope, when they look at it or hear my explanation, the hanging will be included in the exhibition.

I have already sent the photo of the chair, so I'll show them what the cover will look like when it's finished. My hands are leading the material strips and pulling loops as I think about all this. I like the display idea of leaving the worn seat visible with the new cover ready to be attached. In their email reply, they suggested presenting it that way and asked me about transporting the chair.

I assured them, "I can borrow a truck and know a couple of strong young backs who can heft an old but heavy armchair whenever you're ready."

Chance wants back indoors, so I'm forced to move. A cup of tea and a muffin sound like a good break and, what's even better is to take both outside on this lovely June day. The dogberry and birch trees are in full leaf now and the willow is a bright yellow-green with renewed life. On the trail, the chickadees are flitting from one tree to another and the pips on the rose bushes alongside duck pond road are ready to bloom. Even here in the back garden, the sparrows and jays make a farce of the dog's ineffectual attempts to catch them. I can't help but wonder whether the birds are enjoying the game as much as my companion with her jumps and sprints.

The clock on the microwave signals that I need to get things together and head down the road. Chance will have to miss out on this ride, something that will get me a displeased look. Unlike when she first came to live with me, she now knows that I shall return. Ten minutes later, my car is parked.

I'm in through the double doors of the Town Hall and getting directions to the celebration committee office. Right on cue, my contact meets me, and we go into a board room with a long conference table. Her colleague joins us and after introductions, I unroll my wall-hanging so it lies flat on the surface in front of us.

"Oh, wow, that's gorgeous." I sense the unspoken "but" and jump into the story behind the image.

The growing understanding on their faces puts to rest my concern that I've blown an opportunity. Both Adam and Jennifer stop and, almost in unison, they voice a plan to not only include the piece in the exhibition but to put it and the story behind it in a prominent location. I am thrilled about all of it and nearly forget to show them the future seat cover. Its design is much more stylized by comparison and takes a little imagination to recognize the elements of sky, hills, sea and shoreline, but, I quickly add, it's going to be on the seat of a chair. It's not telling a story at eye level.

Their plans for the celebration are well organized and I love hearing the excitement in their voices as we look at the white board covered in potential displays and events from one month to the next. We talk about security and all three of us sign an agreement before we decide on dates for delivery and installation. I add that I'm happy to borrow a truck a week from today.

I'll also have the seat cover completely hooked by then and they can decide how best to, even temporarily, attach it to the chair. My drive home with the car windows wide open feels like I've stepped up my game and put myself into the public arena.

As always, I'm met at the door by a large dog doing her best to both wag her back end and present me with a toy to welcome me home. What more could a woman want?

*****************************

## **Carrie**

Every window in my house is wide open this morning. I'm not one to bounce around and jump up and down with excitement about anything, but now might be a good time to break the mould.

Airing out my house from front to back and side to side is great after it's been closed tight against winter.

When Maisie stopped by with the newspapers just after 8:00, she thought I had a spring in my step that she was happy to see. I wouldn't have said that I've been without one, but that's Maisie for you.

Now that I'm outside and having another look around the place, the buds on the flowers and those on the hedge are getting plump. The past few days have been nice, warm and dry. The woman and her dog went by not long after Maisie and I had finished talking about the fishing gear for the exhibition. She rolled her eyes heavenward and said she'd text Arch about it.

I walk around to the back garden mostly to check that the pole is holding the line far enough off the ground now that the breeze has picked up a little. My hand goes into my apron pocket and feels the seed packets that I bought from the nursery one day last week. Time goes by so quickly that I need to get things planted.

There's a branch blown off one of the bushes, perfect for my purpose. I run it through the soil in the bed to mark out four separate spaces, one for each vegetable. Carrots in one square, onions in another, beets in the third and greens in the last. I saw this design in one of the seed catalogues and it works because I can squat down on any side of the bed and still reach far enough to plant and, later, weed each section.

It takes me no time to make seed holes with the handle of an old spoon saved year after year just for this purpose. Let's hope that with a little water to get started, today's sun will last all month long. There's nothing as good as the veg out of my own garden. What I don't grow, I can always buy from one of the veg stands on the main road. My knees and back are moaning now, so it's time to get this apron off, wash the dirt from under my fingernails and make that run down to the Town office.

Earlier this week, I very carefully hand-washed the tablecloth and laid it flat on my back bridge to dry in the warm air. It not only held together, it looks a little brighter than before and has lain unfolded on my spare bed since then. Now, I gather it gently, wrap it in white tissue paper and take it with me to the front door. My little old car and I will enjoy a slow run this morning. I'm just about to turn the key in the lock when I remember my collection of old knitting patterns. I go back inside, pick them up from beside my chair and turn back to the door.

The drive isn't too bad once I'm through those lights at the top of my lane. The traffic is light without any emergency vehicles, thank goodness, and I have no problem finding a parking space at the Town Hall. The young lady behind the counter gives me directions to an office down on the ground floor, so that's where I go.

"I'll call ahead and tell them you're on your way," she says, and I thank her for her help.

A young man comes across a wide open space to greet me as I make my way down the stairs, introduces himself and shakes my hand. Nice manners pops into my head. We go to a nearby room with a huge window at one end and a long, shiny table dividing the space.

I show him the tablecloth and tell him its story. He puts on a pair of white gloves before he touches a corner. I've seen that done on television. His smile and the nodding of his head tell me he'll use Aunt Maude's handiwork in the exhibit. Then I remember the pattern books in my bag and tell Adam about them.

I'm quick to apologize for springing them on him and won't be offended if they're not of any use for the celebration. Again, he looks interested and is very gentle as he turns one page after another.

"Those were the days when babies wore hand-knitted clothes and pattern books cost twenty-five cents," I tell him.

He'd like to put the pattern books and the tablecloth in one of the glass display cases.

"That way, they won't get damaged."

I hadn't thought about that so I like his plan. I'm looking at the wall across from us. It's covered in white panels with squares like a calendar. We walk over to them and he explains that they're called white-boards, much like our old blackboards in school but different.

The first has a chart of all the submissions okayed for the exhibition. The names or numbers in red are contact information and mine will be added in a specific space. The second board is for artworks and crafts and the spaces needed for each article. The final white rectangle with blue lettering is actually a calendar of events and the groups or people involved.

I see a music festival, parties on the beach, sailboat races out on the bay, so many things to organize. I'm amazed and I tell him so before he walks me back up the stairs where we shake hands good-bye.

I left the tablecloth and the pattern books in his care, which feels rather scary now that I'm driving home. He promised they'd be safe and well cared for so I guess I shouldn't worry. We had both signed a paper that sounded quite serious about responsibilities and dates for when my items will be given back to me. Thanksgiving sounds like a very long time away but I know it will come soon enough and it's not like I won't be able to go and look at things whenever the exhibit is open. That's what I'm telling myself as I go down the lane and into my driveway.

It is most definitely time for tea and a sit-down. This has been a very busy day, quite unusual for me, and I confess to feeling a bit tired by it all. On the other hand, I'm really pleased with myself for doing everything in one day.

The only thing that completely slipped my mind was to mention the old oar-locks and anchor, but they can be part of whatever Arch lends to the exhibit, if he lends anything at all. I reckon I've done my part and that feels almost as good as this cup of tea.

****************************************

## Margaret

Last evening, there was plenty of talk about who's doing what, which farming tools to offer, what we will let out of our sight and what we won't share. It was a long evening, but everyone was, in the end, all of the same mind. Some folks just needed to have their say and that's just fine by me.

The only things for which I now have responsibility are those previously stored in that old margarine company carton, the two special household bibles (my word for them) and the glossy magazines. The email I had earlier in the week from Jennifer said that they had another submission of some old hand-written recipes, so Mother's exercise book stays here at home.

I'm going to catch a ride with my sister-in-law to take my share of the family heirlooms down to the Town Hall. She is off shift for a few days and will be a second set of eyes and ears at the meeting this afternoon. I don't have a car and, in recent years, have no real need for one, so going with Anne will be an outing.

In the meantime, I am opening windows like a crazy woman to get this warm June air blowing through my place. The scent of flowers won't be carried on it yet, but that's okay. The curtains at both the living room and kitchen windows are happily waving at the world.

The down side of a bright, warm day is that every speck of dust is illuminated on just about every surface, as well as the new particles floating in on the breeze. I'm laughing at myself because I can't have it both ways, a dust-free, closed-up home or an airy but dusty one. Today, I'm happy with the latter. There used to be a fridge magnet that read *Feel free to notice the dust; just don't write in it!* That's absolutely appropriate for my place today.

Yesterday, I planted my vegetable patch. Two of the younger children, Rachel and David, came over after school and we had fun poking tiny seeds into the soil. I like their enthusiasm and their disbelief that what they're putting into the ground will turn into something they can watch grow, eventually pull up, and then eat.

The green tops of carrots, beets, peas and onions will evolve and when the time is right, someone will come to help me build a frame and run the twine for the pea tendrils.

Last summer, I remember small hands carefully unrolling the green curls to wrap them around the lines so the plants didn't topple over when they became heavy with pods. Even now, I'm smiling that another generation will understand how things don't simply appear in a grocery aisle and magically end up on their supper table.

After I cleared away breakfast dishes this morning, I laid the magazines and two books out on my kitchen table. Part of me is uneasy about entrusting them to the care of strangers, never mind the idea of leaving them in a public place for nearly four months. They've been cozy in my attic for so long. Cozy? In reality, they've been stored out of sight for years and will now be enjoyed by as many people as care to look through the glass of those display cases.

Anne knocks on my door before she turns the knob and steps into the hall, "Are you ready?" she smiles as I move towards the door.

"Yes, I'm ready and the treasures are tucked inside my canvas bag."

She knows it's a big step for me, so her hug of encouragement feels nice as we walk to the car. I like Anne's little car. It's low to the ground and sporty, a just reward for her long hours of work. The ride down the shore road to the Town Hall is filled with pleasant and easy conversation about her job, the family, gardening plans, and the children's news. When she extends a hand to, ostensibly lift my bag out the passenger door, I thank her.

"My joints and the adjective sprightly no longer belong in the same sentence," I laugh.

Anne has been to the Town Hall for other events, so she knows which way to go this afternoon. At the door, we meet two young people and make introductions as we walk towards the long table dividing the room. They have already looked at the photos I sent and read the story behind our attic discovery but that's where our conversation starts as I put everything onto the table in front of us.

Anne and I have pored over each item and no longer find them as amazing but they are truly novel for Jennifer and Adam standing between us. Their pleasure is contagious and exchanging glances, it's clear we're all enjoying the moment.

We agree to leave the magazines and books in their care sign documents that detail safety, dates, display times and methods (glass display cases), the value of the items and everyone's responsibilities. Anne takes her time, reads the papers carefully and asks a couple of questions, which makes me glad that she's here. I have a tendency to trust people until proven otherwise, sometimes to my disadvantage.

There's a wall full of white boards marked with well-organized notes, names, items, space requirements, times, events and goodness knows what else. I notice it has all been divided according to the subjects mentioned in the media announcements. It's an impressive undertaking.

I hear myself heave a big sigh as we walk to the car. Anne suggests that we deserve an ice cream stop on the way home, to which I readily agree. Trying not to drip soft serve anywhere inside her lovely car, I hear Anne laugh and tell me not to give it a second thought.

"She's cute, gets me where I want to go and cleans up real nice."

Eating a soft ice cream and driving a stick shift is a blast from my past and I'm happy to say that my driver today does it with both skill and pleasure.

As we slow to turn into our driveway, I catch a glimpse of a bright red jeep-style vehicle that smoothly pulls around us and continues over the crest of the hill. Anne stops to let me out beside my house and waves as she revs the engine and pulls away. I think a vehicle higher off the ground, like the one heading up the little hill, would be my current choice of car if I were in the market for one.

However, that's a pipe-dream, one that I've no honest wish to fulfill. Today, I am evidence of the great divide between a four-on-the-floor and a pair of well-worn knees that call out for their own version of grease and oil. It's time for tea.

*************************************

## Ben

The chatter of starlings and the distinctive call of a Northern Flicker wake me. The bedroom window was ajar all night, so the room is fresh as I climb out of bed. On my way to a much-needed coffee, I stop and look at my painting.

I've worked steadily for two days and what I now see pleases me. The feeling of wide open space is there and the shoreline in the foreground brings things back to the edge. I'm letting it sit today. I took a couple of shots of it last evening to email to Rob.

I balance my coffee on the plate beside a piece of toast smothered with almond butter. I'm going to start my day out in the morning air. A woodpecker is quite near but I've yet to locate it over the rim of my mug. I'll take the car out of the garage at Rob's house today and head into town to pick up my prints. The shop is open until 9:00 tonight, so I have tons of time to walk the trail, although my feet, itchy for movement, will get the better of me soon enough.

A flock of starlings suddenly rises up from behind the house and swoops over the roof to land in the grass on the other side of the lane. Even at a quick guess, there must be fifty or more fighting each other for space and chattering non-stop. It's a sea of speckled brown.

My breakfast done, my laptop and charger still in my backpack and, other than keys, phone and water bottle, there isnothing more I need. The birds keep me company as I walk to the main road. The school bus comes around the corner and brakes going down the hill. I step to one side just before it reaches the little bridge and glance up at the sea of faces.

I've never, not even once in my life, wanted to teach in a school. Providing occasional surfing moves on a hot beach is the limit to sharing my pearls of wisdom. Nowadays, walking the trail and keeping to myself are the definition of a life well-lived.

After a moment's pause to set up the music on my phone and put in my ear buds, I pick up the pace. It doesn't take long to work out the kinks from so much sitting, although I feel no guilt for two sedentary days, given what I accomplished. To now stride along the familiar path, see gulls riding the breeze out over the water and smell the salt air is exactly what both mind and muscles need.

Behind a few homes, I see laundry on a line and lawns that have turned from brown to green. As I cross the first shoreline bridge, two dogs run back and forth behind a fence, their sharp barks breaking through the music in my ears. Farther along, at windows facing the water, curtains blow in open windows.

The ducks must be at the far end of the pond this morning because none are here under the bridge and in the distance, I can see that familiar curved tail trotting alongside its human companion. At the eastern headland, I decide to see if my favourite gnarled tree is still clinging to life. Its roots are visible where high tides and strong surf have eroded the bank around them, so I keep expecting it to tumble to the beach below.

The narrow path has shrunk with new branches stretching into the warm sun. I'm glad the material in my pants is tough because, in some spots, wild rose bushes actually block the way. My tree, however, still stands, albeit at an awkward angle that seems incredibly unstable. I don't dare go close enough to touch my fingers to its grey bark. We might both find ourselves at the water's mercy.

The fields of the pumpkin farm are tilled under and I expect seeds have been sown by now. I take the last few turns back on the groomed trail, step onto the short lane and arrive at the house. All looks fine from the outside and a quick look around shows the same indoors, so, without hesitation, I slip the car key off its hook, step through the adjoining door and greet the red machine. She'll take me to town and back this morning before I sit down at the table to look at any emails.

I adjust the seat, my legs being longer than Rob's, check that there's plenty of gas in the tank, open the garage door with the button above the mirror, put her into first gear and out we go. Another touch brings the door down behind us as I pull onto the quiet side road then head into town. It's about twenty minutes or so when there's no commuter traffic or construction, so I open the windows and enjoy the drive. Shifting gears with each speed change comes naturally, even after a long absence from an old habit.

The shopping area is busy but I wait for someone to back out of a space near the print and frame shop. Unlike the departing vehicle, I back into the parking spot, preferring to see what's around me when I pull out to leave.

The prints are ready and they are gorgeous. I'd chosen standard formats so the shop owner and I choose ready-made mattes. Then, from the supply on the wall, we decide on frames that best suit each image. I'm really pleased with how they all look as we put them together and I can't wait to share them with Rob.

"Send him my best wishes," she adds as we carefully place the five wrapped packages into the spacious trunk of the red machine.

I readily assure her that he'll know the finishing touches are her work as soon as he sees the photos in my email. Not wanting to spend any more time in town than necessary, I start the drive home with precious cargo behind the second row of seats.

I must have been a bit uptight because when I finally arrive back into the driveway at the house, I feel relief. It takes me five trips to carry the framed photographs from the car to the kitchen table. The light coming through the big windows is perfect for recording these new possessions before I grab a cold drink, make a quick sandwich, transfer the files to my laptop and sit down to write an email.

The inbox shows one message from Rob and, immediately below it, a reply from the exhibition contact person. Which to open first? Knowing that the celebration email is more time-sensitive, I open his message and am more than a little surprised that he wants to include three of my photos in the Arts and Crafts display. His email goes on to say that the only commitment required of me is to deliver each piece framed, to discuss the installation in person, and to be on-site during the Grand Opening.

I'm not keen on that last item, but I do realize that it's not an unreasonable thing to ask, so I hit the reply icon and then type my thanks and pleasure. I add that those three photos were framed this morning and ask him to let me know a time and place to meet. If he suggests an early morning, I'll plan to stay down here overnight and take advantage of Rob's invitation to use the Jeep again.

Now, on to Rob's email. He's doing fine and was informed

that his four-month stint has been shortened, so he'll be home by the end of August. He says life's pretty routine, but he's met some great people. The next paragraph is just as I expected. His reaction to my having submitted photos to the celebration exhibition is full of multiple exclamation points and many words of encouragement.

There's also a reminder to me that when I become well-known for my work, I must not forget the little people who got me there. So typical.

I start, then stop, read, backspace, and then find the best words to tell him about this morning's acceptance email. I decide to quote the exact phrasing from that message but delay telling him my reaction. I chat about other things, the house, the weather, the trail, and the birds around my place, until several sentences later, I throw in that I've accepted their image choices, have those photos already framed and will meet in person soon.

Of course, I'm enjoying this almost as much as I would were he here in front of me receiving my news. On impulse, I exit that half-finished email and let it save as a draft. I'm wondering whether there's been a quick reply from the Town suggesting a meeting time or any further comment about the photos, so I refresh the Inbox.

Sure enough, there is a reply. It asks to meet tomorrow because time is getting short. I agree to 10:00 in the morning and attach the photos I've taken of the framed prints. I send that reply and re-open my draft to Rob. Reading through it again, I make sure I've given him as much information as he'll want to hear and then add the final touch. I tell him that his email is being sent mere minutes after setting a meeting for tomorrow at 10:00.

I admit to him that I'm feeling hesitant about it all, but, somehow, pleasant anticipation is gaining the upper hand. I spell out my plan to borrow his jeep again to deliver the prints to the Town Hall and hope that's all good with him as he sits somewhere on the other side of the Atlantic Ocean.

I attach the pictures of the three framed prints accepted for the art display and then attach the shot I took of my painting before I left the house earlier this morning. I haven't even told him much about the painting, so that image will be a bit of an eye-opener.

As I sign off, I look at the file names of the four attachments and, quite suddenly, have an uneasy feeling. I send my email to Rob and immediately open the Sent folder. Both the one just gone and the message to the exhibition contact are the two most recent. I open my email to Rob and read the file names again.

Then, I click on the email previously sent and, ignoring the text, look immediately at the attached files. Sure enough, the framed versions of the successful photographs are there, one, two and three. Then I see a fourth file and sit back in disbelief. Toggling back and forth between two different emails is not something I usually do, and now, it's obvious that I'm not very good at it. There, underneath the three intended files, is a fourth attachment. It's the picture of my painting.

What on earth do I do now? Email the guy and apologize, possibly drawing unnecessary attention to the extra file or hoping that his focus will remain on only the files he's expecting. I need to walk away from the laptop, make some fresh coffee, take it outside into the fresh air and calm down.

As I step onto the back deck, the phone in my pocket rings a Marley tune. The display tells me that it's from the Town, so I swipe the answer icon. A voice introduces himself as Adam, a contact for the exhibition, then asks if he's speaking with me. I'm about to ask if he's received my most recent email when he thanks me for my quick reply. Then, Adam hesitates. I hold my breath and force myself to wait until he goes on to say that he noticed an additional attachment.

"Yes," I tell him, "that's a painting I've just finished and I hadn't intended to include it in my email."

I'm hoping he can hear trepidation and apology within my words.

"That is your original artwork?" Adam confirms that he's heard me correctly.

Phone to my ear and coffee unfinished, I turn and walk back into the house as I hear, "That's a fabulous scene. Would you consider allowing us to include it in the exhibition?"

My brain doesn't quite process his words. The idea had never entered my mind, not even for a second. My caller is patiently waiting for a reply, so for a few minutes more, we chat about the possibility. He feels that my painting captures the theme of the whole celebration as well as the true sense of the community itself. Hung alongside my photographs, he thinks it will make an amazing display.

I tell him the dimensions of the canvas and then agree to bring it with me when we meet tomorrow morning. The call ends and I'm not sure what I feel as the cold coffee goes down the drain and I refill the bright blue mug with what's left in the pot.

I decide to send an update to Rob, "I wish you were here in this kitchen right now to help me work through what I've just agreed to do."

It's one thing to put my photographs out there, as he thinks I should, but to bare my soul through my painting is so tough. I will, as promised, take the canvas with me to tomorrow's meeting but right now, to not only have it on display but, in essence, for me to also be on display is nerve-wracking.

Maybe after some more thought and time in the comfort of

my little home tonight, I'll feel better. If not, I can always say no, not an unfamiliar response.

No matter how I word this new email to Rob, I suspect my emotions will be obvious and my words probably disjointed. The subject line reads *To be read after my previous email*. I add that when read in sequence, a little perspective might be provided. I groan aloud at the unintended pun, knowing that Rob will appreciate it.

I decide to stack the framed pieces in a corner of the living room. There's no point in carrying them home and then back again tomorrow. I'll stop by for them on my way to the Town Hall. For now, I close the windows that I'd opened earlier and reset the lighting timer. I'll have to borrow the jeep again to transport that painting in the morning so I'll drive to my place now. The high wheel base won't have any trouble going down my unkempt lane and there's enough room in front of my house for safe overnight parking.

I empty the fridge of any remaining items and do one last check of the house. The car key comes off the rack for a second time, I complete the garage routine and off we go, the red machine and I. The three-hour distance that I walk each day will be covered in less than half an hour if all three traffic lights are in my favour. I'll be home mid-afternoon with enough natural light to do any touch-ups to the scene on my canvas and still be sure that it's dry for transport in the morning. This has been one heck of a busy few hours filled with unexpected twists and turns in my usually quiet, uncluttered life.

As I approach the bridge at the foot of the little hill where my minder lives, I pull behind a fancy little sports car signalling a turn. I shift into second and then pass as it gears down and turns into the long driveway. Given all the other oddities of today, I can't help but wonder if she's the one behind the wheel.

Less than five minutes later, I turn off the main road and onto my lane, avoid the biggest of the potholes, pull the jeep to one side, and tuck it snugly against the base of my land.

*********************************

# Chapter Fourteen

## Sara

A sour dough starter has bubbled overnight so today will begin with making bread. The kettle boils while I put a tea bag in the pot. While the dough is on its first rise, we'll have an hour to walk. Yesterday's sunshine is not with us this morning. The sky is a uniform grey as Chance and I head to the trail in light drizzle.

It's not the bone-chilling damp of a mild winter's day, which makes it relatively pleasant for both of us. The chickadees are out and about in the garden this morning and above us now, there's a long line of starlings perched on the utility wires. Mental note to self not to look up too often, just keep walking to the open air beside the sea.

The dull overcast stretches all the way to the hidden hills on the far side of the bay and the ocean is strangely gentle as it rolls to land. My companion's nose is sweeping the rocks, the bright green bushes and, now and then, a protruding evergreen branch that must hold an exceptional scent. I wonder if smells are amplified by this sort of damp weather. All I detect is salt in the air.

I see a group of seagulls well out in the bay, with only a couple in flight at the moment. Crows are circling above the duck pond in the near distance, but nothing else is on the move. Even my lighter walking boots sound loud to me without the wind. The islands off to the east are barely visible but I know they are there.

A well-written scene floats into my head. I picture a young Quinevere being transported by rowboat through the mists of Avalon to the safety of an island that outsiders have never seen. That's definitely a flight of fancy because I'm pretty certain the water over which that little boat travelled was nothing like the cold ocean beside us this morning.

I check my phone to make sure we haven't lingered overly long. Otherwise, the bread will have risen out the door to greet us. I pick up our pace and apart from my companion's impulsive stops at points of interest, we are back home within the hour. Inside the porch, I attempt to towel off some of the wet fur, but it's really an exercise in futility. My wet jacket will dry more quickly than her water-repellent fur, which is, of course, why that particular aroma lingers for the rest of the day to compete with freshly-baked bread.

My mind wends its way back to yesterday when we loaded the old chair into the pan of the truck and delivered it along with me, my wall-hanging and the potential seat cover to the folks at the Town Hall. I had called ahead to know where to bring it and once inside on the ground floor, a couple of staff people carried it to the display space. The night before, I had written and printed the stories behind the hooking and the old chair to help with the exhibition labels.

This morning, it's quite odd to see a blank wall in my stairwell instead of *Anchored* and the chair no longer occupies a corner of my tiny bedroom. My rug-hooking frame sits in the spare room, awaiting the next project. I haven't decided whether I'll do a covering for the back of the chair. Not as worn as the seat, I might just leave the original deep gold material for contrast, the old above the new.

It's amazing that there's only one more week before the Grand Opening. I'm really looking forward to seeing everything.

The bread is now in its pans, ready to rise a second time before going into the oven and I'm getting a look that indicates some outdoor play time is expected. Once more, I pull on waterproof boots and jacket and step out into the drizzle.

*********************************

## **Carrie**

This is almost fog. I can see, from my chair by the window, that the mist is moving from west to east this morning. I'm not prone to fancy, but you could imagine a giant spray bottle squirting its way along the shore trail. I'm glad it's not snow this third week of June. That's been known to happen and with my seeds already in the ground, if white was falling from the sky, I'd wouldn't be fit for conversation today. Our growing season is short enough without anything cutting it back any more.

I'm working on a new blanket with that navy yarn now that all those squares have gone with Deanne. I'm glad to have something for my hands to be doing of an evening. Yesterday was such a nice day that I washed and waxed all the floors and then put a load of bedding on the line. The fresh air smell on my sheets and quilt was so nice when I got into bed last night. This morning's weather won't see me outside for very long today, I don't think.

There goes the woman and her dog. She's wearing a raincoat and, it looks like, some sort of waterproof pants. Sensible woman, says I, dressed for the drizzle coming down. The dog doesn't look as happy as usual but her nose is to the ground, checking out all it can between my corner and the trail. I see the dog's ears perk up as she spies a scattered duck out on the pond. Her walk, at least, is still a good one.

I think when I'm done with my tea, I'll make some cookies.

Maisie said that Arch was going to put a few things together for the exhibition and he'll take those oar locks of mine. A batch of chocolate chip cookies won't go astray by way of a thank you. Maisie isn't a baker. She's still working in town while Arch, who's older, retired last year. He doesn't mind having supper ready when she gets home, but he's not one for sweets. He likes eating them, just not making them. "Too fiddly," he says. After that, I'll get back to my yarn.

The blanket that I'm crocheting now is a pattern from one of those old books that I put in the celebration display. It's a really simple combination of single, half-double and double stitches so I'll have it done in no time. Maybe, on this damp old day, I'll run up to the little store and get some more yarn.

Come to think of it, I don't have any chocolate chips, so I have to go out. That will give my car a little change of scene after my breakfast dishes are done and I've checked the cupboard to see if I need anything else while I'm up the road.

It's a funny thing. For ages, I never thought about Aunt Maude's tablecloth sitting in the drawer. Now that it's not here, it comes to my mind all the time. The thread is so fine and the pattern so delicate that it must have taken her forever to make. It fits the whole top of the kitchen table. I remember Mother putting it out on very special occasions, but it was always protected from spills by a slippery clear plastic.

That plastic was bigger than the tablecloth and hung down on all sides, so we kids had to be careful not to catch an edge with our knees under the table. My brother admitted, in his adult years, that he was always tempted to give the plastic enough of a tug to topple the drinking glasses just to see where the syrup would run. I'm not sure he'd have survived to tell the tale if he'd tried that.

Enough day-dreaming. It's time to be sensible. I slip my feet out of my slippers and into a pair of outdoor shoes, pull a jacket around me, grab my purse and walk to the car. It's not pension cheque day or two-for-one day, so the store shouldn't be too busy.

As always, I sneak through the back entry to the lot and park far enough away to make backing out easy but not so far that I'm in the drizzle for very long. The layout of the store hasn't changed in donkey's years, so I know right where the baking goods are and the yarn shelves on the far wall.

I don't need anything else because I checked before I went out the door, so it's a quick shop this morning. Two packs of semi-sweet chocolate chips, an extra one for good measure, and two big balls of yarn, one red, one a soft yellow, and I'm all done.

The young lady at the checkout always has a smile and hopes I'll not get too wet on my way home. Little does she know that I've driven here, not walked and I'm not about to tell her the difference.

I just say "Thank you," put my hand through the packed bag that's she holding out to me, and wish her a nice day. I do love the friendliness of our local stores.

Now, I'm back home, going to have a sit down and think about how to work those new colours into the pattern with the navy. Alternating rows of colour might be nice. Then, again, the centre panel could be what I've already done, then go around that to make a bigger yellow area followed by red. What would I want on the back of my sofa, that's the better way to think of it.

Maybe I'll have a look through some of the magazines that Maisie passed along to me. They might give me an idea. Next question, where did I put them the other day when I was so wrapped up in the Town Hall thing?

The exhibition organizer, Jennifer, called me yesterday to ask if I need a ride down to the Grand Opening.

I said, "No, thanks, I'll drive myself."

The tablecloth, she told me, will actually be in one of the glass display cases. The time's gone so quickly since I first heard about the plan to hold an anniversary celebration. Mind you, the last thirty years have also nipped by me. It's crazy that I've lived in this house for nearly fifty years now.

************************************

## Margaret

It's a grey old morning with drizzle lightly tapping at my window as I sit here in my chair, my second cup of tea in front of me. There's absolutely no point in going out to check on the fence right now. I'd get all wet and won't stay long enough to fix it, so I may as well wait for tomorrow. All hands waved and honked their way out onto the main road earlier this morning, so that's all done.

Mother's recipe book, the old-fashioned blue exercise book, is open in front of me and I know that any number of hours can pass me by once I start reading the writing on those pages. Another sip of tea brings my eyes up from the table to the road outside my window. There goes that red jeep that I saw when we came home from the meeting at the Town Hall yesterday.

Now, I'm curious as to whose it is. Maybe one of Emily's or Liam's friends passed their driving test and has a new car, expensive as that will be with the high cost of insurance for a young driver as well as the cost of gas these days. Anne was telling me how much it is to fill the tank in her little car.

It's not a great morning for being out and about so I probably won't see my walker. I feel more than a bit foolish labelling him 'my walker.' I don't mean to be nosy but he is such an interesting person about whom no one knows much at all. Surrounded by family who are in touch with me every single day and who live a stone's throw away, his life seems to be the complete opposite of mine.

He strides along on his own, not stopping to chat with anyone and does it the same way in reverse to a home about which I know nothing. A conversation between us has never happened, but I do wonder what we might have in common, if anything.

Frankie dropped by last evening to tell me that she had found the time to take the dishes and platter down to the exhibition organizers. They were pleased to have them and carried them directly to the line of display cases, chose one, and put our family treasures safely inside. The young man, Adam, told Frankie that while they might rearrange the dishes slightly, none would be removed from the case for any reason. She was happy about that and said seeing them, even randomly displayed, gave her a lovely feeling. For someone who married into our large, crazy family, her attachment is really nice.

My youngest brother, Matthew, Matt for short, spoke with someone about the limited farm tools that we still have in the old barn. Not surprisingly, someone else had already submitted most of what we have, so those things will remain where they are. In some ways, he told me afterwards, it makes life easier. Having fewer things out of our hands for several months allows us to keep a closer eye on the pieces that Frankie and I provided.

I agreed with him, which was greeted with a grin and a smart remark, "The younger brother is finally correct about something."

Apologies, Mother, but I did stick my tongue out at him. Established habits die hard, even at my age.

Now then, woman, stop reliving yesterday and come back to the here and now. That command isn't quite accurate because here I sit, reading recipes from years ago. Here's the Christmas pudding recipe with all its dried fruit and suet. We kids would come home from school at lunchtime to stir the huge bowl of raw mixture, draw an X with the big wooden spoon, hold it up straight with both hands and make a wish.

We each took a turn and hoped to be the one who found the silver coin hidden in the brandy-soaked dessert on Christmas Day. That's when, out of sight in the kitchen, Mother would light the ring of alcohol that surrounded the pudding and carry the plate to the table. Waiting for the flames to die down was always a highlight of Christmas dinner, even if I didn't find the hidden coin.

I turn the page and read her shortbread recipe. I remember that meal and baking plans depended on whatever ingredients were readily available. Shortbread, for example, wasn't the traditional Scottish sweet. Ours was made with brown or white instead of castor sugar and each piece of dough was cut into circles rather than rectangular fingers. Every cookie did have its top pieced by a fork before baking so it looked a little like the picture on the store-bought box.

The upright handwriting jumps off the page at me again. After the chocolate and cream Yule log with its brown bark of thick icing, this is my all-time favourite cake. We called it a Jam Sandwich rather than its correct name, Victoria Sponge. The blonde cake would have some kind of jam liberally spread on the flat surface of the bottom layer with the second sponge laid on top, hence the sandwich moniker. Mother would sieve a little powdered sugar over the surface and as little kids, that sprinkling of white reminded us of snow.

I haven't made this cake in twenty or more years. Today, that's going to change. I'll have to choose from the jars of jam that I put down during the winter to determine what's in the middle of the cake. It could be blueberry, partridge berry, rhubarb or gooseberry, a deep blue or three different shades of red. I think it's time to put on my apron and clutter up my counter.

Good aromas will shut out the grey drizzle bouncing off my flowers and vegetable garden. If any after-school visitors stop in, they'll not go home before trying their grandmother's version of a Jam Sandwich.

*******************************************

## Ben

My first thought upon waking is that I hear something tapping lightly at the window. Up on one elbow, the answer is right there as the water skids down the pane. The one day that I have to transport a canvas full of paint, my first work in many years, it's raining. Lying in bed and moaning isn't going to make one bit of difference, so get over it, get up and get moving. Standing at the kitchen window, I see that it's drizzle not actual rain. The branches outside the bedroom made it sound worse than it is so that's a relief.

Coffee to the rescue, followed by a bagel with cream cheese and the smoked salmon that came home with me from Rob's fridge yesterday. A hearty breakfast that I'll walk off when I make my way back here later today. The red machine looks to have survived its night outside. I can see water beading off the hood. I didn't expect to see anything untoward, but it's still a relief. It's not my car, after all. I'll be glad to get it back within the protective walls of the garage.

I'm going to sit in my chair by the wood burner so I can look at the canvas while I eat breakfast. The image still resonates with me despite the greyness of this morning's light. If anything, the painted weather adds just a little brightness to my cozy room, and once again, I'm glad this is the image I chose from all in my sketchbook. It was my final choice and it's a good one. Others may come off the page and onto canvas at some point, but for now, I'm happy with this one.

That I'm not the only person happy with this image charges into my mind. I'm about to wrap this piece of me against the damp air and share it with two strangers in the outside world. That's a little less daunting this morning after an evening's relaxation and a good night's sleep. The clock on the stove tells me it's already 8:30, so I need to finish breakfast, grab a shower, hope my jeans are good enough for a meeting, wrap the canvas and get it and myself down to the car.

I don't want to be late so I figure an extra fifteen minutes to pick up three of the framed prints from down at the house and get them loaded into the trunk. If I remember correctly, I had the presence of mind yesterday to put those in front of the ones not going to the Town Hall.

I find and slit apart some brown paper bags and tape them together until they overlap enough to wrap around the canvas. Now to protect it with another layer, a highly unprofessional large plastic garbage bag. It's not an artist's best-looking portfolio, but then again, I don't profess to be a bona fide artist and it's all I have on hand, so it will have to do. The shop wrapped the framed prints in butcher's paper, moisture-proof on one side, and I can load them while the jeep's in the garage. They'll be out of the drizzle until I get to the Town Hall.

I've looked at the clock far more often than usual this morning. It's now 9:00 and with my backpack loaded and ready, it's time to make my way down the path, my hands tightly gripping the sides of the frame, fingers under the hanging wire. My feet travel down the damp grass and slippery soil without mishap. My painting now safely stowed on the back seat, I slide myself behind the wheel, give the dashboard a good morning pat, pull a challenging u-turn and start down the lane to the main road.

The commuting traffic has gone and the three stoplights are, as luck would have it, all green on the way to the house. One touch on the automatic garage opener and I back the red machine into the dry air. I'll do all the house checks when I get back so, for now, it's just to collect those three prints.

They are too large to carry all three at once and a quick look at my phone tells me I can make enough short trips from the living room to the vehicle without being rushed. My heart beats a little more quickly with each print loaded and I don't think it's solely a function of caffeine.

All the reading and sending of emails, then the frantic discovery followed by the surprising phone call, was surreal. Even after the morning was done and I drove home, it took until bedtime for my mind to grasp all that had happened, all that I'd agreed to do.

Now, as I sit behind the wheel, I tell myself that, in theory, there is still an option to say no. I fill my lungs with air, exhale a long, slow breath, put the car into first gear and drive into the drizzle at 9:45.

Five minutes before the assigned meeting time, I pull into the parking lot at the Town Hall and text for directions. An immediate reply tells me to pull up to a loading door at the back of the building.

"You'll be mostly out of the wet weather and we will meet you there to help with the unloading."

Easy to find, that's where I park with the passenger side nearest the door. Two people introduce themselves as they lift the prints from the back seat.

"I'm Jennifer and this is Adam." I open the trunk just enough to remove the wrapped canvas.

"The car's fine right where it is for now," Adam adds as we turn to make our way through the double doors, down a long corridor and into an enormous open space.

Despite the greyness outside, there's plenty of light coming through the floor-to-ceiling windows. I notice several large low display cases along one wall, some already with items behind the glass. In one corner of the exhibition room, there's a large table. We unwrap the prints first and, without hesitation, both of my hosts smile and are excited with what they see. They point to an area on one wall and suggest that's where they'd like to hang my photos.

It seems reasonable to me and as we approach, I see that there's a beautiful wall-hanging already installed with a nice old armchair standing on the floor to its side.

"Wow, that's amazing!" I nod at the hooking as they ask if there's a particular order in which I'd like my photos to hang. I assure them that's their decision, and we stroll back across the room to the remaining package on the long table.

I'm not an effusive person, despite my reaction to that rug hooking, so I try to simply unwrap the plastic bag and remove the tape from the brown paper. As I lift it away from the face of the canvas, the young man on my left and the young woman on my right both gasp.

Startled, I look at them and hope I don't see frowns. They're looking at and pointing out the details in the scene, then looking at me, talking again to each other. The voices are happy, amazed and incredibly positive.

"Does this mean that you accept it?" my raised eyebrows and tentative smile ask.

Both my companions are, I think, doing their best to be professional, but their grins give them away.

My trepidation immediately disappears with their pleasure as we lift the canvas by the wire attached to the back of the frame and carry it across to the wall. After a few minutes of conversation, we have all decided upon the position, sequence and where the exhibition labels will be placed. I've printed off a short text about each of the four pieces but leave the creation of formal signage to the pros. I admit to them that it's been really difficult to put myself out there,

"What has been personal and private is now on public display and will be even more so in a few more days."

They seem to appreciate my words as we carry everything back to the table. One of them goes down the hall and returns with an easel. It's quite an impressive object in itself, reminding me of some that I've seen at auction houses in one of my previous lives. They place my painting on its ledge and we all stand back a few feet to look at it. Even I have to admit with a broad smile that this resting place brings a different look than the scrap wood stand back at my place.

I'm quite happy to be sharing my painting with these people, in part because they reflect that pleasure back to me. We read through and sign the appropriate papers, one copy for me and the other for their files. Again, they reassure me that my pieces, along with all the others being lent to them, will be secure and protected.

I ask if I may take a photo of the canvas on its fancy easel for my records and they readily agree. No photos other than official publicity shots will be permitted during the actual exhibition, except those taken by the owners themselves under the watchful eye of security. We shake hands and I stand to look one more time at my painting before Adam walks with me to the loading door.

Sitting in the car before I start the engine, I see my hands shaking. I'm again realizing what I've just done and what I will continue to do in a crowd of people at the Grand Opening. I've told myself this a dozen times, but that hasn't lessened it any right at this moment.

It's nearly noontime, I've a nervous hunger, and I want to be in the quiet of my home. I'll use the red machine once more after today but for now, I want to email Rob with the most recent news and do my house rounds.

*********************************************

# Chapter Fifteen

## Sara

I am not yet completely in step with daylight starting at 6:00 in the morning. It takes time to forget the short days of a long winter when the morning world outside my windows remains dark until 8:00 and returns to dark by 4:00 in the afternoon. However, neither the time of day nor the type of light affects my canine housemate. She's driven by bodily needs and learned routines. 6:00 in the dark at either end of our day makes little difference to her.

I, on the other hand, love putting my feet to the floor with natural light streaming through every window. The sight of a bright sun in a blue sky when I open curtains is a glorious thing and today is one of those days. Our walk is going to be wonderful as soon as breakfast is done. All winter long, my down-filled jacket has one pocket crammed with dog supplies, another with house keys and tissues, and a third keeping my phone warm enough to not die from the cold.

All of those items are now tucked neatly into a pouch with its attached strap going cross-body or around my waist, depending on the weather. If it's raining, around my waist and underneath my raincoat works well, but this morning, I shorten the strap so it sits comfortably over one shoulder, the pouch on my opposite hip. This freedom of movement, unencumbered by layers of clothes, is pure pleasure.

We take the longer route to the shore, sandwiched on the sidewalk between buildings and traffic until we cross the intersection and start down the lane. The ditch is lined with wild roses coming into bloom and the branches of taller trees sway in the breeze. A new bark greets us from the neighbourhood beyond the turn and my companion breaks her focus for just a moment. She hardly pauses to look at the ducks on our side of the little pond.

I smile at a wonderful aroma as we approach the big rosebush hedge in front of the little house on the corner. The drizzle yesterday and the sun this morning must have convinced the buds to burst open. The greenery can no longer hide all the tiny white and pink flowers. I stop, bring my nose closer to a cluster of petals, breathe in their delicate perfume and glance up to see a full line of washing on the clothesline in the back garden.

The ducks are in fine form. Some paddle around the rocks where the stream enters the pond, and others lie in the tall wild grass at the edge of the bank. Half a dozen seagulls perch atop those same rocks and carry on their raucous conversations, oblivious to the disturbance they're causing.

A couple of women wave as they walk over the bridge and we step up onto the old rail bed. They're going in the opposite direction but point skyward beyond Chance and me. Framed against the light blue sky is a large eagle moving in an ever-widening circle while its head points down at the ocean's surface. I am mesmerized by the power in those wings, the flash of black and white feathers and that lethal orange beak.

We walk on as the waves flip and roll to the rocks, throwing up white spray on any that lie slightly offshore. The sides of the path are bright green this morning and tiny bushes sport yellow flowers that are unfamiliar to me. There are flower and vegetable beds newly tilled and planted behind the safety of man-made willow fences. Decks and patios that face the water along this stretch of trail now have colourful chairs ready for remarkable sunsets.

We pass the school playground with groups of children on the swings and slides, others running around on the soccer field, and some moving in and out of the small woods at the property's edge. Not being a fan of high-pitched voices, my companion puts me between her and them and returns her nose to the ground closer to the seaside of the trail.

Little birds flit from tree to tree further along but they move so quickly I can't put a name to them. Too small to be robins or starlings, I'm guessing they're Harris Sparrows, whose call I can't identify. I do hear a blue jay and see crows up in the air. This morning's walk is filled with the sights and sounds that I really miss during the winter.

I'm forced to stop walking at the boardwalk because Chance

wants to stand and watch the ducks splashing their wings in the pond and a few that skim the top of the water to come in for a landing. She's taking it all in, her ears perked up tall and listening keenly, her nose pressed between the wooden palings and her head tilting one way and another.

Our walk this morning has been leisurely and very relaxing after a busy few weeks. The Town's anniversary celebration begins with the Grand Opening this afternoon. That I have a wall-hanging and my friend's chair on display is still a thrill. I hooked for hours to finish that seat cover in time and hope its purpose will be obvious without it actually being attached as upholstery.

It's time to bring my focus back to the traffic and being sure it will stop at the crosswalk before we step off the final curb before home. Chance checks the entryways to several homes along our road to see if the Golden Retriever or the black and white puppy are outside. Then, it's to be sure that the large tail-wagging brown Poodle or the big Bernese Mountain Dog are where they should be. There are a lot of dogs in our neighbourhood, even without counting those on our short side-street. My companion's curiosity is at its finest, all part of her walking routine.

She's out in the back garden now, so I open my laptop to check emails and messages. At the top of the list and sent yesterday is a message from Jennifer. She provides parking directions so, late as it is, I send a simple reply thanking her and that I'm looking forward, with some nervous tension, to being at the Grand Opening.

There's an attachment to her email, and when I open it, an updated flyer fills my screen. It gives the time and location, then breaks the exhibition into categories, each with examples of items that will tell the story of our shore, both past and present.

Under Arts and Crafts, I read rug-hooking, knitting, crochet work, displays of old pattern books, photographs and paintings. The flyer continues to Past and Present with fishing and farming tools, housewares and china, magazines and cookbooks, old maps and even a tablecloth that's nearly one hundred years old. The grounds around the Town Hall will have old farming machinery in a roped-off display as well as a tractor and a dory that are in current use. Under supervision, children will be permitted to sit in the new machines.

Exhibition labels will accompany each item displayed on walls, beside floor exhibits, indoors, outside, and within the glass cases. The donors and creators will be in attendance to answer any questions or provide background stories. That final sentence gives me a moment's pause. I agreed to be there but now, I hope no one asks me any questions for which I don't have an answer. I don't suppose that's likely to happen and if it does, I'll just have to say that I don't know but can try to find out.

I have several emails from friends and family who live elsewhere. All are asking me to take and share photos of the event. I'll have to remember to do that for my items if not for anything else. In the meantime, I can forward the flyer to them. Now, I need to make sure Chance has water and food in her bowls and leave enough time for me to grab a quick shower and make myself presentable. The expected game of keep-away with the soccer ball will have to wait until later.

************************************

## Carrie

What a gorgeous day! This old body practically jumped out of bed this morning with the sun shining through the curtains. That's a bit of an exaggeration, I must admit, but really, I feel quite light of heart. That's not common, let me tell you. While the kettle came to a boil for my first cup of tea for the day, I had clothes in the washer, the table set for one, my bread browning in the toaster and an egg in the pan. It's a grand start to this first day of July for both the weather and me. Happy Canada Day!

I finish breakfast just after eight o'clock as Maisie stops in with the newspapers and another house and garden magazine. Her habit is to read them quickly, unlike in this house where I dawdle away a rainy morning or a tired evening, one page at a time. We both smile about the warm air coming in the window this early in the day and she asks,

"How are you feeling about the big exhibition this afternoon?"

There's a full-page ad in colour in both papers, she tells me, which is good for our town, getting some ink in the city's Saturday issue.

I tell her, "I feel fine about the event, excited really."

I want to see how the tablecloth and the pattern books are being displayed and look at all the other things, too. I lay the stuff from Maisie on the little hall table as she rushes out the door, only to stop and call back,

"Arch made rabbit pie for supper last night from a brace in the freezer. He says he'll bring some over."

That's my supper taken care of for sure. I can hardly wait because Arch's pie is the best, with lots of vegetables in thick gravy and paste biscuits on top.

As I'm clearing my dishes off the table and putting them into the hot suds in the sink, I notice that the washing machine has stopped, so I gather the wet clothes into the basket, slip on my outdoor shoes and go hang it all on the line. There's enough breeze to get it blowing even before the second or third peg is attached. Dry before the afternoon ends is my guess. Shoes off and slippers back on, I finish washing those few dishes and set them in the rack to dry.

I haven't run the vacuum over the place in a few days. That's next. When I had the cat, it was a daily thing, but now that it's just me, there's no fur flying around or hiding in the corners. Mind you, with the windows open more often from now on, the dust will blow in from the lane. My place isn't very big so when I plug the cord into the hall socket, I can do the whole front of the house.

Passing by the window, I see the walker and her dog stopping to sniff the roses that have bloomed. Well, the woman is smelling the flowers, not so much her companion, I don't think. I love it when people enjoy the flowers in my garden and that hedge, when it's in bloom, draws quite a bit of attention from people, birds, and bees.

I unplug the vacuum and spy the things from Maisie. Perhaps, now that the carpet is clean and the line is full of clothes, I could give myself a sit-down to have a look at the papers, just for a small while. I wonder what they're saying about our little exhibition, especially the crowd out in town.

There's a difference between 'in town' and 'out in town' in my mind. The first is us here on the shore. The second is those in the city and suburbs half an hour from here. I remember, as a child, city people asking us if we lived "beyond the overpass" like it was hundreds of miles away in a foreign land.

There's still another cup in the pot, so I leave the magazine but take the newspapers into the sunshine of the kitchen table, bring the tin milk out of the fridge and fix a second tea. I ate a big breakfast not long ago, so this will do while I read. Although I'm curious what the bigger paper says, I feel duty-bound to start with our local news.

It's about permits to build, plans to expand the harbour, people having their say about this, that and the other, all the usual stories until I come to the official Town section. There's a full page, in colour, about the Anniversary Celebration events lasting from July 1st to Thanksgiving Day in October.

It all begins with our exhibition at 2:00 this afternoon and fireworks after dark. There are sections about music festivals, two on weekends in July and two more in August. Lots of the clubs, churches and organizations in all the communities are holding teas, take-out suppers, dances, Bingo evenings and card games. If the weather cooperates, the town is sponsoring barbecues and family picnics at the shore and a carnival company is coming to the old stadium parking lot with rides and games of chance for the kids. I feel that I've read so much, I need to take a moment to sit back and take it all in.

That done, I can now go back to the section about our exhibition. Most of it is inside the Town Hall, but the big things like farm equipment and a fishing boat will be outside on the grounds. Indoors is where the display cases will be, as well as photos and art on the walls, displays of crafts and hand-made things like mitts and quilts, and even some old furniture.

It sounds a lot bigger than I thought it was going to be. I think I'll get there early because, if all the families who provided these things are going, that's a lot of people, never mind everyone who might just come out of interest.

I feel like I've used up my time for sitting, so I flick through the bigger paper until I find the Entertainment section. That's where there's an interview about the exhibition and another copy of the flyer I just read. If a bunch of people drive out to see the start of everything this afternoon, the roads are going to be clogged with parked cars.

I didn't notice this until just now, but the flyer in both papers asks people to donate an item to the food bank as an admission price. I must remember to take something with me. I'd better go and have a look in the pantry right now and put it by the door, so I don't forget. Yes, I am definitely going to drive over there before the crowds arrive and find myself a good parking spot.

****************************

# Margaret

This morning feels like the perfect temperature for a walk around the garden. The Geraniums have little purple buds, several on each sprig, and I'm hoping the Nasturtiums might have begun to sprout. Their wide, deep green leaves often hide the kernels until they burst into colour. First things first, though. Eat breakfast and check on the neighbourhood.

It's Saturday morning, so my crowd won't be tearing out the driveway or making their way to the bus stop. The youngest will be awake by now, the teenagers probably not, and I won't hazard a guess about the adults. Last evening was Friday night, the end of the workweek for most of them, so a scattered glass may have been raised knowing a sleep-in is possible this morning.

I've never been one for sleeping in or napping during the day. My mental clock just doesn't permit it. That's why I'm on the job here at my window with a view of the road every morning. Case in point, there goes my mystery walker. He's dressed in sensible gear and his grey ponytail hangs over his jacket collar. That's curious. I thought he smiled my way just then. I must be imagining it; more likely a trick of the sun on the window.

Mother's apron is hanging on the door to my pantry and as I put my dishes into the dishwasher, it catches my eye. I give it a little pat on my way to the bedroom for a cardigan in case the breeze is a bit chilly. It's early and the night air was cool coming in the window, so the grass is probably wet. I slip on my green gardening boots just in case and go out my back door.

I'm curious to see if any of the seedlings have pushed their way through the soil since yesterday. The children will be thrilled if their efforts have started to show promise. Bending forward slightly, I can see the tiny tips of future onions and a few carrot ferns just above the damp earth.

A hand waves good morning from the door two houses along the sweeping driveway and I, of course, wave back. Someone's up over there. Along the side of my place, the Flox are a good foot tall already. Their tiny flower buds have yet to show colour to the world and, at the moment, I cannot remember which I ordered. I think, maybe, it was a combination packet rather like the wildflower seeds from a couple of years ago. They'll be a nice surprise for me. Flox and heather were Mother's favourite things to grow. She left the vegetables to the farmers in the family, preferring to have colour in a vase on the hall table. I wonder, as my feet go back through the door, what she would think of her magazines and cookbooks being in the exhibition.

I think it's time to open the laptop and visit the online universe for a little while before getting ready to go out after lunch. The sun is so pretty in the living room. I'll sit in my comfy chair instead of at the kitchen table for a change. This little computer makes me laugh because I swear it takes a long time to boot up and then makes me wait before I can type in my password, much like getting my own self started some mornings.

There are ten unread emails staring at me and, at a glance, I can see that only one is anything that peaks my interest for now. It's from the celebration office and came in last evening. It's a reminder about reserved parking behind the Town Hall and that the Grand Opening is scheduled for 2:00 this afternoon. Attached below the text is an extensive outline of the categories and examples of items in each.

Inside the exhibition hall, there will be old farming and fishing tools, photographs, artwork and hooked wall-hangings, hand-crafted goods like knitted mitts and crocheted blankets, old kitchen equipment, cook books and publications related to home and garden, to name just a few. The more delicate items will be protected within glass display cases but I knew that from the meeting Anne and I had with the organizer. Out on the grounds, old and current farm tractors and dories will be displayed.

I don't take the time to click on the link to the flyer that provides details for the whole celebration. This is enough information for now and, besides, I'm getting quite excited to just get there and see everything. I knew people along the shore would pull together to make this a good celebration. My old chime clock strikes twelve and the morning has disappeared, so it's time for lunch and then a wardrobe decision. For a brief moment earlier, I thought I might wear Mother's apron, but I won't.

****************************************

## Ben

I think some work around my place is needed this morning, but, first, a short walk at least down to the little bridge and back, check on the jeep and stretch the sleep from my muscles. When this afternoon's event is finished, I'll walk home from the house in the evening sun. For now, I leave my backpack at home, put my key in a pocket, tie my hair out of my face and go down the path. As expected, the car looks fine, no bird droppings visible and the lane is dry underfoot.

At the turn onto the shore road, a blue jay follows me until he finds something far more interesting and a few of the ducks, having ventured this far from their pond, waddle across the road ahead of me. That fence by the long driveway is tilting and will need a bit of work before it comes completely adrift from its supports. Purple flowers under the front window of the house are beginning to show some colour and while not knowing much about flowering plants, I suspect colour will soon appear between the green leaves in the window boxes.

I stand for a minute here on the bridge to look downstream to the distant bay before I turn to go back up the hill. It's definitely an unusual walk for me, brief but that's all I have time for this morning. Fifteen minutes gets me back up the path and through the front door once again.

Now is the time to clean the chimney flue and make sure there isn't a home for tiny critters behind the metal plate. As always, the amount of soot that catches down there surprises me so I know it needs doing before I light the burner next winter.

That done, the scraper and scoop are back on the shelf in the outhouse turned tool shed. I lift the chain-saw from the floor and can feel gas in the tank. The blade is oiled so, I'm ready to cut up those windfalls. The junks will dry out nicely stacked in the cradle near the back door, at the ready on a cool Fall evening. That half-hour walk was a good idea because wielding the saw and hauling wood when I'm not warmed up is always sketchy. This chore, despite the noise, is good fun.

It's still only 11 o'clock. Time for a shower, hang the two prints that aren't in the exhibition and maybe a light lunch before heading out the road. I think I'll drive directly to the Town Hall. There's not really much point in going to the house. I won't have time to do anything there before I have to leave again. This way, I'll take the jeep back to the garage, check emails, lock the door and then walk back here. I'll need the downtime of the shoreline.

I unwrap the brown paper from the two extra framed prints and prop them on the table for another look. That day at the shop feels like a long time ago, so much has happened since. I'll be glad to have the other three back here. With that in mind, I look around my room to decide where they will all go and settle on putting the brilliant yellow puffballs beside the front door.

Looking at them now, I remember searching the internet with Rob the evening after I'd first come across these tennis balls atop the moss. They looked larger than most of the examples we found online, so I'm still not entirely certain of their correct name. They might be yellow field caps, but that morning on the headland, they weren't on above-ground stems that I could see, and I didn't want to disturb them. To this ignorant eye and now up on my wall, they shall remain golden puff balls.

The second print will hang on my bedroom wall because, if I were forced to choose, it would be my favourite. It's that wonderful bare-to-the-bones tree that stubbornly clings to the eroding bank off the eastern headland path. Facing the sea, the trunk leans with the prevailing winds, marked by mottled salt-bleached shades of grey. I was kneeling on the bracken behind it when I took the picture so the branches appear to stretch helplessly to the blue sky and white clouds well beyond its reach.

One of these days, when the tide is out, I may climb down onto the rocks and try to capture the roots. They must run back into the bank underneath where I knelt that day. The two images would compliment each other on the same wall and they'll catch indirect light from the window. Now, I can no longer procrastinate. It's time to find my cleanest jeans and a shirt fit to wear in the company of all those people.

I am, in truth, looking forward to seeing *Coffee Ice*, *Tracks* and *Perched* from a distance and, with mixed feelings, my painting on that elaborate easel. Perhaps I can blend in with the crowd and spend most of my time among them, looking at all the displays and learning more about the communities through which I walk every day.

# Chapter Sixteen

## Sara

Chance and I walked the shorter loop this morning. It's really a couple of blocks, not a stereotypical loop, but here on the shore, nobody speaks in blocks. We either say the street names or the points of points of interest, for example, school road, the duck pond, the headland, the beach. Everyone will know where you mean and the term block would definitely label you as a townie or a come-from-away. Our walk was mostly to give us both some exercise and allow Chance to have a nap in my absence this afternoon. Needless to say, she will not be attending the Grand Opening.

The remainder of this morning disappeared in small tasks, and now that I've fed us both, it's time to decide on my attire. I expect the hall will be warm enough for a long cotton tunic, light leggings and sandals, easy to choose and easy to wear. The drive down to the exhibition might take a bit longer than the usual ten minutes if there is a lot of Saturday traffic, so I'll leave myself fifteen. I feel the dog's eyes following me as I close the bedroom and bathroom doors and pick up my shoulder bag.

"I'll be back, I promise," I tell her with a rub of her ears before she jumps up onto her spot on the couch.

I was right about the traffic. Pretty weather, weekend flea

markets in parking lots and driveway yard sales bring everyone out along the shore. I drive behind the large Town Hall and see the perfect space between a little beige car and a red four-by-four. There is a steady stream of vehicles coming from the lights at the bottom of the hill, so the Grand Opening will, indeed, be grand. I opt for the second-floor entrance above the exhibition space to allow for an expansive view of the displays below the glass railing.

Everything is arranged in distinct sections along the outer walls with two long rough wood tables down the middle. The scope of the exhibition really is very impressive with plenty of space between displays for people to walk or even gather in small groups to look at items.

The wall across from the bank of floor-to-ceiling windows catches my eye. There are several colour photographs hung at average eye level, a large painting resting on a tall easel, and then my wall-hanging before a series of old black and white prints. Every piece hung along the wall has a notation beside it.

On the floor to one side of my rug-hooking is the armchair with my potential upholstery cover sitting partly on the actual seat, one edge draped over a wooden arm. I can see how it hints at the intended purpose.

People are entering the open double doors downstairs and placing their food bank items in the bins or slipping monetary donations into the antique treasure chest in front of the volunteer. I descend the wide stairs, slip my donation through the slot, and then move towards my rug-hooking on the far wall as the Mayor steps to the microphone.

She welcomes everyone to the best Grand Opening ever created by our communities, then introduces the two people to her left, Adam and Jennifer, the organizers with whom I met. Without hesitation, everyone in the hall gives them a huge round of applause for the amazing event they have coordinated. Then, she asks us to clap again to thank everyone who provided their treasures to make this exhibition so successful.

There's a gentleman coming towards me with a determined look on his face. I wait while he reads the story on the label beside my wall-hanging.

"Did you do this?" he nods his head at the wall.

I tell him that I did. He smiles and goes on to say that he saw it from the other side of the hall and his immediate thought was how the colourful houseboat doesn't belong. I smile in return and listen as he tells me about losing his wife a couple of years ago and that *Anchored* now makes sense to him. We chat for a few more minutes before he wanders off to look at the old farming and fishing tools on the tables in the middle of the room.

My thoughts about the older gentleman are interrupted by a

deep, gentle voice cutting through the general chatter that fills the hall. It's the guy near the beautiful colour photographs of scenes from along the shore. He stands between me and the ornate easel. I turn to accept his compliment on my wall-hanging and to answer his question about the seat cover.

I reach out to shake his hand, "Hi, I'm Sara," as I look up at his face.

He looks familiar somehow but in a small community, everybody looks familiar.

"I'm Ben. Nice to meet you," begins a chat about repairing old furniture and bringing it back to life before I ask about his photographs and say how I've seen seagulls atop rocks exactly as he's captured. He moves away from the painting and explains the frozen pond named *Coffee Ice,* then *Perched*, the seagull who stood firmly on the outcrop of rock while the sea sloshed over its feet.

Several people have joined us now and there's an excited discussion about the location depicted in the painting. The man turns his attention to those gathered near him and it's then that I notice a grey ponytail hanging over the collar of his plaid shirt. There are also people looking at *Anchored,* but they don't need me, so I join those in front of the easel.

I feel my heart skip a beat at what is jumping off that canvas in front of me. It's an intricate rendition of a particular section of the walking trail. One edge of the image is actually where Chance and I step up onto the trail at the end of the lane. If I stand on the bridge where the little pond and sea tide collide, I look into the distance as it appears here, both eastward along the trail to come and north to the hills on the far side of the bay.

I am rooted to the floor. The voices of two hundred people are the murmur of the wind and deep rumble of retreating waves. I'm on that trail, wrapped in its peace. I stare at the details of the beach rocks and the ocean rolling onto them, some wet, some dry, below the verge of the groomed path. There are seagulls in the air and a cluster on the deep blue waves. In the distance, high above the ocean, a black and white speck surveys everything below. The bright dots of houses jump off the far shore and that one naked slice of sheer orange cliff disappears into the breaking sea.

I hear water, the cries of seagulls, the crunch of gravel under my feet and, high overhead, the beat of an eagle's huge wings. My eyes, my feet, my heart walk within the image, from wave-soaked rocks to the line of evergreens, on past the curved outcrop of the headland. I'm there one step at a time. In the east, at a distance, I see two tiny figures, one taller than the other. A shadow moves near me, but there, under a bright blue sky in brilliant sunshine, a person with a dog is coming this way.

Someone is speaking to me. Jolted back to reality, I try to

correct myself. No, those figures are not 'coming this way.' They are shapes on a wide canvas about to walk a magnificent acrylic shoreline trail. I am suddenly aware that the artist is looking down at me, his face showing obvious concern at my silent, motionless reaction to his work.

I breath deeply, find a smile, and say that he has captured everything I love about that trail. I shake my head in disbelief.

"I was right there, right now, on that bridge with my walking companion," I manage to tell him and hope he doesn't think I'm crazy.

His body visibly relaxes and his face smiles back at me. He hesitates, frowns, begins then stops before he finds the words to ask,

"Is your my companion, by any chance, a dog?"

My relief is palpable as I grin and tell him that his turn of phrase is so apt.

"Yes, my walking buddy is a rescued Husky and her name, believe it or not, just happens to be Chance."

I'm sure people milling around us think our behaviour rather strange but both of us are now quite speechless.

It takes a minute, but his "That's you and your dog in the distance" crosses in the air with my question, "You're the walker we pass on the trail?"

Both of us stand in stunned silence. Completely out of context from the path along the shoreline, it's beyond belief that we should connect here in an exhibition hall filled with strangers. His painting and its impact have created so much more than two people offering a brief greeting beside the shore.

Neither of us knows how to continue the conversation, so I offer a "Thank you for this trail", turn and force my attention to a question about hooking upholstery for a worn-out chair.

"Are you in a rug-hooking group?" one of the three women asks, then continues, "We get together for a hook-in once every couple of weeks. You're welcome to join us."

The conversation brings me back to earth when another woman laughs, "Yes, we call ourselves the Shoreline Hookers."

They tell me a bit more about their gatherings and how everyone's style, imagery and choice of materials are a matter of personal preference.

"How did you come up with the seat cover idea?" continues our chat.

Ben smiles and tilts his head in my direction as he walks further along the wall to look at the old black-and-white photos of the communities as they used to be. There are images of the old train stations, the interior of train cars, corner stores no longer standing and the inshore fishery with small boats out on the bay. I see him stop at one of the display cases that holds an old Brownie camera, sleeves of negatives, and a very old hand-held flash before his tall frame moves to the centre table of fishing gear.

Our upholstery conversation finished, I make my way to the display case that protects old cookbooks and glossy magazines. There are a lot of people, mostly women, chatting and laughing that they used to read those ads for the latest steam iron, the best soap flakes for washing clothes, and how it was all geared to the housewife. One of the women looks up at me when she says "housewife," and I agree that it's a term we don't hear any more. She says her nieces and nephews couldn't believe what they were reading when she showed them the magazines.

I tell them about the husband of one of my teachers in the mid-1960s who was referred to as a house-husband because he stayed home while his wife, who loved her job, was happy to go out of the house for work each day. That brings another round of memories from the women as I turn to look at the tablecloth in the next case.

"That was my mother's," an older woman tells me with pride.

I acknowledge the skill, patience and time it must have taken to crochet. She's pleased that I know how it was made and asks if I crochet.

"Sometimes, simple things but I like to hook rugs, mostly," I add before asking to know more about the tablecloth. I learn its story and how it was used for special occasions with plastic over it to protect it from spills.

We chat about keeping our hands busy in the evenings and I point to my wall-hanging and the old chair. I'm introduced to Maisie and Arch standing beside her and Maisie tells me that her long-time friend, Carrie here, made dozens of squares for a blanket project for charities. Arch, bored with crochet talk, excuses himself and wanders off towards the fishing and farming displays.

During our conversation about the tablecloth, Carrie keeps looking at me and seems about to say something more. When Maisie finishes speaking, I wait for a second and it's then that Carrie grins,

"I've got it. I know why you look so familiar to me."

She wants to know if I have a dog, and although it's the second time I've been asked this in the past thirty minutes, I say that I do. I then tell her that Chance is at home right now, patiently waiting for me, but that we had a walk along the trail this morning. She's tired enough to have a nap while I'm here at the exhibition.

"I knew it," Carrie shakes my hand and tells me she lives in the little house on the corner of the lane with the big hedge of rose bushes.

I smile, "I'm Sara," and go on to tell her how nice it is to meet her and that I always hope to say hello and maybe chat about her pretty garden.

More people want her attention now, so I excuse myself, step away from the display case and head back to my wall-hanging and chair.

"Hi, I'm Emily," a confident young woman smiles up at me.

"I'm Ben," I turn with her and look at the old crockery mixing bowl before she shows me the pie plate with the slider that would loosen the cooled pastry from the metal.

Given Rob's love of cooking, I've moved from the farming and fishing gear in the centre of the room to have a look at the housewares and baking display. When I point to the old cookbooks and an embroidered apron, she looks around the room and beckons to a smiling woman.

Emily says, "Aunt Margaret, this is Ben. Aunt Margaret owns the cookbooks, magazines," and, pointing to her left, "the china in that display case."

I shake hands with Margaret and tell her that my good friend is keen on such treasures. He's away right now but will certainly come to the exhibition when he's back. She tells me that the apron belongs to someone else but she has one that her mother used to wear on special days. Margaret is looking at me with an interest that leaves me a little uneasy until she asks if I do a lot of walking.

I'm surprised by the question, but figure my long legs and walking boots might be the reason, so I say, "I don't own a car, and, yes, I walk every day."

She apologizes for such a rude question when we've only just met, but her curiosity got the better of her.

I smile that it's okay and tell her, "The colour photos and the painting on the easel are my contributions to the exhibit."

She then tells her niece to go have a look at my work because it's absolutely gorgeous, especially the painting of the trail. She, too, doesn't own a car, but unlike me, she's not a walker unless it's to look at her flowers in the garden or to check on her fence after the snow all winter.

We both stand with people all around us and arrive at the same conclusion. Margaret is my watcher from behind the window and I'm the walker going up and down her road. Again, she apologizes for being so abrupt with her personal question, but her family is large and known for being rather forthright. Opinions are easily expressed and questions readily asked. I'm happy to meet her and tell her that I love walking the trail every day since moving here nearly three years ago.

It occurs to me to ask, “Did you notice a red Jeep behind you one day last week?”

Laughing loudly, she tells me she has wondered who belongs to that car. “It’s new to the neighbourhood.”

I put her curiosity to rest by telling my friend owns it and that when he’s away, in return for looking after his home, I borrow his car when I need it.

I ask which other exhibits she’s had time to look at and invite her to look at Sara’s hooking on the wall and the potential seat cover for the chair. She is pleased that I’ve been over at the farming display because that’s what her family has done on this shore for two generations, although the items here are not from her family. Their houses, “the family compound,” she jokes, is built on her grandfather and father’s farmland.

We part ways with her inviting me to stop by whenever I see them around the fire pit during an evening, then quickly adds, “as long as you’re ready to meet a dozen crazy, very vocal people.”

A gentle tap comes over the loud-speaker and a polite cough draws everyone’s attention to the podium at the exhibition entrance. Four hours have flown as the Mayor thanks everyone for making the Grand Opening of the Anniversary Celebration such a great success, all those who have come to see the displays, everyone who has so generously lent their family treasures, and the children who enjoyed sitting in the dory and tractor outside.

The representative from the food bank, she adds, is very thankful for the much-needed donations received today. Then, she reminds everyone that the displays will be open to the public from 2:00 to 6:00 o'clock in the afternoons, Friday to Sunday, until Thanksgiving Day.

"Don't forget fireworks at the shore tonight at 10:00."

One final thank you to everyone and a suggestion to watch for all the festivals and family events yet to come. The Grand Opening is declared officially over.

People, still chatting in groups, slowly make their way out the wide doors, past the tractor and the boat on the lawn, and into the crowded parking lot. For those whose items will remain here, it's not as easy to leave. The anticipation of today's event has been unusual, sometimes intense.

A number of us linger still feeling the emotions of family treasures rediscovered, decisions to go public with them, hours spent creating things that are uniquely one's own, and wondering how all will be received by a space filled with strangers.

The young organizers reassure Ben, Sara, Carrie and Margaret that their possessions and the items open on the long tables will be safely covered until each exhibition day and that, without question, they themselves are welcome to visit in private.

"Just give one of us a call and we'll inform security," Jennifer adds as they check the locks on the display cases then begin to unfold a sea of white cloth and carefully lay it over the items on the long tables.

*********************************

ANCHORED

# Chapter Seventeen

## Sara

It has been an incredible day of new experiences, and as I walk to my car, I think it will take quite a few shoreline walks with Chance before I remember all the details.

I see Carrie, my rosebush owner, slowly pull her beige car through the empty space in front of her. She's so intent on the process that she doesn't look my way and I don't want to distract her with a wave. I might see her when we turn that corner of the lane on our walk tomorrow.

I met rug hookers from a couple of different communities beyond the shore who talked with me about *Anchored*, so I return their waves. They had read the story before speaking to me and told me, as did that gentleman, that the houseboat and title pulled it all together. I am very gratified for their approval of my hooking technique and their interest in the notion of hooking a seat cover. A number of them have older chairs that need more than something to hide worn arms, so trying their hand at making an actual piece of upholstery carried our conversations.

Chance has been stuck in the house for more than four hours. It's time for me to fulfill my promise and get back for playtime in the garden.

"Nice to meet you, Sara," comes over the top of my little car as I unlock the driver's door. It's Ben and he's climbing up into that red jeep.

"See you on the trail, Ben," I smile back at him.

Now, to concentrate on the traffic and not lose myself back into this afternoon's amazing experiences. There are plenty of hours in the days ahead for remembering as much as I can while I look through years of rug-hooking patterns, decide on my next project or walk the trail.

I'm greeted at my door by a happy dog, her curved tail swinging and her favourite bone being offered as a reward for my return. I go down to my knees and wrap my arms around her neck as she licks my face.

"Oh, Chance, you've no idea what's happened. We're captured in a painting! You and I will walk the shoreline forever!"

I could just sit here on the doormat for the rest of the day, but someone squirms out of my hug, and bounds for the back door.

Rising to follow her, I laugh. "You're right, it's time for outside", I tell her as we make our way into the July sun shining onto the back deck.

She's off and running. I sit on the top step, and let the feelings bubble up inside me. They're difficult to put into words.

Chance and I, on a magnificent canvas, shall walk the trail forever.

***********************************

## Carrie

Maisie and Arch walk out the doors with me and, although I'm tired, the surprise of knowing my walker, Sara, loves to work with her hands keeps popping into my head. Arch is saying that he was surprised how keen the painter was to find out about the fishing gear and figures the guy has some experience with the ocean from the questions he was asking. Maisie is chattering on about the family who donated that beautiful china and the big Royal platter.

I'm hearing her, but she isn't expecting a response, so I'm thinking about the photographs from the hospital auxiliary of the finished blanket with its navy background and bright flower petals in the middle of each square. It's nice that the organizers took my suggestion and Deanne allowed it in the show.

I am also really pleased with how many people loved the tablecloth that Aunt Maude made for Mother. I don't know how many times I retold the story and quite a few people remembered tables protected by plastic coverings.

Maisie and Arch's car is past mine and as they walk on, I suddenly remember to thank Arch for the delicious rabbit pie that's going to be my supper. My memory is so bad these days, but it's not an issue right now because I do remember where I parked my car four hours ago. There she is beside that red jeep machine and what's even nicer, the spot in front of the beige bomber is now empty. All I need to do is pull straight through.

A lot of the traffic is heading up to the highway, so my run home isn't too bad. The usual crazy people dying to get their coffee at the shop by the lights but I just slow down and let them do their thing before turning down my lane. I seem to be getting more tolerant for some reason.

The sun is still shining so I think I'll put the kettle on and change into my round-the-house clothes. I'll eat that rabbit pie and then, I might even sit out on the step and smell the roses for a while.

I'm exhausted, but it's been the very best sort of day. Seeing those blankets in the photos on the wall was wonderful. I allow myself just a little moment of pride. My colourful crocheted squares are now bringing warm hugs to someone. I hope they know that each stitch holds a little love.

This day, for me, might just end with some red or yellow yarn moving through my fingers. I wonder if Sara and her dog might stop by to look at my vegetable bed tomorrow.

## Margaret

We all pile back into the van and I get to ride shotgun in the front seat this time. Frankie laughs at my pleasure and I tell her it's not quite as exciting as being in her little car, but it is going to be easier for my body to get out when we reach home.

All of us fill the twenty-minute ride with stories about the people we met, what we liked most, and the fun it was to see our magazines, cookbooks and china on display.

Frankie is nervous about leaving things in the exhibition hall, but Emily and Liam repeat what they'd been told by the organizers. Liam had actually spoken with one of the security guards. They'd been talking about what was needed to work in that career.

Emily is excited about how she chatted with Ben, "the guy with the pony-tail," she stressed, when he was at the display case and had said that his friend is a good cook. She told him all about her grandmother's cookbooks and her hand-written recipes that weren't in the display.

Then she adds, "Auntie M. had suggested I go look at his photos and painting. They were awesome."

I chuckle as she teases her cousin about his interest in being a security person while she says in one long breath, "I'm going to do photography and learn how to get an image that's in your mind onto the end of a paintbrush and create something as awesome as Ben's painting."

I am happy that my mystery walker is no longer a mystery. Ben seems very nice, a bit unsure of himself and from what little he said, loves his solitude. Those photographs of animal tracks and the coffee-coloured waves of ice suggest a very keen eye for things others might simply ignore.

Perhaps, after a few brief encounters, if I'm out in the garden when he passes by, he'll dare to join our family evenings around the fire pit. Even if that never happens, it'll be nice to just wave or say good morning in passing.

Now, we're turning into our driveway. I'm the first to climb down out of the van but before my feet touch the ground, the two teenagers slide open the side door and head to greet friends on their way down the shore road.

"Thank you, everyone, for a wonderful afternoon, and, yes, I have marshmallows and chocolate-covered biscuits ready for s'mores."

I sit with a good cup of tea after a busy day and gather my thoughts as the sky breaks into sunset behind the trees and the fire pit is readied. Perhaps one day, we will pull up another chair.

## **Ben**

I want to take *The Walkers* home with me and trade the big ornate easel for its simple scrap wood cousin in the comfort of my cozy home. However, I've made this commitment and, without ready transport to carry it back and forth mid-week for the next three months or so, I must leave it to be safely covered. I feel very much that part of me, an important part, is being abandoned.

Does that sense ever leave, I wonder, as I stand here now to look at something I've brought to life, something that means so much to me, only to turn and walk away. The day that this canvas and three more photographs do come home with me will be emotional, I think.

On a more practical level, they will throw a real splash of colour into my little home and, until that day, I'll have to remember to leave space on the walls.

I join the exodus of exhibition visitors and, like a flock of starlings, we make our way into the parking lot behind and above the Town Hall. A couple of people tell me, in passing, how much they love my work and one grey-bearded gentleman wonders if I'm represented by a gallery.

That almost stops me in my tracks, but he smiles and before I can answer, he asks, "Do you have a portfolio of work?"

I tell him that I've an archive of photographs but this is my first art on canvas instead of on surfboards.

"All the more wonderful to see," he laughs as he turns to his companion.

Sara is about to get into her car when I reach Rob's red machine.

A "Nice to meet you, Sara" and a "See you on the trail, Ben" cross paths in the sunshine of the late afternoon.

A hand waves from the back seat of a family van moving slowly between all the people heading to their cars. I lift mine in reply, although I've no idea who that is. Someone I met today, obviously.

There are still people walking around and a line of slow-moving cars, so while the windows are still closed around me, I pump my fist and relieve some of the tension with, "Yes! I did it! I actually did it."

I was out there in that crowd talking with strangers about my photos, listening to their wonderful reactions to *The Walkers,* enjoying conversations and learning so much about the communities along the shore and those who live in them.

The traffic has thinned along the old road and I'm back at the house in no time. The garage routine sees my ride tucked safely back home and remembering to take my backpack off the passenger seat, I unlock the side door to step into the bright kitchen. I have to admit that it feels like a long time since I was in the quiet of this home, even longer in that of my own.

The geyser within me erupts yet again, "I did it. I put myself out there, big time."

I'm happily drained of any energy as I make a coffee and sit with my laptop to email Rob. I start and stop, write and delete, and then type again as the thoughts and recollections flood my brain. My fingers can hardly keep pace as excitement returns and I recall people's reactions, especially to my painting.

I hear myself, a broken record, as I type, "Yes, my friend, you win. I did it. I put myself and my stuff out there for all to see."

Then, I tell him a lot of the information I learned about the fishing and farming equipment, and the stories behind the cookbooks and the old china in the display cases.

He's going to enjoy seeing it all when he gets home in less than six weeks. I can hardly wait to show it to him.

How, I don't know, but I almost forget to mention meeting Sara, the woman and her dog in the distance of my painting. Her incredible reaction to *The Walkers* and my initial worry turned into relief and pleasure with her explanation. That trail and, after today, its depiction on my canvas have meaning to more than just its creator.

My email is really too long for a single message by the time I think I've written everything I want to say. I tell him the house is fine, the garden is blooming and the Jeep no longer needs to bump over my lane.

I've poured my day onto the screen before reading his email, so my epistle ends with a promise to now sit back, look at what he's written and then provide a sensible reply while I finish the last sip of his good coffee.

I don't have three hours of daylight left, so it's time to start my walk along the shore. Thoughts of my day carry me quickly past the headland, the duck pond, the submerged beach and the eagle's perch. The tightly-wound springs inside my chest continue to uncoil with each stride forward. In no time, I am at the entrance to 'my' community and making the turn up the little hill, the tipsy fence in sight.

The setting sun is painting its own canvas as I pass the house, Margaret's house. Voices in animated conversation and the smell of burning wood float on the air towards the road. I smile and glance at the open lawn circled by homes.

The old fire pit is in action this evening, I see. Perhaps, one day, I'll join them, but for now, as the moon lights my lane underfoot, The Boss sings me back to my quiet corner of the world.

THE END

# About The Author

Tina Mardel Stewart lives in Conception Bay South, Newfoundland and Labrador, Canada, near an endless shoreline trail. She and her rescued dog enjoy walking every day and spending time with family and friends. Tina has been a member of a newspaper Editorial Board, created lesson plans for classes in English as a Second Language, and written training manuals for non-profit organizations.

Her articles and photographs have also been published in an anthology of short stories, in a book about rug-hooking with yarn, and in international rug-hooking magazines. She is a member of the Shoreline Hookers, her local rug-hooking group.

*******************************

www.ingramcontent.com/pod-product-compliance
Lightning Source LLC
Chambersburg PA
CBHW060429310726
48977CB00001B/115
*9781964482378*